Finding Daylight

A NOVEL

MARA DABRISHUS

Finding Daylight
Copyright © 2016 Mara Dabrishus
MCC Books
All rights reserved.

This book is a work of fiction. Names, characters, places, and incidents are either the product of the author's imagination or are used fictitiously. Any resemblance to actual persons living or dead is entirely coincidental.

Dabrishus, Mara, 1981 -
Finding Daylight / Mara Dabrishus

Editor: Erin Smith
Cover: Shutterstock

ISBN: 0996187235
ISBN-13: 9780996187237 (pbk.)

www.maradabrishus.com

Finding Daylight

A NOVEL

MARA DABRISHUS

For Erin,
who got the story right.

Part One:
Off Like a Bullet

November

Chapter One

IF GEORGIANA QUINN sat very still, she could imagine the filly underneath her. The slight pull of the reins when the filly pushed her nose to the earth. The nudge of her ribcage against Georgie's calves with her breath. There was a peace there that Georgie had bottled for herself in times like these—the unknown.

A knock at the door pulled Georgie back into the present, her eyes snapping open. The green room, they called it, was painted beige. A basket of candies sat untouched on the coffee table in front of her, where she sat with rigid posture on a sofa that she suspected had seen questionable use. A car zoomed across lonely, twisting roads on a television mounted on the wall.

"Ms. Quinn?" The production assistant for the *Seth Holmes Show* popped her head into the room, the light from the hallway spilling around her feet. "It's time."

Georgie stood shakily in three-inch heels, the shoes hiking her small stature up to average height. She was used to sturdy boots and chaps, a world away from fleeting manicures and sky blue dresses. The material quivered around her pale knees, and Georgie clenched her teeth to keep from trembling.

"You'll be great." The woman smiled, putting a hand between Georgie's shoulder blades as they walked toward the stage. "Just smile. Be yourself. Talk about Sweet Bells."

Georgie nodded wordlessly. *Sweet Bells. Talk about Sweet Bells. Was there anything else to talk about?*

Toeing the edge of the curtain, Georgie shifted her weight from heel to heel. She resisted the urge to mess with her flaming red pixie hair, swept into a style she hadn't chosen and wrangled into submission. She counted her breaths.

Ten in, ten out. Calm, Georgie, calm.

"Welcome back to the *Seth Holmes Show!*"

The audience gave a roar of approval, and the lights shined down on good-looking, easy-smiling Seth. He sat perched on a stool, soaking in the adoration, an empty stool within reaching distance. This was the stool on which she would sit, and already Georgie had doubts as to how she would climb onto it while being charming and coordinated all at once.

"Tonight, we have a prodigy among us," Seth said, clapping his hands together. "Of course, I'm not referring to myself. You may have seen her splashed all over the news today as the rider of Breeders' Cup Classic champion Sweet Bells—Ms. Georgie Quinn!"

"That's you," the assistant whispered when Georgie failed to walk forward, as if she'd forgotten her name. "You've got this."

Did she? Georgie finished her tenth big breath and figured she might as well act like she did. Who in her position could possibly get used to this?

She stepped out from behind the curtain to applause, summoned and achieved a smile. By the time she climbed the steps onto the stage to greet Seth Holmes, all glittering green eyes and dorky charm, Georgie was almost convinced that she could do this. Seth enveloped her in a hug like they were old friends, and she laughed when he let her go and motioned to the insurmountable stool.

"Oh, boy, you couldn't find something more short person appropriate?" she asked.

"You ride racehorses all day and you can't handle a stool? It looks pretty tame to me." Seth pulled a face, eyeing the stool like it might bite. "Do you need a boost?"

"I'll take all the help I can get," she said, accepting his arm as a brace and letting him lift her onto the stool like it was a racehorse. She settled onto it, hooking her feet around the legs, and grasped the wooden disk in both hands as she blinked at the audience staring back at her.

Their applause was polite, maybe charmed. Georgie was getting used to applause—the rowdy kind, drunk on victory. This was different, coaxed. Peppered with laughter. It was reactive, earned. She'd have to work to gain approval here.

"This must be a whirlwind for you," Seth said. "How long ago did you win this race? The Breeders' Cup . . . what was it called?"

"The Classic. That happened Saturday afternoon," Georgie said, waving a hand nervously in the air. "There's been no sleep since then."

"Everyone wants a piece of you, I imagine," Seth said, grinning.

"No, not really," Georgie shrugged a shoulder. "They want a piece of Sweet Bells."

Seth laughed, tipping his head back and shifting toward her.

"If that were the case, we'd have your horse on the show instead of you."

"You'd find she's not exactly a talker."

"How about you?" Seth asked. "You haven't been a jockey very long."

"Oh, yeah," Georgie shifted. "I've been doing this for about five seconds compared to everyone else out there."

"Five seconds?"

"Six months," she admitted, ducking her head when Seth's eyes bugged.

"Well, it's longer than five seconds," he allowed. "But what is it like to ride a horse like this, right off the bat, who hasn't ever lost? Her record is amazing, and she's being ridden by a seventeen-year-old kid with six months of experience."

Georgie opened her mouth, and shut it again, looking out at the lights and the crowd watching her keenly for the answer.

"It's phenomenal," she said carefully, lingering on the word. "It's beyond anything I ever hoped to experience. As far as I'm concerned, I'm lucky to have gotten caught up in her, and I hope we run like this as long as we can."

"Is this a career now?"

"Lately it's more riding than school, so I guess I'm not a good role model," Georgie said, her chin tipping up.

"Speaking of role models," Seth said, pointing to a projected image behind them of the *ESPN Magazine* cover with Georgie's face front and center, freckles and splatters of mud adorning her nose. The headline *The Face of Horse Racing* in bold, white type cut across her parted mouth. "This just came out on newsstands today. How does it feel being called the face of horse racing?"

"It's wild," Georgie admitted, a wave of heat crawling up her neck as she looked at the image. The headline refused to sink in all the way, like it was someone else's life and she was an impostor living in it. "I don't think I've deserved it yet," she said, "but I want to live up to the title."

"You've got time, right?" Seth asked, shrugging a shoulder like it was no big deal.

"Totally," she said, mimicking him, like she had it in the bag. "Tons of time."

"Well, I think you have a pretty awesome horse," Seth told her, rocking forward to lean his elbows on his thighs.

"So do I," Georgie whispered, almost conspiratorially.

"But you're probably more awesome," Seth told her, winking. The blush flooded over Georgie's face before she could say anything. Seth broke out into laughter and turned to the approving crowd. "She's bashful, too!"

"I'm glad fame and glory hasn't gone to your head," he said, standing up as the theme music ended the segment and Georgie found Seth lifting her off the stool, depositing her safe and sound on the stage floor. Applause shifted them into commercial, the camera lights dimming.

"No promises," Georgie found herself saying.

"Come and visit us again soon, okay?"

"The very next time I come to Los Angeles," Georgie promised, knowing there wouldn't be another reason to come back to California until the Breeders' Cup landed at Santa Anita Park. The horses Georgie rode simply didn't go west, not when she primarily rode for Sweet Bells' co-owner, Tupelo Stud.

Georgie collected her things in the green room and was escorted down the elevator to the open lobby doors. Los Angeles waited for her outside, bathed in saltwater air and bright light. Lynsey Armstrong stood next to the sleek black curves of a limo waiting by the curb, her dyed blond hair tumbling around her shoulders in thick, ironed curls. She was all fashion and strings of pearls, oversized sunglasses perched on her pointy nose.

"You were so amazing!" Lynsey cried at the sight of Georgie, who cuddled her bag to her chest and walked into Lynsey's enthusiastic hug. Layers of tension slipped off of Georgie as she let Lynsey bounce against her, babbling nonstop about getting the backstage tour and sitting front and center during the show.

"Even Harris smiled during your interview," Lynsey gushed. "I have photographic evidence I will share with you later, because I know you won't believe me."

Georgie hiked her bag onto her shoulder. "Maybe I don't want to see. I'm used to his scowl. Knowing there's a smile under there might wreck my focus while he's watching me on the track."

Lynsey scoffed and pushed an errant strand of gleaming gold hair back into place, the compass tattoo on her wrist flashing deep and dark. "What doesn't kill you makes you stronger."

"So they say," Georgie said, squinting into the sun as she looked up at her best friend. Lynsey had five inches on her in bare feet, making her positively normal next to Georgie's munchkin height.

"Prepare yourself," Lynsey whispered, putting her hand on the limo's door handle. "Everyone has been celebrating."

Georgie shrugged, used to the Armstrong family's love of all things shiny and bubbly. "Let's do it."

Climbing into the limo, the champagne bucket immediately

caught her attention. A sweating bottle sat in the ice, two empty bottles discarded on the bar. A slender flute of bubbling amber flashed in Samuel Armstrong's fingers as he helped Georgie and Lynsey into the empty bench seat.

"Hello ladies," he smiled gentlemanly at each—one his granddaughter and one his prizewinning jockey. His large, warm hand clasped Georgie's fingers until she settled on the leather seat.

Through the dark interior, Georgie could make out the faces of Lynsey's father, Oliver, and his new wife, Mabel. Mabel smiled winningly, waving at her with charm bracelet tinkling and blown out brown hair bouncing. Oliver, always the handsome, be-suited president of Tupelo Stud, barely afforded her a moment of acknowledgment in favor of his phone. That was fine by Georgie, who could not count all the reasons why she did not want to converse with Oliver. Her eyes fell on the corner across from her, where Harrison, Lynsey's older brother, whispered against his newest girlfriend's neck.

Georgie couldn't remember her name, and figured she didn't need to know. Diamonds sparkled on the girl's ears, and her lipstick stained the champagne glass perched between her thumb and forefinger. Her nails were painted gray. In the dim lights of the limo, Georgie could only make out the straight line of Harris' jaw and his dark hair. He stroked one farm-tanned hand through the girl's bright hair, and the other plucked at the edges of his nearly empty glass.

The girl put her gray-tipped fingers on Harrison's knee and laughed softly, her eyes darting over to where Georgie sat as the limo cruised seamlessly away from the curb and entered Los Angeles traffic.

"Here's welcoming the girl of the hour," Samuel announced, raising his glass and leaning toward the ice bucket in one fluid movement, lifting the bottle by the neck. "I call a toast. Lynsey, fetch two glasses."

Tupelo Stud, Georgie thought wryly. *Proudly providing alcohol for minors since our founding in 1943.*

"Grandpa," Lynsey started, receiving a look from the old man.

"Don't start, Lyn," Samuel told her, his voice leveling out, revealing the do-as-I-command racehorse owner. "No one in this car gives a good goddamn about your age. Get the glasses."

"Yes, sir," Lynsey said, picking up the glasses and holding them out for him to fill. The champagne fizzed up to the rims as Georgie took hers from Lynsey's slender fingers, sniffing the sweet liquid that popped and tickled her nose.

"I am sure this will be the first of many toasts celebrating Georgiana and Sweet Bells," Samuel said, lifting his champagne and showing off his white teeth, his blue eyes bright behind his delicate glasses. "Thanks to Georgie, Sweet Bells will be up for Horse of the Year come January. To Georgie."

Mabel's enthusiastic clapping filled the limo, while Oliver and Samuel took healthy swigs. Lynsey and Georgie traded a look over their champagne as they took dry mouthfuls, swallowing down the bubbles. Harris drank, dark eyes on Georgie as the Gray Girl whispered against his shoulder.

"It's all Bell," Georgie said, clearing the champagne from her throat.

"That's generous of you." Samuel leaned back in his seat. He was a tall man, broad in the shoulders and lean everywhere else, honed from years on horseback. His hair was a shock of white, and had been since Georgie was a child, when her family's Red Gate Farm was Tupelo Stud's equal.

"Maybe it's all luck," Harris offered from across the limo, drawing glances. Lynsey gave him a pointed stare, because surely now wasn't the time to rain on the parade. Gray Girl settled into her seat next to him, looking self-satisfied. "Our filly is ridden by the girl on the farm next door. Where would we be if not for Red Gate?"

Georgie sat perfectly still, smoothing her hand over the skirt of her dress before she looked up at Harris. He smiled at her and winked.

He knew exactly what he was doing, pushing all of her buttons.

"Then I would count your blessings I'm your girl next door," she replied. Lynsey smiled into her champagne. "Besides which, she's not all your filly. You always seem to need reminding."

"Semantics," Harris said, unruffled. Samuel shot Harris a warning glance across his champagne, and just like that the mood turned sour. Mabel glanced between them anxiously, earrings dangling. Oliver kept his attention on his phone, tuning them out while letting them have at it.

"Hardly," Georgie bit, settling when Lynsey pressed her shoulder against hers. She let go of the tension that was building in her chest, letting out a slow breath. "The second Red Gate sells its half-interest in her, that's when you can talk about semantics. Until then, you know why I'm here."

"Obviously," Harris said, turning his attention from her, finished. The Gray Girl stroked her fingers down his arm.

Georgie tightened her grip on the champagne and leaned back

into her seat. Lynsey tossed her hair over her shoulder and gave her a sympathetic look, her hair shading her face from the rest of her inscrutable family. Georgie lifted a shoulder halfheartedly, because what could she expect? That was Harris for you, always there to show everyone their place. She took another sip of the champagne. Larger this time. The bubbles raced down her throat and popped.

Harris Armstrong hadn't talked to Georgie with anything more than barely tolerated condescension for over two years. Georgie told herself all the time that she shouldn't be surprised, but somehow it still felt jarring, like a piece of her life had come loose and she couldn't fit it back into place. Family history dictated that this wasn't particularly surprising. When the Armstrongs and the Quinns trail-blazed into Ocala, Florida with their horses and their money, they publicly sparred when they weren't quietly colluding, creating a cloud of gossip so thick it was sometimes hard to distinguish fact from fiction.

Harris and Georgie—fact or fiction? With the whispered rumors running rampant, sometimes Georgie didn't even know anymore.

Georgiana Quinn, Georgie had overheard in the paddock before riding her first race, nearly turning to answer before she realized. *Didn't her mother and Oliver Armstrong have a thing?*

Before Lilliana, the poor dear.

She'd walked up to her mount in a hurry after that and rode like a wild thing to the finish. She'd felt frenzied since, a ball of utter resolve working to erase the comments and stares, trying to replace them with something so huge she wouldn't have to listen to the whispers threading from person to person, all the way back to her. Something like the Breeders' Cup Classic. Nothing could be bigger. Now it was talk of Eclipse Awards instead of shifting glances.

The Gray Girl looked her way again, leaning toward Harris to murmur something between her painted lips. His jaw tightened, dark eyes flashing, but he laughed softly under his breath nonetheless.

Georgie watched them, unabashed.

Maybe whispers never ended.

Chapter Two

THREE DAYS AFTER landing back in Florida, Georgie stood by Tupelo's training track, waiting on her ride.

"There's no rest for the wicked," Reece Holloway said in his famously English accent.

"I thought Bell was going to rest on her laurels for a couple of months," Georgie said, pushing a wireless radio into the waistband of her jeans.

Reece afforded her a sideways look from his tablet while they waited for Sweet Bells to be brought out of the training barn. As the head trainer for Tupelo, he was always synonymous with the work that clung to him. Cell phone at his hip, tablet computer always running, his fingers always tapping out work times and notes only he understood. Georgie felt dizzy just looking at him.

"This, sweet girl, *is* rest."

"Could've fooled me." Georgie turned her attention to the training track as a monster-sized gray colt thundered past, black-to-silver mane and tail whipping behind him. The colt leapt and bucked, yanking his head down and opening his mouth against the bit. Luna, his regular exercise rider, yelled at the horse to change leads and responded with a sarcastic *gracias* when the colt complied.

Further down the rail, Georgie caught sight of Harris. His arms were folded across his chest, dark hair catching the morning light and momentarily glinting bronze. Jeans slung low on his hips like his belt needed tightening, and a white T-shirt stretched over his shoulders. He looked rumpled, like he was dressed in the clothes he'd found on the floor when he woke up. To Georgie, it was almost a reassuring image. Like Harris was still, somehow, *Harris*.

Still. He looked like an irritated Greek god sent to survey Earth's creatures, and he wasn't impressed. As the colt galloped by, his eyes trailed after him. A foot down the rail, the Gray Girl mimicked his posture, spine straight as a post.

"Looks like Harris' toy is coming along," Georgie observed, pulling her attention away.

"He's calling him Roman the Great." Reece didn't bother to look up from the tablet. He knew the colt better than anyone, had gone to the Keeneland sale in Kentucky last year with Harris specifically to pick out the colt out of hundreds of shiny yearlings. It was the deal Harris had made with Oliver and Samuel—pick out a young racing prospect and make something of it instead of going to college. It was the first baby step up Tupelo's ladder of command.

The first test.

Roman the Great. It felt right, exactly the assuming name Harris would call something of his own. The colt slowed smoothly and lowered his head into the weight of the reins.

Reece stopped tapping on the tablet, looking up as another

fleet of horses arrived from the barns. Most had riders already up, but Sweet Bells did not. Miguel, her groom, held her to a raucous jig. Blue bandages covered all four of her white legs, pale hooves raised high with each step. Bell lifted her head up, her ears flicking forward, and her red-rimmed nostrils blew at the smells of the training track. Georgie's heart did a small stutter step at the sight of her.

"She's ready to tear a hole in the wind," Miguel told her through a toothy smile. "Prepare yourself, girl."

"Definitely no rest for the wicked," Georgie laughed, putting a hand on the filly's withers and letting Reece lift her effortlessly into the exercise saddle. The filly immediately bounded forward, not waiting for Georgie to gather the reins.

"Jog her twice around." Reece's voice came through Georgie's head set, tinny and clear in her ear after she made it to the track with the others. "She's still technically resting."

"Yes, sir." Georgie ran a hand down Bell's black mane and lifted herself up to balance over the filly's withers. Bell huffed and settled into a ground-eating trot, energy coiling like a spring into the reins. Miguel was right. If the wind could be torn apart, Bell was eager to try.

"Okay, baby doll," Georgie said to the filly, who flicked her ears back to listen. "No shenanigans today."

Bell snorted and eyed a horse that galloped past on her inside. *Jog, girl, jog,* Georgie thought, but Bell exploded into a perfect, high-action canter instead.

Georgie twitched her fingers on the reins, leaning her weight back. The filly lifted her head and dropped back into a jog, chewing on the bit so a wash of white froth dripped from her lips and splattered down her chest. When they circled into the backstretch, Georgie caught sight of Roman the Great trotting out ahead of them, head low and stride even. Luna, his rider, cast a quick glance over her shoulder and nodded.

"Outside," Georgie called, and let Bell out a bit more. The filly came even with the colt, who quickened his tempo automatically, eager to stay in front. It was a mark of a good racehorse, those that wanted to run and stay ahead of the competition. Bell flattened her ears and shook her head, aggravated at Georgie's firm hold.

"Sorry," Luna grunted, fighting the colt into a slower pace. "This one has very firm priorities."

"Wouldn't have it any other way," Georgie said, giving the filly rein. Bell jumped forward for two beats, putting the colt well behind her and then settling back into a trot. Georgie threw a look over her shoulder and caught Luna's wave.

"Nothing to it, huh girl?" Georgie said to the filly, smacking Bell's shoulder and bringing her to a walk, finally letting herself rest in the saddle.

Bell arched her neck, her mane and tail ruffling in the light breeze. Further up the track, Georgie caught sight of the gray next to the outside rail. Roman the Great walked calmly, and Harris matched pace along the opposite side of the rail, talking with Luna. After a moment, Luna picked up the reins and rode off. Harris watched her go, eyes on the gray, until he looked to Bell.

A wave of self-consciousness rolled over Georgie, along with that shiver down her spine that never quite made sense. Bell was finally relaxed, playing with the bit instead of trying to strangle it, and had her head dipped low. She wasn't going to ruin that because Harris Armstrong simply looked at her.

Gray Girl murmured something Georgie had no hope of hearing, eyes cutting quick to Bell and down to her half-moon nails. Harris shifted, gave the Gray Girl a look Georgie knew so well—annoyance shot through with disdain, like he didn't want to be bothered anymore.

This had to be the beginning of the end. She'd seen enough of Harris' breakups to notice the signs.

"Felicity," Harris said, loud enough to be heard, "is there ever a moment where you really, truly know what you're talking about?"

The Gray Girl—Felicity—turned an impressive shade of scarlet, whirling on him with an indignant squeak. Georgie sighed and settled into the saddle, resigned to passing the escalating argument on the way off the track.

On her approach, Bell rose into an agitated trot. Georgie collected the reins, brought her back down to a mincing walk.

"Harris," she said, casual as she could with Bell's trembling body jigging underneath her. "How about you take the inevitable breakup elsewhere? We're all bored with the scenery at this point."

The corner of Harris' mouth turned up in amusement. Felicity's jaw dropped.

Georgie rolled her eyes and pointed Bell toward the stables, done with the show. The filly's hooves clattered over the gravel on the way to the training complex, a grouping of three barns interspersed with round pens and green yards overshadowed by live oaks. Hotwalkers led cooling horses in circles around the barns. Their sleek coats shined in the fall light, and steam rose in misty tendrils off their backs.

Tupelo stretched across the Ocala hills, yawning across a thousand neatly manicured acres. The breeding operation sat separate from the training end, green pasture and black fences spacing out clusters of barns that held hundreds of mares, a star-studded roster of stallions, and thundering herds of unruly weanlings and yearlings.

The farm's colors—a deep blue and pale, summery yellow—could be seen everywhere, from buckets to heavy machinery. The Equi-Cisers spun in yellow circles. The farm-owned pick-up trucks' blue paint never saw dust. Horses walked under blue coolers with yellow piping. It was all so detailed, so monogrammed and spotless. Georgie felt a little dirty looking at it, like it was all too pristine for her presence.

Which was ridiculous. She'd only been coming to Tupelo since forever ago.

Georgie halted Bell in front of the first barn, ready to hand her off to Miguel so they could join the line of walking horses.

"Did she tear a hole in the wind?" Miguel asked, taking the filly by the bridle. Bell huffed happily at him, lifting her head to press her muzzle against his cheek.

"Of course," Georgie said, scrubbing Bell on the forehead and mussing her properly combed forelock. "Was there ever any doubt?"

Directly across the road, Red Gate stretched out all gold-tipped green in front of Georgie. It faced Tupelo, white fences against black. Live oaks lined the lanes, dripping with silver-gray Spanish moss. They grazed over Georgie's head as she walked. Every so often the early morning silence would be broken by the hoarse whinny of one of the mares screaming for breakfast.

In the middle of the property sat Ennismore, the great brood-mare barn, cross-shaped like the end of a treasure map. Its sisters, Sunlee and Tall Trees, sat further off, empty and showing their age. All three were white, trimmed in red. On Ennismore, paint flaked in spots, peeling up to show the weathered boards underneath. Blown dandelions left their empty stalks around the open doorway. A rusted weather vane creaked in the center of the sloping roof.

Gravel roads spiked away from Ennismore like spokes off a wheel. One road headed to the empty stud barn with the dust-encrusted chandelier still hanging from the ceiling. Another road wound off to the weanling and yearling barns, two long stables set as far from the broodmares as they could manage and still be on the property. The third went straight to the back of Red Gate, winding up to the old house that sat on the land when it was cotton fields.

Georgie stopped within Ennismore's open side door, peering into the dim light. Lucas and Santino, Red Gate's duo of brood-mare grooms, were already at the feed cart situated in the center of the aisle. Despite the majority of the work falling on their shoulders, the concrete aisle was swept clean and Red Gate's mares dug into breakfast right on time.

"There she is!" Santino called from the furthest stall, dumping the grain into a grateful mare's bucket. "Miss Outstanding Jockey!"

"Hardly," Georgie laughed, stopping to hug Santino and wave to Lucas, his quieter cousin, who busily measured out the right feed for the last mare in the row. "I'm still an apprentice."

"Oh, excuse me," Santino chuckled, putting his empty feed bins back in the cart. "Miss Outstanding Apprentice Jockey."

Georgie blushed, and he grinned. "You're too modest for this business, girl."

"It's been said," Georgie shrugged. "Dad around?"

Santino nodded. "The office."

The farm office smelled like leather and horses, a light coat of dirt covering the items that weren't well used. Old win photos coated the walls, their images shifting from sepia to fading color, frames bumping into each other. Behind the ancient desk, a giant oil painting of the farm's foundation sire, Bird Book, hung in all its dusty glory.

Georgie took in all seventy years of Red Gate's history, and then let her eyes drop to her father, who was hunched in front of a laptop, steaming mug of coffee sitting by his good hand, the one that didn't shake so much. His shirt was wrinkled, dark hair askew. The small desk plaque that proclaimed him *Thomas Quinn, President* had been pushed so far to the edge of the desk by the paperwork that it threatened to fall off.

"You look like you're burning it at both ends," she said into the room. He looked up at her and cracked a smile.

"You and me both, sugar," he said in his smooth, Southern accent. She slipped in, pressing herself up against his shoulder as he gave her a squeeze. He smelled like he usually did—cologne, coffee, and the warm bite of whiskey.

"Getting good work done?" she asked, pressing her cheek against his hair. He sighed, taking his glasses off and rubbing his eyes.

"Not nearly enough," Tom said, then beamed a smile up at her. He rifled through a stack of the farm's unopened mail, pulling out a *Sports Illustrated* with the Classic on the cover, the image a close-cropped photo of Sweet Bells crossing the finish line with her mane fanning against Georgie's face. "You get one more cover this week and you'll be even with Secretariat."

Georgie snorted. "Yeah, give it a few more weeks and all of this attention will die down."

"Can't say it's a bad thing." Tom studied the magazine, thumbing it open to her story. "Imagine if we'd had this happen while we still had the stallions."

Georgie bit the inside of her cheek and let her father run through the what-ifs. He liked to imagine all the wonderful opportunities that could have happened instead of face the farm's increasingly empty bank account. It was like plugging your ears and singing while the world ended.

She lifted the magazine out of his hands, and made her way back to the door. "I'll take this up to Mom."

Her dad nodded, picking up his coffee mug, still lost in thought as Georgie trudged up the road to the plantation mansion, its heavy white columns dingy with age. Live oaks nestled next to it, their tiny, dark green leaves trembling in the breeze. Weeds poked up through the crumbling front steps. No one had fixed it yet, so caution tape had lined off the entire grand front porch for over a year.

Georgie jumped up the back stairs to the kitchen in the rear of the house. She paused at the screen door, looking out over the farm's abandoned training complex, saplings rising proudly from the old training track.

Active racehorses hadn't set foot on Red Gate's property since Sweet Bells' dam took the short journey across the road to Tupelo. She had been their last winner, a brilliant bay flash under red and blue checkered silks. That was so long ago Georgie had to strain to remember it, had to push herself to dredge up memories of what it felt like to see a Red Gate horse in the winner's circle.

It seemed so impossible now.

Georgie shook the fatalistic thought off her shoulders, trying to remind herself that Sweet Bells *was* a Red Gate horse, however draped in Tupelo colors.

Her mother looked up from the dining room table when Georgie pushed through the kitchen's screen door. Files and papers crowded the table, pedigrees and breeding analysis sheets written in her mother's looping longhand. A laptop glowed on top of it, her mother's bloodstock agency logo floating across the black surface. They hadn't eaten a meal on that table for two years, not since her mother started using it as an office.

Claire Quinn knew Thoroughbreds. As an industry insider she kept her finger to the pulse of the market. She stalked the auctions for days on end, saw lines and angles in gangly yearlings when other people were overwhelmed by flash and potential. Claire bought or sold on the slope of a young horse's shoulder, a slanting cannon bone, the ease by which a horse was put together to form the whole.

"Morning," Georgie pronounced, heading to the coffee pot, still half-full. She rinsed out a mug and poured a cup.

"Don't I know it," her mother said, putting down her pen and standing up, stretching her back and then carding her fingers into flaming red hair that had gone too long without a cut.

"How's Tupelo?"

Georgie paused, blowing on the top of the coffee and watching the ripples.

"Good," she said, swallowing a mouthful of coffee. *Vibrant.*

"Shouldn't I be driving you to school about now?" Claire looked at Georgie critically over her mug. "You're missing a book bag, and maybe you could ditch the work clothes. Something with fewer smears of horse slobber, I think."

"I'm going." Georgie gulped down another swallow of coffee, putting the mug in the sink and jogging up the stairs. The house creaked with each rough step, the door to her bedroom squeaking on its hinges when Georgie pushed it open. She crossed the weathered floorboards to her overflowing dresser, pulling out fresh clothes. As she changed, her gaze fell to her book bag, kick-starting the sudden memory of a test.

Today.

With a groaning curse, Georgie rushed to change, grabbed her bag and thundered down the stairs.

The wall clock seemed stuck. The minute hand trembled on the ten, taking forever to make up its mind about moving time forward. Georgie eyed it with increasing impatience, finding it hard to draw her attention back down to the essay in front of her. She rubbed the blue book's corner between her fingers until it tore, rolled the pencil eraser back and forth across its flimsy paper, and finally dug her short fingernails into the palm of her hand in efforts to remember something significant about the Enlightenment so she could turn in her test with something more than a deepening sense of foreboding.

She knew she'd forgotten something while she was in California. The something in question was a World History midterm chock-full of essays that wouldn't even allow her the promise of guessing her way to the right answers. No, Georgie was instead faced with blank pages and a worryingly blunt pencil. The urge to sharpen it skittered across her thoughts, but as she looked at the bowed heads of her classmates Georgie nixed that idea and tried to think.

Her phone buzzed, a muted vibration in her bag. She glanced down at it, wincing when it hummed again and again. Mrs. Blevins looked up like a hawk, zeroing in on Georgie with the increasing impatience of an overwrought babysitter. There was nothing to do except let it vibrate, so Georgie kicked her book bag underneath her desk and ducked her head, wishing her hair was longer so it could at least cover up her distress.

But no, she'd had to chop it all off after she started race riding. On the whole, it wasn't a decision she regretted. Now? Now she just wanted to hide, and when the bell rang she hastily slapped her booklet closed and stood so fast her chair shrieked.

Half the class looked up, staring at her with wide, befuddled eyes. Georgie swallowed, attempted a smile, and dragged her bag out from under the desk as the rest of her classmates unfolded slowly out of their chairs, as if the test had drugged them or they didn't want to be free quite yet. There were bonus questions to answer, opportunities for extra credit. Georgie saw nothing of that. She just wanted out of Mrs. Blevins' World History class.

She dropped the booklet down on Mrs. Blevins' desk. Her teacher pulled the wire-rim glasses down from her nose and folded them carefully in front of her, looking up at Georgie with a squint.

"I saw you on that comedian's show," she said, waving her hand like she could conjure the name from thin air. She shook her head, giving up. "They showed the race. That's a talented horse you have."

Georgie smiled, the kind that come along despite yourself. It was only after her lips curled up that she put a stop to it, because Mrs. Blevins wasn't finished.

"Hope you remembered to study," Mrs. Blevins said with a beatific smile, tapping the growing stack of blue books. Students were clustered around Georgie, turning in tests, jostling her to get out of the room while her ears burned.

"Don't I always?" she asked, backing toward the door. Mrs. Blevins raised an eyebrow, because she knew. Of course, she knew.

Before Georgie could be accosted by more of Mrs. Blevins' doubtful face, she spun into the hallway and joined the flow of students on their way out of Belleview High School. Her heart thumped into a normal pattern that didn't have her on edge. The test was a wash, but that was easily pushed to the side now that she was free to dig into her bag for her phone. The hallways were rivers, kids washing up against lockers and pouring down stairs. Georgie huddled against her locker, spun in the combination, and ducked behind the open door to check her phone in relative peace.

A flurry of texts greeted her, mostly from Angel, her agent. A former jockey, Angel knew everyone in the business, right down to their shoe size. He left Georgie typo-ridden, expletive-laced texts every few hours with new races for her to ride, filling her race cards with good horses that weren't owned by Tupelo. Sweet Bells might have gotten her on national television, but she was really the cherry on top of a career painstakingly sculpted by Angel.

Names of horses and trainers glowed up from her phone, lists of races that they were running in over the next month providing her enough *real* homework to get started on. Forget Mrs. Blevins' World History. Georgie had horses to study.

She scrolled through the names, taking quick note of the new trainers Angel had sweet-talked into giving her a ride, probably throwing her magazine covers and Breeders' Cup win in their face until saying no didn't make sense anymore. That was Angel for you. No wasn't an answer he accepted easily.

Then she hit the last message.

Castellano Senior has a maiden colt for you in Tampa. Name of Little War.

So he'd done it. Georgie laughed to herself, looking up at the photos she'd carefully taped to the inside of the locker at the beginning of the year to keep herself sane. Smiling images of Lynsey and Nick Castellano at his father's training farm outside of Ocala. All of them—Harris included—sitting on the fence at Tupelo with a herd of curious weanlings at their backs.

Once upon a time, Georgie thought. She brought up Nick's number up on her phone and hit send.

"Yes!" she shouted into the phone as soon as he answered with a chipper, I've-been-awake-too-long greeting. Several people gave Georgie the side-eye on their way down the hall.

"I'm assuming you heard the news?" Nick asked. "My dad, of the No Apprentices frame of thought, finally said yes to you."

"How did you get him to agree?"

"Considerable, lengthy nagging," Nick told her. "You would be so proud of me."

"I am." Georgie grinned again, hardly believing it. "This was the dream, you know? You train them, I ride them. How often did we talk about this?"

"Every day during lunch for eight years," Nick said, chuckling. "Harris insisted he'd get you on a horse first, but it looks like I'm going to win that argument."

Georgie wrinkled her nose as Roman the Great galloped through her thoughts, his white-tipped tail trailing like a wisp behind him. Harris and Nick weren't far off from each having a runner soon, in their own way. They'd talked about it so much before, clamoring over each other with their imagined accomplishments. It was always Nick and Harris, the horses they'd train, the horses they'd race against each other. And always Georgie would ride for them.

She remembered laughing at their proposals, rolling her eyes, always saying *yes, of course, ask and I'll be yours.*

It was ridiculous then, but now it was happening. A joke was coming true.

Exactly what they'd planned, only with a twist.

"I'll be there," Georgie assured him, pushing Harris out of the picture, where he'd resided of his own free will for quite some time. "Bells will be firmly attached."

"Good," Nick answered, voice scratchy over the phone, like he was talking over a great distance. "I wouldn't want you there without your bells."

"So I can declare Nick the winner, is what you're saying."

Lynsey pushed her shoulder into the heavy double doors, shoving herself into the brilliant Florida sun with Georgie at her heels. The student parking lot buzzed like a hive. Georgie envied their celebration, since she only had a few hours before heading to night school to clear up the credits she missed in the morning when horses took center stage.

"Suppose so," Georgie said, stifling a yawn as she followed Lynsey into the sea of ancient, beaten-up hand-me-down cars that revved their engines like an exclamatory cheer to another day done. Lynsey's pristine Audi sitting delicately in the cluster of rust buckets looked out of place. She stopped short as a rumbling truck careened past, coming to a screeching halt at the line of cars that collected at the stop sign at the mouth of the lot.

"Harris and Nick haven't spoken since they were juniors, though," Georgie added, giving the truck a wide berth. "I can't see it mattering."

Lynsey threw Georgie a look over the roof of the Audi, opening the door and throwing her bag into the backseat.

"It's like you don't know my brother at all," she said. "He'll notice, he'll say something, and that something will be offensive. I guarantee it."

"You're right," Georgie sighed, opening the car door and letting the thick November heat escape before she climbed inside. "He started breakup procedures with Felicity this morning, so he can't be in a good mood."

Georgie settled into the passenger seat, dropping the heavy book bag between her feet. It toppled onto her foot like a club, reminding her of how behind she'd fallen. Two months into senior year, and she was already playing catch up.

"First," Lynsey said, dropping into the driver's seat and holding up a finger in Georgie's face. "Harris doesn't respond to normal human emotions like heartbreak anymore. Second, you are the flame, he is the moth. Only he seems to like catching fire. It fuels his inner rage."

Georgie stared at her and took a deep breath. "Was Harris swapped at birth?"

"Nope," Lynsey said. "Totally related."

Lynsey's eyes trailed down to the inside of her wrist, where the compass tattoo completed a circle on her pale skin. The dark ink spiked out of a filigreed, eight-point starburst. A delicate N sat in the hollow of tendons defined by Lynsey's grip on the steering wheel, pointed toward her fingers. Georgie had gone to the tattoo parlor with Lynsey two years ago, holding her free hand while the ink buzzed into her skin.

"The kicker is sometimes I get where he's coming from," Lynsey said, pulling her eyes off the tattoo. "It wasn't easy after Mom."

No, Georgie thought, *it wouldn't be*. Lilliana Armstrong's absence was a deep, dark gulf. Visible, remembered. Lilliana was the yardstick by which Lynsey evaluated herself and never said a word about how she thought she measured up.

"But," Lynsey continued abruptly, "I think it's always been apparent I'm the most mentally robust Armstrong."

Georgie made a face.

"Not funny, Lyn."

"What?" Lynsey twisted the key in the ignition, looking ahead at the wall of cars blocking them in. "I'm not allowed a little dark humor?"

Before Georgie could answer, Lynsey laid on the horn in a warning blast and wedged the Audi's nose between cars, forcing herself into the line while waving off the cacophony of shouted curses.

"Only because it's you," Georgie told her, and Lynsey nodded sharply.

"Damn straight."

The honking and yelling didn't let up as Lynsey resolutely kept to her path, turning on the car's stereo system and letting the thumping bass drown out the outrage as she tapped her fingers against the steering wheel. Georgie sank into her seat and closed her eyes, let the music wash over her and drum along her skin. It wasn't long until she was out cold, sinking into the exhausted, restless sleep of someone who knew they had better things to do. Of someone who wanted to be awake for fear of what they'd find in the dark.

She felt heavy, the memory of slippery leather sofa cushions at her back and her heart in her throat dragging her down. The columns of Tupelo's main house shifted out of her conscious, dim gray in the night. Harris' face was all panic, like he couldn't believe what he was seeing even though he already did, was trying his hardest to stop it. Water trickled over the side of the tub, sloshing onto the tile and fanning toward the door in a rush. Georgie with the phone in her hand, her fingers cold, clumsy on the keypad. The spinning lights flashed one after the other repetitively, inevitably, so fast Georgie thought she would be sick.

Red. Blue. Red. Blue.

No.

Weightlessness lifted through her chest, like a soft intake of breath. Her eyes popped open, revealing fence lines streaming along in an unbroken blur.

"Hey," Lynsey said, looking over at her softly. The car rose up one gentle hill, speeding by the Ocala farmland on their way home.

The school was long ago, like a distant world Georgie had launched off of and couldn't remember anymore. "You're exhausted. Go back to sleep if you want."

Georgie shook her head mutely, pushing herself up and rolling down the window, letting the warm autumn breeze hit her face, keep her from falling back into that place she couldn't tell Lynsey about. She would sound like a lunatic, and Lynsey seemed so far beyond that.

Better than all of them combined.

So Georgie turned her face into the Florida wind and breathed deep.

December

Chapter Three

IN THE WOMEN'S changing room, Georgie chewed relentlessly on a piece of gum and bounced on the tips of her toes. Her lightweight jockey boots squeaked on the linoleum, a sound she knew must irritate the room's only other inhabitant, Silvia Zambrana, who was deep in warrior pose on a yoga mat with pink and white flower designs, which was not exactly what Georgie would have expected from the weathered local jockey.

On the opposite side of the wall, pool balls clacked together in the common room, the sound echoing through the thin wall. Georgie didn't have time to join in the game, so she kept to the changing room. Lockers, benches, and personal clutter surrounded them as she kept bouncing and Silvia kept finding her breath.

Georgie tucked her white sleeveless turtleneck into her equally white riding pants and looked down at the solid yellow silks lying in a crumpled ball on the bench. Outside, her valet had already gone to help tack up Little War. Nick was out there assisting his father, Senior, with last-minute adjustments to the girths. He'd straighten and tighten, stretching out the colt's legs to make sure he was comfortable. The colt would be led in a fastidious circle under the bright Florida sun, his chestnut coat glinting.

Georgie blew out a breath. Zipping on her safety vest, she shrugged into the silks, tucking them into her pants and rolling up the sleeves. Thick rubber bands kept the flapping cuffs in place around her wrists. Then she dug her helmet out of her bag, pushing the yellow slip cover over the utilitarian plastic.

Behind her, Silvia stopped her meditation and began her own preparation in her typical silence, pulling her sleek black hair into a low ponytail at the base of her neck.

Then there was a knock at the door. Silvia opened it, coolly observing the track official in his regulation polo shirt and mustached smile.

"Ready, girls?"

Silvia pushed her helmet on, flicked her riding crop up along the back of one arm, and strolled out without acknowledgment. Georgie afforded him a small smile and slipped out behind her, joining the stream of pixie-sized men walking down to the paddock in their colorful racing silks. They looked like walking bits of wrapping paper, bright reds and neon purples, icons and images proudly sewn across their backs. Georgie fastened her helmet as she walked, falling into step next to Dean Hayes, who took one look at her out of the corner of his eye and smashed his shoulder against hers.

"For the love of Christ, Dean," she growled, shoving him back as he laughed, bouncing away like it was nothing. Dean Hayes had left his apprentice jockey license behind two months back, riding the big names as a journeyman—a professional, full-time jockey—without a hitch yet. It was one more thing to add to his cocksure attitude—that he'd taken to journeyman status like a fish to water when so many other jockeys found that the apprenticeship's weight advantage had been greater than their raw talent. They worked themselves sick to be a journeyman, only to get there and fall face first.

Dean had the talent, was so chock-full of it he pushed his chances to the edge, taking opportunities no one else in their right mind would ever attempt. Georgie clenched her teeth whenever she was on the track with him. One day, his recklessness was going to wreck that wide smile of his, and Georgie wanted no part of it.

"Just giving you a good preview of what this race will be like," he said, waggling his eyebrows at her.

"Oh, like all the others then?" Georgie shot back. "When was the last time you rode a clean race?"

"Always, baby," he said, dancing out of her reach. He jogged a few steps forward and spun, walking backward with that same aggravating grin on his face. "It's why my name's up there with yours for that Eclipse Award."

The Eclipse Award for best apprentice jockey could also be known as the award given to the jockey with the largest earnings next to their name. Talent and professionalism were assumed, not an objective requirement. Dean had started riding before her, and burned hot at each meet. But Georgie had Sweet Bells, and that was more than enough to turn the tables.

"Think you still have a shot at that, do you?" Georgie asked, unable to stop herself. Dean sucked in his cheeks, his narrow nose flaring with a deep breath.

"Stick around for the last race," he told her. "I'm on that gray colt of your boy's. He's a monster, that one. Wonder why the *face of racing* didn't get the ride."

Georgie rolled her eyes, because of course Harris would put Dean on Roman the Great. "Haven't the faintest. It may be that assholes are magnetically attracted to each other."

Dean pulled a sour face, although nothing could ever stop his mouth. "Why you gotta be like that? Aren't we destined to be together? All Romeo-and-Juliet-like?"

"Of course we are," Georgie replied dryly. "We are obviously soul mates and are meant for each other because somehow I manage to not bind and gag you in the common room every day we are within shouting distance."

"Damn," Dean whistled. "Kinky."

Georgie just shook her head and left him at the paddock gate on her way up to Little War, the chestnut doing a prancing walk as his onlookers beamed.

Nick stood with his father, his bright brown eyes firmly on the colt and his sun-bleached black hair tousled by the Florida breeze. He was dressed up for the race—shiny leather shoes and a tie that featured little silver horseshoes on a sea of yellow. Next to him, Lynsey stood in a shimmering blue sun dress, all ruffles down to her knees. Her high heels gave her a boost so she stood at Nick's height, but no more, her blond ringlets tumbling around her shoulders.

Even from here, Georgie could catch snippets of Lynsey's rapid chatter. Her hands fluttered through so many animated gesticulations that she nearly caught Nick in the face.

"There you are," Nick said as soon as he caught sight of Georgie, throwing an arm around her shoulders and giving her a little shake so she'd fall into him. She let herself fall. It was easy to let things slow down around Nick, who was all lackadaisical smiles.

His persistent laid-back attitude was a blessing before a race, which was usually a time of hyper horses falling apart around shredded nerves. It was easy to grab onto Nick and surf into calmer waters.

Georgie closed her eyes and let the autumn breeze rush over them. It smelled like sea salt and thunderstorms. Rain was coming, announcing itself with towering clouds on the horizon. But that was far off. It didn't concern the race, and it didn't concern Georgie.

"How's training treating you?" She pushed back from Nick, nudging his arm with her crop hand. "You wouldn't shut up about it at school, and here you are, four months in. Is it everything you dreamed it would be?"

Nick rocked onto his toes, widened his eyes for effect. "I am living the dream, Georgie. I even got you riding. What more can a guy ask for?"

"A little fashion sense, maybe?" Lynsey plucked at his tie, showing him the horseshoes. "What is this? Who did this to you? It's okay. You can tell me."

He made a fake grab for her, and Lynsey expertly darted away with a laugh. It was so practiced Georgie had to smile.

Behind them, Little War shook out his thick red mane and bowed his head into his groom's hold. The colt towered on lithe legs, muscles bunching under his coppery coat and belly tucked neatly into his hindquarters. He looked like he could out-leap a deer, and Georgie felt a little tremor of excitement race up her spine at the thought of finding out.

"Ready?" Senior asked, patting Georgie between her shoulder blades. He looked down at her with that peculiar way adults had, as though he was astonished they were here together. A year ago,

Georgie was just the girl with aspirations bordering on obsessions that he nodded at, humored her with a smile. Now here they were, dreams realized.

"Ready." Georgie shot a shivering smile at Nick on her way toward Little War. The paddock judge called for the horses to assemble into an orderly line, the nine horses in the field beginning to move in a loop around the perimeter of the paddock.

"Remember," Senior said as they walked along Little War, who danced and tossed his head. "He's hotheaded, and he'll try to go for the lead. This is seven furlongs, so let him. We don't have enough time in the race to get stuck in an argument."

"To the lead we go," Georgie said, gathering the reins with one hand at the base of the colt's neck as she walked. With one bounce, she was airborne, throwing a leg over the colt's back. She slipped into her smooth racing saddle, barely a scrap of leather on Little War's back. At the added weight, the colt did a quick stutter-step, and arched toward the inside of the paddock. The colt's groom was there to meet him, pressing the heel of his hand into the colt's shoulder in gentle reminder. Georgie put her feet in the stirrups and nodded at him.

"Thanks."

He offered her a fist bump, and she touched her knuckles to his.

"Safe trip," he said as he led Georgie and Little War from the paddock.

The colt's walk ate up ground with a purpose, and Georgie patted him on the neck as she got herself situated on their way to the track, where the pony riders casually waited for them. Little War was the six-horse, near the back of the line and reacting to every sight and sound. The first horse in the line spooked at the minor crowd, and it cascaded down to Little War, who skittered sideways from his pony rider and tried three bouncing half-rears with his head twisted over the pony's withers. The pony laid back his ears and kept trucking forward, acting the model citizen in the face of upset baby Thoroughbreds. Little War settled in the post parade, giving Georgie a moment to breathe before taking off into a rousing warm-up. The colt kicked up his heels and pushed forward, throwing his head in the air and fighting the pony rider's hold on his mouth.

"We're good," Georgie said, and the pony rider let her go, leather line swinging. Little War exploded up the turn, lowering his head into Georgie's hands. Georgie perched over the colt's shoulders, her feet nestled against his ribcage through the saddle, and guided them into the backstretch. The gate was positioned at the head of the seven-furlong chute, *Tampa Bay Downs* emblazoned across the top in bright green letters on a white placard.

Little War took one look at the gate and held his head high, huffing excitedly all the way in, the doors shutting with a sharp click behind them. Georgie went through her mental check list, pulling her goggles down over her eyes and setting her feet firmly in the stirrups. Her assistant starter perched on the gate near the colt's neck, one hand clinging to the bars and the other holding Little War's head straight. It was Georgie's job to get Little War out fast and positioned well early. She expected to be riding a tornado, one that wouldn't put up with obstacles in its path.

The last horse loaded, and Georgie tightened her grip on the colt's mane, making sure the reins were loose enough so she wouldn't catch Little War in the mouth on the break.

The bell rang, and with a sudden clang the front gates burst open. Every single horse jumped, a tremor of adrenaline spiking through their bodies. Then they plunged, and Little War was out of the gate in two strides, hindquarters digging in and launching forward. His ears laid back flat, eyes rimmed in white like he was saying *what the hell is happening?*

We're racing, Georgie told him, hustling him up through the wall of horses.

One more stride and Little War had the advantage. Georgie clucked to him—the universal code for *speed now, thank you*—keeping herself stationary on the colt's shoulders and twitching the left rein when the colt got clear. Little War took a straight path to the rail like he would have learned in training. From there, Georgie sat and waited, listening to the colt's breaths and the rolling thuds of his hooves in the dirt. The horses fell back behind them, Little War in the clear lead, with Georgie counting mile fractions in her head.

One one-thousand, two one-thousand, three one-thousand.

The striped pole zoomed toward them, was left behind in a hurry.

Eleven seconds. Georgie shifted her weight back, seeing if she could slow the colt down. Little War didn't pay attention, and Georgie considered it a blessing that her next movement got the requested lead change. The colt shifted to his left lead, legs stretching, collecting, stretching, collecting. His strides were sure, happy, energy streaming along ceaselessly in that way that made Georgie hopeful.

They'd get to the end.

In the homestretch, Georgie sat icily in the saddle. The rest of the field became louder, breaths blowing hard and hooves rumbling on their heels. They were coming, but she waited to change leads.

Waited.

And then *whoosh*.

Georgie glided down low over the colt's back, pushing her arms up the colt's neck as she threw the first cross. The reins flapped out like she'd dropped them, loosening in that one split second to give the colt room. Little War shifted into a line, his legs blurring as they shot forward with speed to spare. The thunder kept coming, kept rolling up next to them, but Georgie couldn't let it pass, so her fingers deftly lifted the crop and arced it down. It bounced off of the colt's hindquarters, and Little War flattened his ears back, jerking the reins through her fingers when she threw him another cross, and another, working to get the colt to the finish line.

This is mine, the colt seemed to say, his breath coming in blowing snorts. *Mine and no one else's.*

The finish loomed ahead, the harrowed dirt sliding under their feet. To her right, Georgie caught the sight of Dean's neon green colors, and she gritted her teeth.

Mine.

She pushed the colt again, arms and thighs burning, and Little War kept coming, the energy never stopping until they were under the wire and his head was still in front. Georgie stood in the saddle, her toes gripping the colt's sides and her hands brushing through Little War's flame red mane. She grinned so hard it ached.

"Don't get cocky, baby," Dean shouted at her as he rumbled by on his mount. "It's not a good look on a girl."

"No one ever said it looks any better on you," she yelled after him, swinging her weight back and convincing Little War to slow into a canter, letting Dean go laughing up the clubhouse turn.

~

"Roman the Great is going to win by daylight. Look out for this one next year, folks!"

The announcer was positively beside himself, the small crowd that had held out for Roman's debut letting out cheers along the grandstand for a colt who would be in the future betting pool for the Kentucky Derby about two seconds after he crossed the finish line.

Georgie pressed into the rail, holding her Styrofoam coffee cup out over the track as Harris' gray colt thundered past the finish line. He was lengths ahead, the second place finisher so far in his rearview that Dean peeked under his arm to check out the distance they had opened up on his rivals. Dean slapped Roman on the neck, galloping out around the first turn.

"Harris will be happy," Nick said, sipping his coffee as nonchalantly as you please, like the sight hadn't been something he'd talked to Harris about endlessly for years. Georgie rotated her coffee in her hands, wondering what Nick regretted.

Nick and Harris had lived their friendship through *Call of Duty* bouts as they elbowed each other in front of the massive flat screen in the Tupelo mansion. Lynsey always rolled her eyes at them, saying they were a textbook bromance. But that was then. After Harris came back with his second, shiny BMW, Nick simply hit the pause button on their friendship.

"He's working through some shit," Nick would say every time Georgie asked him about it. "I choose not to be around while he does it."

Georgie didn't get it. At all.

Nick looked up. Georgie followed his gaze, right up to the Tupelo viewing box. She could see the flash of smiles, Harris shaking Reece's hand, each thumping the other on the shoulder. They would be down in the winner's circle soon, Lynsey flitting around them like a bejeweled fairy.

The horses returned to the grandstand, Roman and Dean jogging along behind them. Georgie watched over her shoulder, not reacting when Dean waved his crop at her, tongue held indelicately between his teeth. Nick shook his head, but Georgie knew just by looking at him that he was as impressed as she was by the colt. You had to be when a maiden won by opening up, leaving the field like they weren't there to begin with.

"Stakes next?" Nick asked, like he might be talking to himself.

"Of course," Georgie said. "Colt like him? Harris knows what he has."

Nick looked down at her. "And I know what I have. You and Little War in the Holy Bull."

Georgie sucked in a breath, a laugh rising halfway up her throat where it died out at the seriousness written on Nick's face.

"No allowance?" she asked, wondering if this wasn't rash. There were better ways to ease a three-year-old onto the Derby trail, and Little War may have won his maiden, but he was still figuring out what they wanted from him, still figuring out how to rate—still determining if he *would* rate. Besides, winning maidens usually went on to win allowance races, which lead to stakes races that went up the hierarchy of talent and ability. Little War was talented, maybe even able, but a stakes so soon?

Georgie wasn't sure about that.

"The Holy Bull will be on top of us in a month's time," Nick said. "The distance and time will be right to try our hand. We want to see what we have."

We. The colt's owners, Senior, and Nick. Georgie just rode and gave her opinion when asked. Otherwise sit down, shut up, and ride. She was good at that. Georgie nodded, shrugged her shoulders.

"You have me when you need me, Nick."

He smiled, offered her his hand like it was a business transaction completed. She took it, folded her fingers around his. A surge of noise around the rail brought her attention back to the race, to Roman, who entered the winner's circle with Harris there to greet him. Dean raised his hand for a high five, and Harris eagerly accepted. Harris with such a fuzzy glow around him didn't feel right, like he'd taken on an alternate personality that so completely changed him it was impossible to reconcile this Harris with the Harris she knew by heart.

The crowd lined up for the win photo, the colt's sides still heaving with Dean's hand resting lightly on his damp neck. Afterward, Roman strolled out of the winner's circle, his sweat-streaked shoulders glistening on his way past. The colt snorted, nostrils still blown wide in excitement, veins tracing up his neck. He was a definitive winner on his first try, and Georgie felt a little thrill at it for Harris. Felt some measure of pride. This was what he'd wanted, and if nothing else had worked out for him in the last two years at least he had this.

Harris caught her eye from where he stood in the emptying winner's circle. Her grip on the coffee cup tightened, the tips of her fingers tingling from the pressure as she waited for Harris to tilt the earth out from under her feet. She'd been waiting for it ever since she agreed to ride Little War for Nick, waiting for some comment, some quip, something to raise all her hackles. He was Harris, after all. And she was Georgie. This is what they did now.

Then Harris lifted two fingers to his temple in a half-hearted salute. Cold sluiced down Georgie's spine. It always felt like a punch to the gut, the very second she allowed herself to think positively about Harris, even through an innocent, winning colt, and reality would always insist on rushing back in. She pushed her heel on that swell of pride and crushed it down where it belonged, in the pit with all her other hopes that clustered close to Harris, for some future that would never come.

Harris rocked back on his heels, shook his head like her presence there amused him, and was gone.

Chapter Four

WHERE? WHEN? HOW far? Against *which horses? When will Sweet Bells be ready?*

Do you think she'll get the Eclipse Award? Will you?

Georgie shrugged her shoulders at the questions, self-consciously smoothing a hand over her silk dress. She couldn't stop nervously touching things, fiddling with her earrings and tapping her heels against the hardwood. When she found herself by Samuel Armstrong's twelve-foot Christmas tree, she slipped her fingers along the soft needles, setting the ornaments jangling.

It had to be a side-effect of being in Tupelo's main house, at one of the parties she never wanted to attend. The old plantation home was a cavern full of people, mahogany gleaming and dresses sparkling in the holiday cheer that had been strung over every eave and door frame by someone paid handsomely to make it look like a magazine cover. Even with Lynsey cruising through the crowd like a big cat on the prowl, Georgie didn't feel quite like she belonged. It was as if the whole room was a lion, and she was the lone antelope, jumpy and itching to run.

"Red Gate used to have parties like these." A whisper floated through the air, and Georgie spun to follow it, zeroing in on a group of women ensconced on the opposite side of the tree. "I just don't know what those people are thinking, letting it get to such a state."

Georgie pulled a needle off the evergreen, the sap sticking to the tips of her fingers and setting the whole thing shaking. The whispers kept hissing through the tree, unperturbed, like they usually were. This was Ocala. It was horse racing. The talk never stopped.

"After Oliver bought most of their stock, I thought they might at least restore that crumbling house. The façade is a shame. A damned shame."

Georgie rolled her eyes, the tips of her ears pink. Catching a glimpse of Lynsey's elegant white gown headed up the grand staircase—no doubt in escape—Georgie slipped into the crowd to follow.

"Georgie."

Her stomach dropped. Caught. Pressing her lips into a thin smile, she spun to acknowledge Oliver in the best way she knew how—feigned interest.

Oliver stood there, suited in charcoal and sporting a red tie like he was ready for a presidential debate. He smiled at her, white teeth and a pull of lips that was so like Harris it was hard not to do a double take.

"Oliver."

"I'm glad you could make it to our little get-together," he told her, his lips twisting in amusement, since they both knew Tupelo did not do *little* get-togethers. They held parties high society would gladly kill to attend. There was a difference.

"Couldn't very well turn down the annual Christmas bash, could I?" Georgie asked, although, god help her, she had wanted to do just that. She'd stared at the invitation long enough that she thought the intensity of her gaze might light the heavy card stock on fire.

"I haven't seen your parents this evening," he said, looking across the crowded house as though he honestly expected them to show up. Georgie breathed deeply through her nose, struggling to keep her smile in place when all she wanted was for Oliver to simply cease to exist.

"You know them," she said, beginning to slip around him. "Busy bees, no time, etcetera, etcetera."

He watched her curiously, like he didn't know what to make of her.

"Send your mother my regards," he said, like that Southern gentleman charm ever worked for him. Georgie forced herself not to wince. Forced herself to smile and nod.

"Of course," she replied, perky enough to sound like a squeak.

Oliver nodded, seemingly satisfied.

"Merry Christmas, Georgiana."

He turned his suited back on her, leaving Georgie scrambling for the base of the steps. She struggled to breathe, finding herself irrationally angry at her mother, because she was the one who always left her to confront these events alone. Two years had passed and Claire wouldn't show her face at a Tupelo party even if Oliver offered to fix all of Red Gate's problems as a reward for her presence.

Georgie shook it off and dashed up the stairs, taking them as fast as her heels would let her. It was impossible to grab the banister for the thick ivy garland, so she trailed her fingers along the wall to steady herself. She took care not to tip the framed photos of smiling family members. Samuel and his long-dead wife, Oliver and Mabel, Lyn and Harris. Lilliana.

In the hallway, she paused next to a photo of Lilliana on horseback, her dark hair in a tumble of waves behind her, and a chubby toddler version of Harris sitting upfront with clumps of mane in his tiny fists. Georgie had seen it before in the multiple times she'd been in this house growing up, but passing it now felt like walking through a ghost. The hall would go cold and her hands clammy at the sight of something her family helped ruin.

Because hadn't they?

She backed away from the photograph and quickly turned the corner into the old billiard room, which was crowded with boys milling around the pool table. Above their heads, black-and-white win photos dating back to the farm's founding cluttered the walls. The Christmas decorations wound into the room like roots, pine garlands infusing the air that otherwise smelled of too much cologne. Georgie wrinkled her nose, a move that didn't go unnoticed by Harris, who leaned on his cue stick by the pool table and shook his head at her, like he wondered what she was doing there.

"Nine in the corner pocket," someone said, the crack of the ball spiking through the room. Georgie ignored Harris and found Lynsey by the liquor cabinet, pouring fingers of port into two crystal tumblers. She wordlessly put one in Georgie's hand, taking a healthy swallow of hers.

"It is far too dull down there." Lynsey squeezed her eyes shut, letting out a breath. "These experiences have convinced me that party planning makes me a bona-fide crazy person. Next time I'm making Mabel do it."

Georgie raised an eyebrow, wondering how that would go. "She'd probably like the opportunity," she said, perhaps too charitably by the look Lynsey shot her.

"Good," Lynsey griped, then sighed, rubbing her forehead. "No, not good. It's just that she married my father, so I naturally don't trust her decision-making capabilities."

"I ran into him downstairs." Georgie sipped the port, letting the liquid warm the back of her tongue before swallowing it.

"My apologies."

"He asked about my parents."

Lynsey finished her drink in one swallow, turning back to the bar for another pour.

"Typical," she said, spinning around with a new glassful. "Did you tell him to go screw himself? Because that's what I would have done."

"What's this about telling off Dad?" Harris asked, appearing before Georgie could tell Lynsey that telling Oliver Armstrong to go screw himself was professional suicide. For Harris and Lynsey, she assumed it was all in a typical day.

"Dad was doing some friendly inquiring about Georgie's parents," Lynsey said. "Only when I say 'parents,' I mean to say 'Claire.' It's always Claire."

Harris looked like he'd swallowed something bitter and wanted to spit it out. Georgie figured it was a testament to their relationship that she didn't know whether it was in reaction to Oliver or her.

"What did he say?" he asked Georgie.

"Does it matter?" Georgie parried.

"It doesn't," Lynsey decided, nodding firmly, draining her second glass of port and putting it on the bar with a flourish. "Now, the strings are playing a song that was not on the approved list, so I'm going to have to go back out there."

She paused, looking between Georgie and Harris.

"Will one of you tell me which race we're running Bell back in? That will be at least one question I can answer without wanting to punch myself in the face."

Georgie shook her head. "I know nothing."

At the same time Harris said, "The Donn."

Georgie blinked, standing up straighter and focusing on Harris. "Who said anything about the Donn?"

"Grandpa, Dad, Reece, and yours truly," Harris said, rolling the cue stick in both hands and bouncing on his heels. Georgie narrowed her eyes at him, sensing he was gearing up, searching for something. She rose to the challenge.

"Why is it that I don't know these things?"

"Since you decided to be a jockey, not an owner," Harris replied with a shrug. "We get to call the shots. Last I checked, you just ride 'em."

Georgie's mouth fell open, and Lynsey sighed, knowing what was coming. The pool game in the background, Georgie noticed, went silent.

"It seems to me that you might want to come to the quick realization that I get to call the shots during the race. You know, the thing that makes you money?"

Harris shrugged, hardly perturbed.

"Jockeys *are* replaceable. If you start becoming burdened with opinions, finding another jock is easy enough."

Georgie jerked her head back, laughing softly.

"Seriously, Harris, that's enough." Lynsey's peacemaking query fell on deaf ears.

"So, what, you'll just kick me to the curb?" Georgie asked. "You already did it once, why not do it again, right?"

Harris tilted his head at her, looking at her so curiously that it reminded her of Oliver.

"Is that what you think happened?"

A flush rushed swiftly across Georgie's skin, the urge to run biting at every bit of her. She ignored his question because she had to. There was no other option.

"Try to replace me," she said, gritting her teeth. "See how well that works out for you with Samuel. See if it works out for you at all."

Georgie put her tumbler on the table and spun on her heel, shoving past Harris. In the hallway, the cold memory of Lilliana's ever-smiling photo dug into her as she passed.

⌐

The sun had been bright that day, when everything ended. It beat down on her shoulders as she stood in the yearling paddock, her hands carding through tufts of Sweet Bells' wild yearling mane. The filly glowed a burnished bronze under the brilliant blue sky. Georgie couldn't stop looking at her, couldn't stop seeing all the Red Gate bloodlines flowing across the filly's muscles. Tupelo already pinned its hopes on her gangly legs and filling chest, but for Georgie she was a reminder that maybe Red Gate wasn't done after all.

Not with this filly.

Sweet Bells ripped at clover, shouldering into Georgie with all the grace of a steamroller. She shifted with the filly, resting one arm over her withers and thought to putting a saddle on the filly's back, to training, to racing her so fast her eyes would tear and she would gasp for breath in the wind they made.

She thought *forward*. It was so much nicer than looking back.

A shiny black BMW pulled up behind her, top down and Harris grinning behind the steering wheel like he'd caught the canary.

"Oh, no," Georgie said, looking over her shoulder at the car's gleaming lines. The filly's head jerked up, ears swiveling.

"Oh," Harris said, drawling the word, "yes." He put the car in neutral and pulled up the handbrake, lazily relaxing in the drivers' seat, arms resting wide. "Who wants to joy ride?"

"Your dad is letting you roam around freely in that thing?" Georgie asked, raising a skeptical eyebrow.

"As you can see," Harris said, motioning to the car with a flick of his hand. "The man isn't here. He's following from the dealer and it looks like he's taking his time. We can have all the fun we like, George."

George. His nickname for her made Georgie blush, and Harris knew it.

"What do you say?"

Georgie considered it, cocking her head and pushing a long strand of hair back into her ponytail.

"I don't think I'm clean enough," she said, and he shrugged.

"The car has to be christened sometime," he told her, wide smile refusing to leave his face. "Get your dirty jeans in here."

"Well, since you ask so nicely." Georgie gave the filly a parting pat and climbed the fence, landing on the other side. She sank into the passenger seat delicately, careful not to swipe horse hair across the leather or dig dirt into the floorboards. The car smelled so new, like promises.

Harris laughed at her hesitancy, like it didn't matter at all to him, and put the car into gear. "So where do you want to go?"

They hit the drive between paddocks, and Harris opened up the engine, sending a plume of dust in their wake. Horses peered at the car as it passed. A group of new weanlings dashed up the fence after it, keeping up for a moment before upcoming fences forced them to veer off in a flurry of hooves and mane.

"I thought this was a joyride," she yelled over the wind, laughing when he took a tight turn and headed up to the main road, coming down to a quick stop at the end of the farm's property. Ocala spread out in front of them, Red Gate's fences sliding along the other side of the road.

"Yeah, well," Harris said, looking down at the gearshift and fiddling with it, rocking it around in neutral. He looked nervous all of a sudden, like he couldn't quite find the words he was looking for. "Dates usually have destinations, don't they?"

Georgie's heart seemed to stop, and then began to beat furiously just as quickly.

She swallowed thickly and said, "Coming a little out of nowhere, don't you think?"

"How long have we known each other?" he asked her.

"Forever," she answered, not even having to think about it.

"This was coming, wasn't it?"

Like a freight train, Georgie thought, but she only nodded haltingly. She'd never been on a date before. What did dates consist of? Hadn't years of teen movies prepared her for this moment?

She stared at him, wonderingly. A swift heat slipped over her skin, gathering into her tingling fingers. Every part of her body felt suddenly alive, as if she'd toed up to the side of a cliff and was looking down.

He smiled and shrugged, then let go of the gearshift and ventured out to hook his index finger around her pinky. So many nerve endings fired at once Georgie found it hard to sit still in her seat.

"Yeah," she breathed, giving his finger a squeeze. "A date. Now, as to where . . ."

Georgie looked up at the inviting blue sky.

"Ice cream," she determined, and nodded her head sharply. "It can only be ice cream."

He laughed, put the car into gear.

"But I need to change out of these jeans," she said. "I can't go sauntering around in public smelling like horse."

"Hasn't stopped you before." He looked at her knowingly as he pulled out into traffic.

"I wasn't on a date before."

"Fair point," he said, turning into Red Gate's main drive.

Georgie couldn't stop smiling, like the edges of her mouth were permanently affixed in glee at the thought of *date, this is a date*. How did this even happen? Harris maneuvered around Ennismore and up the drive, pulling up behind a familiar car. Oliver's Mercedes SUV, shiny black and empty.

"That's weird," Harris said, giving the SUV a puzzled look. "Is there a horse for sale?"

"Isn't there always?" Georgie asked as Harris turned off the engine.

They both got out of the car, Georgie motioning for Harris to follow her around the side of the house to the kitchen. She'd only be a minute for new jeans and sandals, eager to shed clothes in the oppressive August heat. Georgie rounded the side of the house and put a foot on the bottom step, looking up through the screen door, and stopped in her tracks.

Harris ran into her shoulder, and she automatically reached behind her and found his hand, turning to drag him away.

Except it was too late for that.

Oliver's back was to them, half hiding Claire as his hands trailed up her sides, into her hair. They seemed fused together, too consumed to notice anything else. They didn't see Georgie, didn't know she was even there. She could slip away, immediately scrub every image of this from her brain, but Harris refused to move. He planted himself, and she could feel the tension in him coiling, his hand tightening on hers. She pulled desperately to get him to turn around.

"We have to go," she hissed. "I can't . . . *we* can't be here."

No response. She dug her ragged nails into the side of his hand and came close to him, going up onto her toes. "Harris," she whispered quickly, "I can't see this. I can't keep standing here. Come with me now."

He turned to look at her like she was someone he didn't know. And then even that smoothed away, replaced with a sudden rage that prickled against her and made her shrink back.

"Please, Harris." She took a step toward the driveway, stretching his arm out with her and tugging softly. He allowed himself to glide toward her, shaking his head mutely as he leaned down and put both hands on her face, making her look up at him.

"Georgie," he said, coming so close to her she could feel the heat on him, warming her. He was trembling, and his jaw was set. She reached up and put her hands on his wrists.

"Please," she said again, her heart racing. She only wanted to run away, go back to their plan, forget, even when she knew it was impossible.

He let her go. "I can't."

Harris turned around and walked up the steps, and Georgie sank down onto the grass, her legs refusing to hold her up.

Then the screaming started, and Georgie covered her eyes. She heard the screen door screech, obscenities tumbling out onto the lawn and rolling over Georgie like a tide. There was a crash, glass breaking. When the door opened again she looked up and found Harris, his shirt collar torn and eyes watery.

"Let's go, Georgie," Harris said, leaning down and grabbing her elbow. Her legs shook, ears ringing with Oliver's hoarse voice. The screen door squeaked, but she scrambled toward the car, hitting the door and yanking it open as Harris cranked the engine.

They spun out of the driveway in a cloud of dust, a scatter of gravel, leaving a disheveled Oliver in their wake while Georgie's heart pounded in her throat. Her hair whipped around her head at will, catching between the fingers she kept clamped to her mouth.

What is happening?

She wanted to scream it, but her throat was closed. Tears sprang up in frustration, streaking across her cheeks. Harris shifted the car up into sixth gear, the engine roaring as they sped past the speed limit. They passed Tupelo in a spinning whirl, Harris pushing the car faster until a ragged gasp climbed out of Georgie's throat.

"Stop," she managed, clinging at the door handle. "Harris, stop the car."

His hands were pale on the steering wheel, choking it in a strangling grip as he yanked the car off the main road so suddenly Georgie screeched, sinking into the seat and bracing herself. The tires hit gravel and the car skidded onto a side road with a whine. They came to an abrupt halt, dust drifting past them and clinging to Georgie's lips.

For a moment they were both silent, staring out the dust-smeared windshield in mutual astonishment before Harris punched the steering wheel so hard she heard something crack. Then he was out of the car, leaving the door open to ding plaintively while he stood trembling in the middle of the road.

Carefully, Georgie climbed out of the car. She walked up to him, arms firmly crossed over her chest. Standing in front of him, she focused on the tear in his collar and tried to think of something to say. She groped for words, found them scattered all over her thoughts that simply could not be arranged into anything more coherent than a simple question.

"What are we going to do?"

Harris reached for her, pulling her up to him in a crushing hug. His arms clasped around her shoulders, hand against the back of her head. Georgie burrowed her nose into his shirt, wrapped herself around his chest like a vise.

She didn't know how long they stood like that before he said, "I'm going to tell my mom."

Georgie pulled back so she could look up at him, nose brushing against his chin. "Are you sure?"

"I'm not keeping secrets for him," Harris said firmly. "Are you going to tell your dad?"

She stiffened and he pushed her further away to look at her hard.

"Georgie?"

"I don't know," she blurted. "I can't know, Harris. This just happened."

"I think it's been happening," Harris said. "For a while."

"We don't know that," Georgie told him. "Would it matter?"

"No," he said after a beat. "Not for me."

Georgie tried to corral her thoughts, but all she could think about was Lilliana's devastation. Her father's devastation. It wasn't their place, and she wanted to say no, absolutely not, but the way Harris looked at her made the words stick to the roof of her mouth.

"Do what you need to do," he told her, letting her go. His hands fell to his sides, and Georgie went back to hugging herself fiercely, as though she could warm up the part of herself that had gone cold by looking at him. Harris was set, all hard muscle and strong lines like a fighter ready to walk into the ring.

Georgie was nowhere near ready for that. If there was a rock big enough to crawl under that would be her option.

She started to ask if they could just forget, just reset, but the words died before she could put them there between them. It was stupid to ask such a thing. They couldn't unravel the past, couldn't fix it. Georgie focused on the tear in Harris' shirt and wanted to wish it back to being whole.

She reached out, drew her fingers down the ragged edge of torn cloth. When she felt skin he flinched, and she dropped her hand.

"Okay," she said, wanting to do something, say something to

make this right again.

"You'll tell your dad?"

She nodded haltingly, because he was right, wasn't he? They shouldn't have to keep secrets. He took her hand and led her back to the car, a pact drawn between them.

January

Chapter Five

IN HALLANDALE BEACH, Gulfstream Park glittered under floodlights. Red carpets rolled through the arched outdoor walkways that flanked the saddling paddock, its central oblong fountain cascading through colored lights. Lasers bounced chaotically into the sky, catching clouds and turning them sickly shades of green. The salmon pink grandstand arched over palm trees that sprung and popped in dark fronds around the track.

A line of black limousines slowly cruised to the entrance, people spilling out of them to welcoming camera flashes. Georgie crossed and uncrossed her legs, wiggling her painted toes in the tall heels Lynsey had talked her into wearing. She nervously flicked her pinky nail underneath her thumb, creating a *click, click, click* that Lynsey stoically reached out to silence.

Stop, she mouthed at Georgie, who settled for tapping her foot against the floorboard and clinging to her friend's hand. Lynsey beamed out at the rest of the limousine, while Mabel stared daggers at Claire, who sat on Georgie's other side and heroically pretended not to notice. Tom stared out the tinted window, Gulfstream's lights glazing over his eyes. Oliver didn't seem perturbed in the least, hand resting casually on Mabel's knee.

Harris sat across from Georgie, glaring at her like she had caused this rather than Samuel's irrational decision-making process and desire to present a united front between the two farms in the face of the press and the cameras. Everyone was watching, and everyone would see two farms, peaceful and serene, united for the cause of Sweet Bells.

This was Georgie's worst nightmare come to life.

Gossip ran amok through racing. There were newsletters, opinion columns, Twitter feeds and forums dedicated to it. Of them all, *Uncle Moe* reigned supreme. It was all trash talk, crude cartoons, and witty commentary that could be had around any racetrack. Scathing stories filled it to the brim, and for two years Claire and Oliver were the perpetual stars, always providing a cheap laugh. And where *Uncle Moe* stopped, the whispers slipped through barns, skipped from track to track, farm to farm. Everyone knew each other's business, and one limousine shared between Red Gate and Tupelo was downright scandalous. Clearly Tupelo needed a better public relations person.

"Remember," Samuel said as their limo pulled up to the curb, "there will be questions about Bell's next race. We intend to announce that she'll run in the Donn during our acceptance of her award. I will break the news on stage."

He glanced across the limo at Georgie. "Keep playing clueless until then, Georgie."

She managed to nod just as the door opened, sucking in fresh air and a flurry of camera flashes. Photographers stood on each side of the walkway, more than Georgie remembered there being in the past. Lynsey squeaked excitedly and threaded her arm around Georgie's, her glittering dress set aglow in the flashes as the rest of their party exited the limo without killing each other. More than a few photos would have her hovering by Lynsey's shoulder, watching her parents separate themselves politely, if abruptly, from the rest of the group.

"What do you think Mabel was envisioning the whole way? Death by glare?" Lynsey asked, tugging Georgie through the crowd of camera flashes and glimmering sequins.

"My money's on throwing Claire out of a moving vehicle," Harris said flatly, walking behind them. Georgie cast a disparaging glance at him as they walked up the stairs.

"I didn't say it was *my* fantasy," he said, holding up both hands.

"That's comforting," Georgie responded, deadpan.

Tables packed the theater. A stage occupied one end and a rise of cameras crowded the opposite side of the room. A second stage near the entrance housed the HTV anchors—two men in suits and flashy ties talking animatedly behind a desk about the entries and their past accomplishments. She caught sight of Dean across the room, casually flipping her off and mouthing *suck it* at her through his inability to stop smiling.

Even though he was a journeyman jock, Dean had spent the majority of the year as an apprentice, so Georgie had the great luck of being his competition in the same category. Ignoring him like a champ, Georgie dropped into her chair between Samuel and her mother, closing the circuit of tension that ran around the table. Mabel spoke into Oliver's ear, Oliver watched Claire like a hawk might watch an unsuspecting rabbit, and Claire wound her hand around Georgie's fingers hard enough to leave marks. Lynsey batted at Harris as he stole a bite of her filet mignon, talking to Reece about Roman's work that morning as Samuel looked on like he'd accomplished something great.

This was something to be proud of, two farms at one table with enough rumors to fuel them to outer space and back. Tom reached for his whiskey, throat working around a hearty swallow. He didn't look up when the lights dimmed, or when Georgie's name boomed across the hall, winner of the Eclipse Award for Best Apprentice Jockey.

Cheers erupted under rolling applause, people craning their necks to look toward their table. Georgie stood, her heart stuttering in her chest, and paused long enough to shake Samuel's hand. Claire pulled her into a hug, then handed her off to Tom, who put trembling hands on her shoulders and mustered a watery smile like this was all too much, but damn it he was proud. Georgie ducked her head on her way to the stage, wondering what everyone must be thinking. Wondering what they were saying even more.

By the time Georgie had done her media rounds, from *Daily Racing Form* to the *Miami Herald*, she missed most of the awards and didn't feel like going back to the table for fear of what she'd find. She took off her heels and padded barefoot over Gulfstream's balcony, seeking a quiet place to take ten breaths and close her eyes, hoping to pop back into normal life as Georgiana Quinn, Eclipse Award recipient who can handle anything, even a table full of crazy people with too much history between them. With a drunk as a father and a social pariah as a mother, Georgie figured she could allow herself those breaths.

Rounding the corner, she stopped short at the foot of a bench she'd hoped to find empty. Instead there was Harris with a beer in his hand, caught mid-sip. She stared at him hard, and he slowly lowered the beer, swallowing a healthy mouthful.

"Who did you sweet-talk to get that?" she asked, which seemed to surprise him because an eyebrow quirked up.

"Bethany the waitress likes me," Harris supplied, and took another drink. "Want one? I'm sure I can weasel more out of her."

"I don't think I need to add to my family's already questionable alcohol intake," she said, already starting to turn around in search of a free, non-Harris infested area to sit.

She heard the sigh before the bottle made a clinking sound on the concrete. "I should say congratulations," Harris said to her back, and Georgie stopped, looking at him over her shoulder.

"Should?"

"It's just that it seems like the obvious thing to say," Harris told her, leaning forward and resting his arms on his knees. He'd taken off his tuxedo jacket, tie still impeccably tucked into a black vest and shirt untouched.

"What would you prefer to say?" Georgie asked. "I have a feeling you've got some treatise on how I don't deserve this locked away somewhere."

He laughed and said, "You know me too well, you know?"

"I do," Georgie said, and eyed him suspiciously when he nodded to the bench, offering her the seat.

"Come on, sit," he said, picking up the beer bottle. "I've cased the immediate vicinity, and this is the only bench not occupied by people who really need to get a room. I'm not moving until I feel like it, so . . ."

"Yeah, yeah," Georgie interrupted, sitting down and putting her shoes and the award between them. "Just don't talk for five minutes, okay?"

To her shock, he honored her request while she shut her eyes and pretended for three hundred glorious seconds that she didn't have to get up and witness what was happening inside the theater. Her dad wouldn't be working on his fourth whiskey, and Mabel wouldn't be attempting to pry confessions out of her mother via death glare. Oliver wouldn't be present at all. Perhaps he'd be in Paris, screwing some other mistress to his heart's content. Here, there was no Oliver, no whispers, no table filled with cutting looks.

After five minutes sailed by, Harris said, "You can tell me what you know."

"Did you time that?" she asked, eyes still closed.

"Of course." He huffed, the beer sloshing in the bottle. "Who do you think I am?"

"A man of many mood swings," Georgie muttered, opening her eyes. She looked at Harris as though through a haze. The normalcy dissipated, leaving her in the stark disappointment of the bench on which she sat.

"What are you thinking?"

Georgie narrowed her eyes at him, wondering exactly what she was supposed to say.

Harris leaned forward, resting his elbows on his knees. "If we're going to keep being pushed into this united front bullshit, I'm owed."

"Obviously this is going to be a shock," she said, "but I don't know what you're talking about."

Surprise passed across Harris' face, quickly covered by a dark annoyance. "Seriously?" he asked, sitting back and digging for his phone. "How can you not know? What do you think this is all

68

about? The shared limo, the table?"

"Okay, let's back up," Georgie said. "How about you enlighten me concerning your insane raving?"

"Do you ever read *Uncle Moe*?"

"You know I don't read *Uncle Moe*," Georgie snapped at him. "For obvious reasons."

"Put it on your reading list," Harris told her, handing his phone out to her. She took it hesitantly, as though afraid it might bite.

The most recent edition of *Uncle Moe* stared her in the face, its logo of a horse smoking a cigar puffing the title in lazy bubble script. The first story was a simple paragraph.

The Floridians Saga Renewed! Just when you thought those two kids had called it quits, news out of America's Retirement Community puts Claire Quinn and Oliver Armstrong at the Keeneland January Sale. When found in Hip #291's stall, Mr. Armstrong and Mrs. Quinn insisted they were "inspecting each other's bloodstock."

A shot of adrenaline slid down Georgie's spine at light speed, and her fingers clenched into fists in her lap to keep herself grounded. Her first instinct was denial. She would deny until she was blue in the face and gasping.

"First," Georgie said, "*Uncle Moe* doesn't differentiate truth from rumor. Most of it is fanciful crap based on speculation. That's the whole point of the newsletter."

Harris looked like he had a point to argue, but Georgie bulldozed over it.

"Second," she continued, "why are you showing me this?"

"Because I know that both of our dear parents were at the Keeneland sale this week," Harris said, like he was bored having to explain it to her. "And I know where your loyalties lie."

She couldn't help the laugh that burst bitterly through her teeth. Just because Georgie refused to actively hunt for Claire's secrets didn't make her their keeper. That had always been the difference between her and Harris. He'd wanted to know everything, and Georgie wanted to know nothing.

And after Lilliana, what did any of it matter?

"It's almost like you think I want my mom to keep screwing your dad, as if there's some side benefit in it for me other than abject humiliation. It would be hilarious if I didn't think it was completely true."

"That's not what I think," Harris said, standing as she struggled to find her balance to put on her shoes, hiking herself three inches taller so she didn't feel utterly minuscule next to his stupid height. He towered over her, a lean giant full of muscular angles and suntanned skin. She hated herself for even noticing.

"You could have fooled me," she snapped at him.

"I only want someone to be honest here," he said to her. "With this shit coming back up again . . ."

"You need someone to tell you it's not true?" Georgie broke in, peering up at him. He let out a heavy breath and shoved his fingers through his hair, the product in it doing him no favors. Georgie poked him in the chest, making him twitch. "I can't know what happened because I wasn't at the Keeneland sale. Despite what you may think about my family life, my mom and I don't exactly sit down and gossip over tea or whatever it is you think we do, so I can't tell you what you so desperately want to hear."

"That's not what I want you to say," he glowered.

"So what *do* you want?" Georgie asked, exasperated. "I've never lied to you."

He looked down at his feet, eyebrows drawing together like he couldn't quite make out the Italian leather. Georgie didn't hold her breath, and picked up the trophy. She spun on her heel and took two steps when she heard him say, "Do you need reminding?"

The hairs on the back of her neck stood at attention and she came to a dead stop.

"What did you say?" she asked, rounding on him.

"Lying by omission, Georgie," he said, clear as day. "That's a thing."

"What?" she hissed, walking back up to him.

"I'm happy to talk about it if you are," he told her, opening his arms in invitation.

"No, you're not." Georgie recognized the trap, sidestepping around it. "When are you ever happy to talk about anything with me?"

A muscle in his cheek twitched. She pushed on.

"But fine, since you brought it up, let's talk," she said, her face heating up, turning pink with pent up frustration that she couldn't purge no matter how hard she tried. "I admit I didn't tell my dad. I didn't do it because I wanted to—"

"Pretend," Harris said, finishing the sentence for her.

"To keep my life from crumbling," Georgie pressed. "Nothing would have been the same."

"Nothing *was* the same," he broke in, keeping his voice quiet when she knew he wanted to yell it in her face. "Everything went to hell anyway. You left me holding the bag, George. You left it all to me."

Georgie pushed the tips of her fingernails into her palms. She realized she was holding her breath, and forced herself to raggedly exhale, draw in air through her clenched teeth. It wasn't so easy, she thought, to fight against Harris when he was right. She had left it all to him. She had pretended, and all for what? Their lives had gone to hell anyway.

"I did what I thought I had to do," Georgie said haltingly. "If you don't believe me now that's your business. I've never *lied* to you, Harris."

"It's amazing, the things you tell yourself," he said, shaking his head, just as the approaching clack of Lynsey's heels echoed over the concrete balcony.

"There you are," Lynsey said, appearing in all her glittering glory. She stopped and put her hands on her hips, eyeing the two of them like a disapproving grade school teacher in a dress of glinting, silver sequins. "I've been sent out to find you, since, you know, the awards are basically over. Bell's up for Horse of the Year in five. Let's go."

"Yes, ma'am," Harris said, mustering his best Southern gentleman accent and draining the rest of his beer.

"Do I even want to know why you two are conspiring in some dark corner?" Lynsey asked, leading them back to the theater. "Since neither of you is bruised or bleeding, I'm hoping the world isn't ending."

"Far from it, Lyn," Harris said, smiling like a wolf when Georgie made an audible snort. "Can't say it isn't getting more interesting, though."

Georgie firmly pushed past Harris, her thoughts whirling with all the unsubstantiated rumors she'd ever heard about her family over the past few years. Auctions teamed with people, ran on strict schedules, leaving no time for Claire to whirl off with Oliver in front of the entire horse industry. It would be far too stupid a move for either of them.

Although Georgie had to admit, they'd made stupid moves before. They'd gotten caught, for one.

When they walked back into the theater, Lynsey's dress flashing like a disco ball under the lights and the trophy heavy in Georgie's arms, there was no time to think. The presenter ripped open the envelope in front of a hushed audience.

"And the Horse of the Year is Sweet Bells."

Then there was nothing but the roar of the crowd in Georgie's ears.

Part Two:
Running Rank

February

Chapter Six

GEORGIE BURROWED UNDER the covers in her hotel room near Gulfstream Park. Fuzzy memories pulled at her, slick and ghostly, shivering in a dream that dragged her down, pressed her back into smooth cushions. Her eyes closed tight, breath coming quick. In the dream, Harris had his weight carefully held above her, hands pressing dents into the leather, catching in her spreading hair. His head dipped, and that was all it took.

Georgie woke up in a rush, embarrassment pink in her cheeks, heart jackhammering in her chest, and lungs racing to catch up. The sheets twisted around her legs like they had been trying to keep her from falling off the bed.

She pulled the sheets back into place, checked the glowing alarm clock again, and rolled onto the cool side of the bed, telling herself to think of nothing. Think of nothing and maybe that's what she would get. When dawn threatened to break, Georgie finally fell into the sweet, dreamless sleep she yearned for. Mindless, numb, blank, devoid of Harris looking at her in disbelief, without Lilliana not looking at her at all.

An explosion of knocks against the door yanked her back into her dark hotel room.

"Georgie!" Nick called through the door. "We don't wait for daylight to start burning in this business, and you know it."

Georgie groaned into her pillows as another round of knocking hammered through her skull.

"I will get the key," he threatened.

"Okay," she shouted and staggered out of bed. Pulling on clothes, she arrived at the door with one boot on and one boot in her hand, hair sticking out at all ends. Nick smiled winningly at her, a habit he had when he was annoyed, and shoved a cup of coffee in her hand.

"You are soulless," Georgie muttered, sipping at the strong, black coffee. "But I accept your offering and will ride your horse in exchange."

"You were already going to do that," Nick told her, blazing the way to the elevators and pushing the button impatiently. Georgie limped after him, leaned into his arm to pull on her boot. "You look like you could sleep another day."

Georgie shrugged, letting him pat down the wild tufts of her hair. "I haven't been sleeping, so thank you for your observation, Captain Obvious."

Nick shot her a look as they shuffled onto the elevators. "Why?" he asked, because now was as good a time as any to figure out if she should be riding his horse in the Holy Bull. Georgie wanted to tell him to mind his own business, but it was Nick. The words babbled out of her before she could stop and think.

"Because *Uncle Moe* is at it again," she said, showing him her phone, the newsletter still cued up on her browser.

"No one really believes this crap," Nick said, scrolling through the story. He handed the phone back to her and pulled out his keys as the elevator slowed to a stop in the parking garage. "Even if they did, their opinion doesn't matter. It never mattered."

"I'm not worried about their opinion," Georgie corrected him, stopping at his truck and climbing inside. "It's whether or not it's actually the truth that's the problem."

"You think it is?" Nick asked, giving the truck a loving pat on its dashboard as it coughed to a rumbling purr.

"I don't know. Harris thinks it is," Georgie said, "which he was more than happy to tell me."

"Come on, Georgie," Nick said, pulling out of the garage and bumping onto the road bound for the track. "You can't tell me he didn't already think that."

"Because everyone thinks it," Georgie muttered, staring out the window at Gulfstream Park, barn lights twinkling in the dark as the moon still reflected a half-arc on the ocean. Dawn was still far off. "What's a little reminder?"

Nick grunted, out of ideas. They drove in silence, the coffee warming Georgie's cold fingers. She tried to shift her thoughts to something else. To Little War in the afternoon's big race, to the flood of ride requests Angel forwarded to her in expletive-laden glee, to the homework that—god help her—she wasn't doing. Nothing worked. Her mind just fell back on Claire and Oliver, Harris' face when he asked her to be honest with him, just this once.

Then, like it always did, back to that damn sofa. And after. Georgie shut her eyes, opened them, wiped it all away when they rolled through the open gates to the backside. There was work to do, horses to ride. This would be a busy day, one that didn't want or need introspection and questions.

Nick parked the car in front of the Castellano barn and considered the shedrow, with its horses shaking bedding out of their manes, grooms prepping for feed, lights winking on and off in the dark.

"What will you do if it's true?" he asked. Georgie stared hard at the barn, wondering what she *could* do. Even when she had pushed it away, it always came roaring back.

"Does it matter?"

She opened the cab door and dropped down into the crisp January cold.

⚡

Georgie fiddled with the rubber bands around her wrists until they laid smooth, keeping the cuffs of her silks properly pinned down. That was the down side to the one-size-fits-all mentality. You wound up wearing rubber bands on your wrists to keep your sleeves from covering your fingers. Georgie buckled her helmet as she walked up to Little War's station at the far curve of Gulfstream's paddock fountain. The water tinkled cheerfully, catching in the warming January afternoon light. Nick sat at the edge of the fountain, Lynsey resting her head on his shoulder.

"Aren't you fraternizing with the enemy?" Georgie asked her, sitting down next to Lynsey, who scoffed.

"Harris knows better than to tell me what to do," Lynsey pointed out, lifting her head from Nick's shoulder to cast a glance back up the fountain, where Roman stood surrounded by Tupelo,

Harris and the fleet of friends Georgie wasn't sure how he'd managed to keep. The gray colt's groom held his head as Reece's assistant tightened the girth, Roman kicking out a hind leg and pinning his ears.

On their side of the fountain, Little War walked in a circle like a tightly wound ball of nerves, like he was begging to pick up a trot and only the firm hold on his lead shank kept him from his goal. His chestnut coat glistened, orderly mane sitting along his neck in one long line.

Georgie cast a look over the paddock, at the eight horses and their clusters of people. Most were local horses, although that wasn't saying much since so many national trainers wintered over in Florida. The rest had flown in from New York to escape racing through the seagulls and the bitter cold. Blissful blue skies domed over Gulfstream. Georgie couldn't blame anyone for leaving gray New York.

Her eyes fell on Reliance, fresh off of winning his own Eclipse Award as best two-year-old colt after his win in the Breeders' Cup Juvenile. He was an unexpected entry, shipped in from New York and looking even better since she'd last seen him. His dark chestnut coat was a burnished bronze, mane braided like a show horse, his four socks gleaming like they'd been whitened. They probably had been, given the braids. Some trainers were sticklers for appearance. Georgie always found that amusing, since every single jockey set to work unraveling those braids the second they landed in the saddle.

You had to have something to hang on to at the break.

"Georgie." Senior's shadow fell over her, and she stood up like a bolt, ready.

"Hi, Mr. Castellano," she started, offering her hand again

like they hadn't met thousands of times before. It was just how you acted in the paddock. Shake the trainer's hand, meet the owners, shake the owners' hands, listen to the instructions, get on the horse, ride the horse.

All in a day's work.

The corner of Senior's mouth turned up, but he took her hand all the same and walked with her to the colt. Little War came to a tentative stop, craning his neck up to study the crowd.

"We've been working on rating him since his maiden win," Senior told her. "But honestly he wants no part of it. He's got natural early speed and he's a jerk about it."

"Go figure," Georgie said, patting the colt on the shoulder. Little War swiveled one ear toward her, still standing like a shivering statue and looking at the paddock like he was casing the joint.

"Go to the front," Senior told her, boosting her into the saddle at the call for riders up. "Otherwise he'll tire fighting to get there."

She nodded, watching the line of horses trail around the paddock fountain out of the corner of her eye. Roman's gray coat flashed between onlookers, Dean perched in his saddle as he waved to a group of girls clumped against the rail.

The walk to the track and the warm up to the gate was Georgie's quiet time. She liked to sink into the feel of the horse, listen to Little War's huffing breath and move with the slide of his muscles. It was her moment to find out what she had to work with before the gates clanked closed around them, the assistant jumping onto his shallow perch with a hand on the colt's forehead.

Little War pricked his ears at the track. Georgie felt him take a deep breath, ribcage rising and falling, rising and falling, until the doors burst open and like a shot they were gone.

With a few quick shoves, ears pinned back and head down like a bulldozer, Little War cleared the way to the front and kept plowing. The wind brushed his mane off his neck, forelock whipping up off his face and catching on his ears when he finally looked up and swiveled them forward like he'd just now noticed he was in front.

Just where they wanted to be.

"Okay, boy. We got there, it's okay," Georgie murmured, easing him onto the rail as they passed the grandstand. She heard the rest of the field behind them, promises rumbling out under their feet. Little War could lead the way, but that didn't mean he'd finish in front. Georgie tested bringing him back, taking a firmer grip on the reins, sinking her weight back, feeling the pressure the colt answered with as he used her strength to push into the next stride, then the next.

They cleared the three-quarter pole, galloping down the backstretch like life was a breeze. Racing? Easy. Little War kept galloping with his head down, nothing but the wind and the track in front of him as they hit the far turn and the rumbling behind them became a roar.

She chirped to the colt, a noise like a kiss. Little War's ears swept back, his stride changing, power channeling down his legs. One stride, two, and Georgie sank into him, felt the colt's mane slap her skin as she sighted between his ears and gathered the reins in preparation to push. The thunder was on top of them now, a jumble of noise that they surfed against on their way through the turn, past the quarter-mile pole, down the beginning of the homestretch.

A breath on their neck, the shock wave of a body rushing up on their outside, and Little War responded eagerly. The colt accelerated like a rocket with all thrusters lit and burning, and Georgie shoved herself into the stream of him. She gathered the reins, pushed her hands up his neck, gathered, pushed, flipped her crop up and past his eye, brought it back and down on his hindquarters. The colt responded again, again, kept finding more speed to throw at their challenger who wouldn't stop coming.

Georgie looked to her outside, saw Reliance in full run, and swung her attention back to the finish line that loomed in front of them. The dark red colt was dirt-splattered, and he was coming with everything he had.

Within another breath, he was even with them. With one more, he was half a length ahead. Little War rallied, stretched, leapt at the finish line like he could fling himself over it. Whatever it took, Little War wanted to make it happen. Georgie could feel it in him, the shuddering need to keep going, even as Reliance was under the wire first.

She eased off Little War, rose over his back and stroked a hand down his mane as she crooned his name. He tipped his ears back, listening, only halfway convinced that it was time to slow down. When he broke into a trot, Georgie let herself sink back into the slip of a racing saddle, rising and falling to his beat all the way back to the grandstand.

Nick stood there in the dirt, watching her ride back to him with a smile stretching across his face. A laugh bubbled up into her throat.

"What are you smiling at?" She reined the colt in, Little War shoving his head down into Nick's nice dress shirt.

"Second time out, and he managed a second to the best juvenile colt in the country." Nick scrubbed the colt between the ears.

"I'd be a fool to be disappointed."

Roman trotted by, sloppy with dirt and dark with sweat seeping across his neck. Dean jumped off him before the colt even came to a stop in front of his groom, pulled the saddle off Roman's back and walked off without a word. Harris was nowhere to be seen. He was in the stands, perhaps, playing owner to the third-best horse in the field.

Stop it, she told herself.

Thinking about Harris was forbidden right now, when she was on Little War with good things around the corner. Georgie shook Harris from her head, even as she watched his horse walk back to the backside with a swing to his step, dirt falling off his hooves, blowing out a breath that felt like *next time.*

Chapter Seven

ELEVEN HORSES WALKED the Donn Handicap post parade, their burnished coats shining under perfect Florida sky. People pushed against the outside rail, hanging their arms over the partition, hands occupied with programs and half-filled plastic cups of beer. It was a common sight at the track, men puffing silently on cigars and circling picks in cheap ballpoint pens before going to the windows with their bets. Losing tickets littered the grandstand like forgotten white confetti.

This Saturday, girls clustered in small groups along the rail, squeezing through the hardboiled bettors to beam and point cameras at the horses. Sweet Bells walked with her exaggerated extended stride, stretching one leg out and tapping her hoof against the dirt once, twice, before letting her weight sink down. Georgie hooked her fingers in the filly's mane and sat her strut, listening to the crowd hoot its approval.

This was Sweet Bells' war dance, something she always did coming into the paddock before a race and in the parade before the post. It jostled Georgie side to side, up and down, but she didn't bother to correct it because it was part of Sweet Bells saying *I'm here. We're going to win this together. Let's go.*

The filly arched her neck low and snorted at the ground, pulling the reins through Georgie's fingers as she tap danced her way up to the gate and in.

They were in the five stall, given ample time to collect themselves as the other six horses filed into line. Georgie pulled her goggles over her eyes and gathered the reins. Their assistant starter crouched on the small metal beam between them and the solid gate wall, pushing Bell's head toward the middle of the stall so she was forced to look out at the straight away. She pricked her ears and chewed the bit, white froth lining her lips like cream.

Next to them, Dean Hayes whistled low from the back of the four horse, a giant dark bay named Stonecutter. "Girl, have I ever told you watching your butt is one of the best parts of my day?"

Georgie didn't even feel ruffled, which in any other situation might concern her. But this was racing, so she traded a knowing look with the starter and said, "It's pretty telling that my butt is always in front of you, Dean."

The bell rang over Dean's reply, the doors opening with a sudden, spring-loaded shock. Sweet Bells jumped and launched, taking two big strides onto the track before Stonecutter bounced sideways and hit them so hard the filly fell to her knees. Georgie tightened her hold on Sweet Bells' mane as the filly pushed herself up with a spray of dirt, grabbed the bit in her teeth, and shoved Georgie off her neck like a rag doll. The filly was a quivering set of determined nerves as she took off after the field, Georgie working to keep up with her. There was ground to make up.

Sweet Bells ran last going into the first turn and Georgie

tasked herself with what might be impossible: turning a stalker into a closer in the space of a minute and a half. The filly sped up behind the last horse, and Georgie let her drift wide, passing and plunging up the clubhouse turn with their sights on the horse ahead. Dirt pummeled the filly's chest and stung against Georgie's cheeks, splattering across her goggles. Up ahead, Dean held Stonecutter steady between horses, biding his time as they turned into the backstretch. A wave of rage swept through Georgie, heat flushing across her skin and setting her teeth on edge. There was simply no way she was going to allow this to be the race Sweet Bells lost because of *Dean Hayes*.

As they ran up the backstretch, Georgie silently checked the filly's movements, found her going easy under the hail of dirt flying up from the horses ahead. Her strides were long and low, not wasting energy in an effort to hold herself above the spray.

"Good girl," Georgie called into the filly's mane, and felt a little spike of energy in response. She smiled, and the half-mile pole slipped past in a blur of candy red and white.

They were going to win this thing.

The pace quickened, seconds ticking by as the inside rail slipped by in a rapid rush. Dean chirped to Stonecutter, scrubbing his fists lightly up the crest of the colt's neck. Stonecutter moved up, sending his considerable bulk through horses. Georgie sat icy still on Bell, letting the filly drift up without urging, moving on her own time. Dean took up reins, scrubbing again as the field plunged out of the far turn and hit the homestretch.

Pulling down one dirty pair of goggles, Georgie peered through the clean set and saw her mark—a hole in horses that could provide a path straight to the front, if she was lucky. If the hole didn't close before they were through. Georgie lowered herself over Sweet Bells and pushed her knuckles up her neck, telling the filly under no uncertain terms to *move*.

Sweet Bells switched leads, a quick flip of her legs, and became a blurring surge. Other horses could have been standing still for all Georgie was concerned. She pointed the filly at the hole, and Sweet Bells plunged through it like a bull, her ears back and her body flat as a line as they swept past horses and drew even with Stonecutter at the eighth pole, the finish line approaching so fast Georgie didn't have time to think about gloating. She lifted her crop up and flicked it past the filly's left eye, then brought it down on her hindquarters once to say *more, more, more.*

Ragged bursts of breath from Stonecutter faded behind her as Sweet Bells pulled clear in a hail of hooves. She hit the wire a length in front, pulling away.

Georgie lifted herself up in the stirrups, and bent down to slap the filly on the neck. Bell lowered her head, snorting and flicking her ears, off the clock but happy to keep going if that was what Georgie wanted.

All Georgie wanted was to get back to the winner's circle and give Dean a piece of her mind.

She slowed the filly to a quick trot and turned back to the grandstand, cuing her up into a canter. On her way, there were smiles from the smattering of local jocks who had made it into the race. The national riders were less interested, professionally guiding their mounts back to their grooms, Dean among them. He left Stonecutter to his groom and pulled off his saddle, wiping at the mud on his face as he crossed to the scales.

Tupelo streamed into the winner's circle. Dean bounced off

the scale and nearly ran into Harris in his haste to get back to the jocks' room. Georgie sat back in the saddle as applause peppered across the grandstand at their arrival. She waved to the crowd, slowing the filly and letting Miguel clip his line to her bridle.

"Iffy start," he said to Georgie, telling her all she needed to know. Dean's epic bad break would be chalked up to just that. Iffy.

"Certainly didn't feel iffy to me," Georgie said, shaking her head. Miguel led Sweet Bells into the winner's circle, up to the hedge that separated them from the rest of the track, and into the open arms of Samuel Armstrong.

"Well done," he said, all brilliant white teeth. His suit and tie were immaculate, hair combed into submission. He looked like he was poised to jump out of his skin and was containing it so perfectly that he hummed with excitement. "What a race after that start!"

"A crap start," Harris observed helpfully. He watched her with that emotionless mask, making it hard for her to tell if he blamed the stumble on Dean, her, or simply fate.

"Dean cut in," Georgie said, pulling the rest of her goggles off and letting them dangle under her chin. She wiped at the mud on her nose. "Took two strides and decided he wanted to be where I was, so he did it."

Samuel's grin morphed into a pinched frown, the news a dark cloud on his shiny day. "We'll review it. If I see anything, I'll bring it up with the stewards."

Georgie wanted to tell him not to bother. Bumping and rough riding was so common she'd had to nearly elbow her way through in Sweet Bells' first few races. Not only was she a newbie, but she was a girl, and that meant some extra special antics thrown her way. Stewards knew what was deliberate and what was dangerous, and acted accordingly. They suspended jockeys, reordered fields, disqualified runners, but it had to be obvious and there had to be a consequence. All ended well today, so the stewards would turn a blind eye.

Tale as old as time.

Georgie posed for the win photo and jumped off the filly, kissing her on the nose and taking her saddle to weigh in. She jumped on the scale, waited a beat for the weight to register, and bounced off, handing her saddle to her valet on her way out of the winner's circle, eyes set ahead, ready for the argument she was already preparing in her head.

The hand that landed on her arm yanked her out of her thoughts, tossed her back into the present where Harris stood in her way.

"Excuse you." She stepped around him, but Harris didn't loosen his hold, pulling her to the side so they were no longer blocking the flow of happy faces leaving the winner's circle. Georgie stumbled over her thin boots, coming to a restless stop entirely too close to him.

"Slow down, Rambo," he said. "Take a breath before you go pummel Dean."

"I'm sorry, but your precious jockey almost knocked us out of the race." Georgie forced herself to keep her voice down. Harris rolled his eyes, and her hackles went straight up in response. "Don't start, Harris. Dean was very close to putting me on the ground, and he has to know that."

"I'm betting he already knows that," Harris said, "not only because he was there when it happened, but because I already told him to cut the shit. He's got an issue with you? Fine, but he won't have an issue with you when you're on our horses. Not again."

Georgie stuttered to a halt, narrowing her eyes in an attempt to fashion words around such a blunt statement. Harris calling Dean out wasn't something Georgie thought she would ever see, much less when Dean was riding for him.

"Think you can open that statement up to include the races I'm not riding for Tupelo?" She crossed her arms, looking up at him expectantly.

Harris laughed, tipped back on his heels and rubbed at his forehead with the knuckle of his thumb.

"Don't push your luck, George."

He left her there before she could respond, slipping past her like she was someone he didn't know, hadn't just pulled aside in some half-baked attempt to calm her down. So Dean wouldn't mess with her when she was riding for Tupelo, simply because Harris said so? What was that to her when there were so many other horses to ride, when there was Little War waiting to run against Roman in the Fountain of Youth?

Would it be open season then?

Turning the corner into the hallway to the jocks' room, Georgie slid to a halt at the sight of Dean chatting up two girls, signing their programs and writing something on the palm of the shorter girl's hand. The giggles drifted down to Georgie, who was moving again before she could tell herself to stop.

"Dean," she called, voice echoing down the bare hallway.

Dean craned his neck, caught one look at her, and grimaced. With a flashing smile to the girls, he ducked into the jockeys' room. Georgie followed, leaving the girls' befuddled expressions in her wake. She caught up to Dean halfway through the common room, and scurried in front of him, blocking his way to his locker.

"You do that again and I will make it my life's mission to make sure you never get another ride."

"Damn, baby," he said, shaking his head like he was sorry for her, really he was. "I'd hate to know what you'll do when something intentional happens. That was a mistake. Lucky for you it turned out well enough, right? You got another win photo to add to your pink dream horse scrapbook and everything."

"This is not a game, Dean," she said, and added as an afterthought, "nor do I scrapbook."

"No, you're right, it's not a game," he said, becoming serious so suddenly Georgie almost experienced whiplash. "And I'm not about to be lectured by someone who treats it like one."

Georgie couldn't help laughing, almost in awe that she was finally seeing a side of Dean Hayes that wasn't busy making slick moves and writing his number on the palms of girls younger than her.

"I do this every day and you roll in here when you're running a big name, so don't treat me like I'm less."

Then it stopped being funny. Every bit of Georgie recoiled.

"Wow, that was uncalled for."

"No, the scrapbook comment was uncalled for," Dean took a step back, like he'd come too close to the fire. "Everything else, that's true. So stay out of my way, Georgie, and I think we'll be just fine."

Before she could argue, he pushed past her, leaving her with the sudden realization that the entire Gulfstream jockey colony stared her way. Georgie spun around, pushing into the women's changing room with bottled frustration boiling in the pit of her stomach.

She pulled off her boots and sat down with a rush, realizing for a quiet moment that Dean wasn't wrong. He was invested, self-made. Being a careless asshole certainly hadn't slowed him down, not when it so easily translated to gutsy riding. He lived and breathed this sport, and seemed to be doing just fine. Georgie had Sweet Bells paving her way, and she could barely nail down school and Red Gate at the same time, much less riding.

She pushed the thought aside, compartmentalized it, and took a deep breath.

Ignore the asshole called Dean Hayes, Georgie told herself firmly. It wouldn't work, but it didn't hurt to have a mantra for herself. Already she was calming down, heart slowing to a dull thud in her chest.

Georgie untucked her silks and pulled them over her head, wadding them into a ball and leaving them discarded on the bench. She was needed on the backside soon, and the showers were calling her name.

Sweet Bells shifted under Georgie, walking down the last glistening, dewdrop carpeted hill toward the stables. The filly chewed on the bit, white froth lining her lips, her ears swishing front to back, listening, stepping, snorting at the sounds of the training track that echoed toward them. This was their post-race downtime, a handful of days spent walking the open hills like they hadn't just won hundreds of thousands of dollars in purse money, hadn't just done that very thing in front of a nation eager to see more.

Lifting her face into the bright, orange sun, Georgie took a deep breath and the filly matched her perfectly with a rise and fall of her ribcage against Georgie's calves. Bell blew out through flared nostrils, pressing into the reins the closer they came to the track, where horses streamed on and off, riders chatting to Reece as they went in a current of misting breaths that hung warm and cloudy in the cold.

Quivering as a horse rumbled along the inside rail, Bell let loose a yearning whinny and rocked onto her hind legs in preparation to run.

Georgie shushed her. Collected the reins in a swift gather and sat back, sank her weight down, and then nudged her forward into a soft connection, the filly lowering her head and shaking out her mane with a huff as though saying, *fine, be that way.*

"I admire your constant energy," Georgie told the filly, scrubbing her fingers into her mane and pointing her to the training barn, losing herself in the clop and scrape of hooves meeting gravel, the swish of the filly's tail slapping with a fine crack against her flanks. Bell halted square at the training barn door, ears forward like antennas looking for friends.

Swinging down, Georgie collected her saddle and let Miguel lead the filly off for the warm water faucet, humming his Spanish lullabies the entire way. Georgie cuddled her saddle against her chest, watching them go. A line of horses to ride and she found herself wanting to take a warm sponge to Bell's coat instead.

Then, just as quickly as the impulse hit her, Georgie rolled her eyes at herself. Her Eclipse Award sat on the mantel at Red Gate next to the four statuettes the farm had received decades before, back when breeding graded stakes winners had been all they ever did. Ride requests popped onto her phone every few minutes, hitting her from all sides, from all corners of the country, from a few countries across the globe. Angel could barely keep up, could hardly stop laughing when he called to tell her which big name trainer wanted her next.

And Georgie just wanted to keep riding Sweet Bells.

Shivering the thoughts off her back, Georgie started off in the direction of her next ride, stumbling to a stop as Roman and Harris clattered out of the barn. The colt's dappled coat glinted silver and black in the morning light. Harris held him to a bouncing, trembling walk, Roman all attitude in his attempts to yank on Luna's hold on the reins. With an impatient squeal and a hard toss of his head, Roman reared up on his hind legs. Luna folded against the colt's back, going with the rise. When Roman fell back down to earth, Harris kept the colt moving, looking up at his rider as he pushed a row of knuckles into the colt's shoulder to keep him on a straight path to the track.

"We're good, boss," Luna said from the colt's back. Georgie leaned into the barn, wondering if that was really the case, but Harris seemed satisfied and let them go. The colt danced his way down to the track, all energetic snorts and fanning mane. Luna sat the skitters and leaps, threaded him through the gap onto the track, and set off treading up dirt down the outside rail. The colt's head came down, ears forward and legs setting a two-beat Georgie knew by heart.

Harris watched from the rise outside the barn. He looked rumpled—jeans hung low on his hips, held in place by a leather belt that hadn't made it into all of its loops. His long-sleeve shirt was partially tucked, the light down vest he wore on top of it already smeared with fresh horse slobber, probably courtesy of Roman. He pushed a hand into his tousled hair, past the brink of an acceptable hairstyle and into mayhem.

Of course, it looked good on him. Georgie glared at his back and thought about all the horses she still had to ride, thought about why it was she didn't seem to want to move. He hadn't noticed her there, and this was one of the rare moments she had to look at him without his knowledge. Like she could peer in on his private moments and see . . . what?

What was she even looking for?

Her phone began to chime from her back pocket. She jumped, nearly dropping the saddle in her haste to shut up her phone and dive into the barn at the same time. The display read *Mom*, a red flag if there ever was one. Claire didn't call her during the works, especially when Claire was in Kentucky, consulting for a string of breeding farms.

She answered the phone with a question. "Mom?"

"Thank god, Georgie," Claire said breathlessly. "I wasn't sure you'd pick up."

Georgie took a few steps into the barn, further from Harris, who had to know she'd been there, voyeuristically watching his back like some sort of socially awkward crazy person.

"What's happening?"

"Your father," Claire said with the type of sigh that let Georgie know how not well this conversation was going to go. "Did you see him last night at all?"

Georgie wanted to ask why, but she was too afraid it would come out like a garbled scream of frustration. Besides, she knew why.

"No," she said, falling into the barn wall and staying there, preparing herself for what was coming next. "I assumed he was at the barn when I left for Tupelo this morning."

"I hate to ask you this, Georgie," Claire said, her voice dropping. She didn't want anyone to hear, and Georgie wanted to tell her not to bother. Everyone already knew their business, even all the way off in Kentucky. *Uncle Moe* had seen to that.

"What do you need me to do?" she asked quietly, lowering her voice out of habit and finding it funny that she was doing the same thing as her mother. It must be instinct now. She almost smiled before she remembered and ducked her head, squeezing her eyes shut.

"Currently, I need you to go pick up your father from the police station," Claire whispered into the phone. "He tells me he has his court date already, and just needs to post bail."

No doubt through some old friendship, a favor called in.

"That's great. And while I'm picking him up from jail, maybe I should go ahead and grab some groceries while I'm at it. What are we out of? Oh, right, sanity. And maybe common sense," Georgie said pointedly.

"Georgie," Claire admonished.

"It's true," Georgie said. "How many times have we had to do this?"

"There will be a time and a place for that conversation."

That meant never. They never talked about this.

"Fine," Georgie muttered. "I'll figure something out."

She hung up on her mother's goodbye, pressed the phone against her forehead, and let out a little groan.

"Bad news?" Harris said behind her. She wheeled around, suddenly very aware that he had clearly listened to the whole thing. Shame fluidly washed over her, coloring her cheeks pink and coating thickly on her tongue. Then she had to push it all away, because it wasn't like Harris couldn't identify.

"Tell Reece he needs to find another rider," she said, pushing the phone back into her pocket and taking off the radio, handing it over to him. "Think I can borrow a farm truck?"

Harris narrowed his eyes at her, taking the radio. "The first is doable," he said. "The second is not freaking likely."

"What?" Georgie asked, not in the mood. "Afraid I'll total it?"

Harris huffed out a disbelieving laugh, shaking his head at her like she'd only gotten in the way of her own intentions. "You have a strange way of asking for help."

"And you heard me on the phone," Georgie bit out. "You know what I need the truck for, so don't *pretend* like you don't."

He stared at her for a beat and finally pulled his keys out of his front pocket, turning on his heel.

"Hey," she called to his back, jumping to keep up with his longer stride.

"If you think you're driving one of the trucks, you are so completely mistaken," he said over his shoulder.

"I ride your farm's horses," she shot back at him. "I think those are more important, and I manage that just fine."

"It's really not comparable," he said, unlocking his BMW.

Georgie stood by the car for a moment, its sleek black curves shining in front of her like they had on that day two years ago. Only this wasn't that car. That car was wrecked past saving. She put her hands on her hips and felt ridiculous, remembering something like that now. It was just a car.

Harris started the engine and rolled down the passenger window, leaning over the console and peering up at her.

"Get in, Georgie," he said, opening up her door and swinging it toward her. She caught it and held it for a moment, her head swirling in a potential future of Harris having seen her bail her father out of the drunk tank. She was dead sure she didn't want any part of that future, but Harris was already there, car idling and jaw set.

"If you tell anyone, I swear I will make every morning we work together miserable for the rest of your natural life," she said through her teeth, sliding into the car. Her dirty boots pressed prints into the floorboard carpet as she secured the seat belt. Harris tilted his head back, looked down his nose at her and put the car into gear.

"You know the Armstrong family well enough to know that hiding secrets is our great talent," he said through a sardonic grin, backing out of the spot and kicking up dust on their way to the main road. The car skipped off the farm's driveway and onto solid pavement. "Far be it from me to break with tradition."

"That's incredibly well-meaning of you," Georgie said, rolling her eyes, "but you guys are terrible at hiding your dysfunction."

Harris shrugged, as though the fact didn't bother him when Georgie new damn well that it did. "But that's *our* dysfunction," he said, putting a hand over his heart like it was dear to him. "We don't have time to care about anyone else's problems. So you've got a drunk for a dad, Georgie. That's bush league."

"That's not exactly how I would describe it," Georgie replied, gripping the armrest as they blew past the Ocala city limits sign. Harris didn't contradict her, letting the car dip into silence as they slipped through the city and arrived at the police station in record time. Georgie sat for a beat longer than necessary after Harris turned off the car, failing to immediately release her seatbelt and scurry into the station like a good daughter doing her mother's bidding.

"Hey," Harris said, making her jump.

She dragged in a deep breath, and undid the seatbelt, doing everything quickly. The faster she moved, the sooner this would be over.

"Hold on, Georgie," Harris said, catching her hand before she could fling herself from the car. She startled to a stop, heart in her throat as she looked at his fingers around hers. Just there, like he touched her all the time and thought nothing of it when she was hyperventilating.

"I'm coming in there with you."

"What? Why?" she asked, finding words and spitting them out.

"Because maybe you'd like the help?" Harris shot back at her, raising his eyebrows.

"If you come in there with me can you refrain from reveling in the heinousness of this situation?"

Harris just stared at her, a kind of weight that dragged Georgie back to those days just after Lilliana. She knew where he'd been back then, and knew all about the why.

"Well?"

"I'm not saying anything to anyone because it's not anyone's business but ours."

Ours.

Georgie fell back into the seat with an audible thump, so exasperated with him that she didn't know where to begin. *Sure,* she thought, *now the repressed crazy person suddenly insists on being helpful.*

Georgie didn't know how to handle this.

"Let me help, George," he said, and for all she knew he was sincere, and she was so far out of her depth.

"Okay," she said. "Okay, you can come with me. Just stop talking."

"Gladly," he said, and let go of her hand.

Ocala wasn't a sleepy town, and its police station looked like it ran solely on caffeine. Stale coffee filled the air, made Georgie wish for a cup of the good stuff straight out of Reece's office in the training barn. As they waited for her father to be brought out from detention, she sat on the edge of one stained chair and watched Harris' knee bounce up down, up down. She wanted to reach over and stop it, but that would mean touching Harris, which she'd already done once today through no fault of her own and wasn't eager to do again.

So she let it bounce.

And she tried not to think.

Invariably, she gave up. There was no way sitting next to Harris in the middle of a police station wasn't going to garner some thoughts. It seemed so fitting, like a twist of fate. Every time an officer walked by that knew Harris there was a moment she got to watch him sink into his chair, nod to the officer's request that he stay out of trouble.

Yes, Georgie thought. *No more cavalierly breaking luxury cars for Harris. My, how he's grown since his last visit in this very station.* She kept the thoughts to herself.

"You can ask," Harris told her, making Georgie wonder if he hadn't also discovered how to read minds while on his straight and narrow path.

"I wasn't going to ask anything."

"I know," Harris told her. "Which is why I'm telling you that you can."

"I wasn't looking for your permission."

"Which is just how you would spin this," he sighed, shaking his head. Georgie wished her father would appear soon. As in *now*. So she didn't have to sit with Harris, who insisted on being helpful and was instead *not*.

"It wasn't that bad the first time I was here," Harris said, volunteering information Georgie didn't want to know. She already knew enough without having to look into the horse's mouth for the full version of events. "A ticket, a fine, a few precious hours of alone time. It was the second go-round that was actually the best."

"What second time?" Georgie asked. "I distinctly remember Oliver throwing around some money and you landing in rehab for a month."

"That month was amazing," Harris said. "I'd probably be right back there if I hadn't moved into the farm's guest cottage after I checked out."

"Why are you telling me this?" Georgie asked, swinging around in her seat to glare at him. He stopped, looking at her like he was surprised when he couldn't be. There was no way he was that stupid.

"Because you want to know why him and why here, deep down," he said simply. "Things aren't going to stop sucking for a while, because we all know Red Gate isn't pulling itself out of that pit, and maybe he just wanted to be someone else's problem."

"That is absurd," Georgie said. "How does any of this make him not my problem?"

Harris shifted toward her, making Georgie cringe back. "Because," he smiled, "you don't understand what it's like to have people you know, people you even love, asking you how you're doing. All. The. Time. And they won't stop because nothing you can ever say will convince them to stop asking. It's offensive, and then it's hilarious, and then you just want to leave, through whatever means."

Harris sat back in his chair, victorious in that careless way of his that made her want to reach inside of him and bring *Harris* back.

Her Harris.

"I remember when you came back from rehab," she volunteered, a blurt of information popping out of her mouth because this was not Harris victorious. This was sad. He looked at her out of the corner of his eye, waiting.

She tapped her finger against the wall, at the parking lot beyond it. "You were driving that car. I was walking to the yearling barn, and you went flying past in that thing. You drove straight past me, looking at me all the while like you were making a point. There was no me anymore, not to you."

It was like he hadn't even seen her, like she was mere air.

"So maybe don't tell me how great it was to not be around the people who cared about you," she said. "I was one of those people."

He sighed, looked up at the ceiling like he was studying the water marks. "It's really not about you, Georgie."

"No," she agreed. "But you twisted it that way."

That got his attention. He shot her a dark look, and she thought *good, live there for a while and see how it feels.*

The back door to the holding cells swung open, and Georgie stood up like a shot. Harris lifted out of his chair at the same time, stepping into her peripheral just as her father slowly pushed out the swinging partition that separated the station from the waiting area. He was rumpled, hair askew, green around the gills and far too pale.

"Morning, Dad."

Tom nodded to her, rubbed the back of his hand against this mouth. He smelled sour.

"He might want some hair of the dog," the officer at the desk advised Georgie, all good ol' boy grin before he directed his attention to her father. "We'll be seeing you, Tom."

Georgie opened her mouth, a comeback so swift to her tongue that it was nearly past her lips when Harris' strangled grunt caused her to rein it back in. She swallowed it down, even as she desperately wanted to unleash some of her frustration. For a moment she felt rooted to the spot, her body still clinging to the desire to tell someone how screwed up this was.

"Georgie," Harris broke into her raging thoughts, prodding her into action. "We're done here. Let's go."

She blinked at him, watched Harris put one hand on her father's shoulder and guide him toward the doors. Lurching after them, she followed Harris' lead out into the brilliant Florida light. It shone down on them like a stark morning flood, crisp air pouring down her throat, filling her up, trying to make her feel better.

And for a second, she did. Then Tom bent forward, coughing up meager bites of breakfast all down the front steps of the station. Harris put a hand on the back of Tom's head, let out a disbelieving huff of a laugh. Something within Georgie spasmed, shriveled into itself, wanted to die but just couldn't quite manage it.

Something like her heart.

She shut her eyes, counted to three, and said, "Let's get out of here."

Then she took the first step toward home.

Chapter Eight

IN THE CORNER of the stall, Sweet Bells ripped at her hay net, shifting only occasionally and lowering her head to check out Georgie's knees. She rubbed her muzzle against Georgie's worn jeans, then swung her head to one outstretched leg to rub away the material's itch on her lips, and dove back into the hay. Georgie smiled without looking up, turning the page on *The Odyssey* as it sat propped against her legs. She was so close to finishing the book, scrambling to soak up the story for the extra credit she desperately needed to pass English come June, but the words swam across the page and she rubbed at her bleary eyes.

Maybe if she just shut down for a moment, took a power nap in the hay at Bell's feet. She'd have some energy after that to get up and walk back to Red Gate, help with the evening feed, and finish the book before passing out after a typical fractured Quinn family dinner that would involve her parents being even more silent than usual. Ever since her father's DUI charge, Georgie was fairly sure no one had spoken above a hissed whisper. There was still an empty whiskey bottle in the trash every other night, which meant business lurched on as usual.

The filly huffed, dropping a scattering of scraggly hay strands across the book. An invitation to *hey, look at me*. Georgie absently pulled a mint out of her coat pocket and handed it over, the sweet smell drifting down to her while the filly crunched.

She shut her eyes, replaying the weekend's big race in her head like a loop of stuck film reel, Little War leading gate to wire and dragging Georgie around the track with an insistence that bordered on manic. When Reliance came at him in deep stretch, his heaving body moving so much faster, she was relieved to find a spark in the colt's reserves. She asked him for more, and Little War gave, straining forward just as the finish flashed over.

Little War takes the Fountain of Youth at the wire!

Reliance blew past them too late, his jockey standing in the irons and sawing back on the reins far into the clubhouse turn. If the race had been another quarter of a mile, it would have been no contest. Give Reliance a distance like the Kentucky Derby and Little War had no chance. She could feel that in the exhaustion shuddering through the colt on the way back to the grandstand, in the way he blew out in the winner's circle like he was searching for air.

She cued up the race on her phone, watched through the glow as Reliance took his time firing all engines, gathering himself for his big run as she worked at Little War, telling him to keep the lead. Somewhere mid-pack, Roman sat behind horses, covered in dirt with nowhere to run. Footsteps in the barn aisle made her pause the video, the tinny announcer's voice disappearing into the quiet.

"Congratulations," Harris said, leaning over the open partition. Bell crunched her peppermint, the air spiked with sugar.

Georgie looked up at him, the race in which his horse magnificently lost glowing up from her hands. She hastily shut it down.

"How magnanimous of you," she said. "I thought you might just pretend the Fountain of Youth hadn't happened."

"Nah," he said. "It's very much in the front of my mind."

Harris paused for a beat, shifting on his feet as they stared at each other over the partition. Then he unlatched the stall, the bedding rustling under his feet.

"Of course, I hadn't anticipated visitors," she remarked.

"You see the new *Uncle Moe?*" he asked, like he hadn't heard her.

"I told you . . ."

"I know what you said." He pulled a light green piece of paper out of the back pocket of his jeans and handed it to her. She unfolded it carefully as he settled against the wall next to her, stretching his long legs into the bedding.

Attention Floridians: Tom Quinn, embattled Red Gate Farm owner and lover of fine Kentucky mash, has been suspended from the road for six months. No word yet from Tupelo Stud on whether or not this makes things more difficult for Oliver Armstrong's late night Red Gate liaisons.

"That's disappointing." Georgie handed the newsletter back to Harris. "You need to stop reading these."

He laughed, shoving the paper into his pocket. "Yeah, I probably should. It's like I can't stop caring or something. What's your secret?"

"I'm not talking about this right now," Georgie snapped, getting her tired legs underneath her and pushing to her feet. She'd ridden sixteen horses over the weekend, and her body felt loose, like it had been stretched too far.

"Yeah, probably best to let it keep stewing until someone blows up," Harris said, nodding. "That sounds like an awesome plan."

"You're paranoid," she accused.

"And you're deliberately playing dumb," he shot back.

She took a deep breath that did nothing to calm her down, her heart already jacking into a wild race in her chest. Georgie forced herself to wait for a beat, forced herself to take a different track than the one she always went down with Harris. The snipping at each other about something neither of them knew for certain wasn't doing it for her this time around.

If it ever had. It wasn't like this was quality time.

"If you can bring me anything else about Oliver and my mom, some concrete proof that isn't this bullshit out of *Uncle Moe*, then maybe I'd consider believing you," she said, watching his eyes narrow because she knew he didn't have it. Neither of them did. "Until then, stop. Just, *please stop.*"

Silence. Georgie clutched her book to her chest, gauging how awkward they could be on a level of one to ten. She figured this was a healthy eleven.

"You're right," he allowed, and she let her head fall back in relief. "The *Uncle Moe* stuff is a joke, but the fact that I saw your mom over here . . . when was that?" He looked up at the ceiling, screwing his face up like that would help him remember. "Oh yeah, looking at the yearlings this week with Oliver. Never too early to start sales prep."

A finger of cold dragged its way down Georgie's back, dug into her spine. Claire wouldn't come to Tupelo, wouldn't set foot on the grounds, not after everything.

"I'm sure whatever you saw . . ."

"Was definitely my dad, your mom," Harris said, pulling himself to his feet just as Georgie's already tired knees felt like they might give out on her. "I looked into it later, and turns out the farm was looking for a new bloodstock agent. Oliver went on something of a firing spree, and guess who turned up soon after?"

"Shut up," Georgie told him, quivering.

"I wish I could, Georgie."

"It still doesn't mean anything," she pointed out. "Selling and buying horses for someone doesn't mean . . ."

"You're right. It doesn't." He pushed off the wall and came to a stop too close to her. She could feel the excited heat coming off of him, the urgency in the way he held himself. She wanted to take a step back, but it would only put her against the wall, so she stood her ground. Georgie only dimly realized he was agreeing with her. Instead of being happy about it, she wanted to throw up at their feet.

"It just means that if you see something, say something. That's all I'm asking," he said, and she jerked her eyes up to him, wondering how she was going to do that when she didn't even know her mother had walked onto Tupelo's property for the first time in two years, ready and willing to do business like nothing had ever happened.

"Then what?" she asked, wondering what any of it was worth. What did knowing matter when she couldn't do anything about it? "Let's say they are doing everything you imagine. What will you do then, Harris?"

He just stared at her for a beat, which made her wonder what it was all worth to him. Was knowing all he needed? Like it would make everything that happened with Lilliana make sense? Because it would never make sense, not for Georgie. The pieces would never fit, and it would never be okay. Nothing about this was okay.

"Just do this for me?" Harris asked, so close Georgie felt her skin prickle with impending warning. The tips of his fingers found the inside of her palm, touched feather soft. The bolt of adrenaline that kicked into her system made her pull away, push past him for the stall door.

"I'm going home," she announced.

"I'll drive you," he said, recovering swiftly and following her out of the stall. She spun around, holding a finger up between them so he stopped in his tracks, looking at her.

"I will tell you what I find out," she told him. When he started to say something she pushed on. "That's it. No hunting for information, no trying to catch them in lies. I'm opening communication with you, but that's it. That's all I'm doing."

"Did you know she was here?" he asked.

"What the hell sort of question is that?" she snapped at him. "Of course not."

He nodded. "Then that's already one lie you've caught. Think there will be others?"

"You're such an asshole." She turned around, stalking out of the training barn and into the early winter night. Harris jogged up behind her, caught her hand in his to slow her down. Another red hot bolt shot up her fingers. She dropped the book and wheeled around to tell him to knock it off. He couldn't just keep touching her. He wasn't allowed to do that anymore, and he knew that.

She had told him.

He handed her the book and fished the car key out of his pocket, showing it to her.

"A ride," he said. "I really actually meant to drive you home."

"Why?" she asked, and he blinked at her, confused.

"Because I can be nice sometimes?"

"When you get what you want," she told him. "Sure, then you're an angel."

"Do you want the ride, or . . ."

"Shut up," she growled, stalking over to the BMW and opening the unlocked passenger door, folding herself into the seat and staring straight out the window as he drove them down to the main road, gravel rumbling under the tires and covering up Georgie's icy silence. She pressed her knees together, pointed them toward the door, as far from Harris' hand on the gear shift as she could possibly get.

"Little War looked good," Harris offered mid-drive, shifting into third and speeding past the paddocks.

"Should I pass that on to Nick, or do you think he'll care what you think?" she asked, risking a look over at him to see if the barb hit its mark.

"Jesus, Georgie," he sighed. "I *think* that was a compliment."

"You think?"

"Positive, actually," he said, and shook his head, like he couldn't believe he was having this conversation.

"I'm sure he'll be thrilled," Georgie said. "What happened with Roman? I read what Dean had to say after the race—"

"That Roman lacks the will," Harris interrupted. "Sometimes initially promising maidens tank when faced with real speed. It certainly wasn't Dean's fault, that's for damn sure. That's what you read, right? The interview where it's all the horse's fault and not his?"

"I'm taking from this outburst that Dean is no longer riding for you."

"That's about the long and the short of it." Harris stopped at the end of the driveway, the headlights cutting across the road and illuminating a stretch of Red Gate's white fence. Instead of pulling onto the main road, Harris pushed the car into neutral, sitting back in his seat.

Georgie stared at him, felt the moment stretch out two years to that day on what felt like an entirely different timeline. An alternate reality, really, of when they were different people leading softer lives. She could feel the moment stretching out, see what could have happened had they just not turned out onto the road in front of them, and every time she thought that would have been the better outcome. If she had just never gotten in the car that day, everything would have been so much easier.

"What is it?" she asked, felt that softness creep into her voice without meaning to draw on it. She wanted to leave it in the past, where it wouldn't get bruised and broken.

Harris cast an uncertain look at her, and she knew in a flash that he felt it, too. Felt the moment stretch past them and boomerang back. Then he said so quickly she had to strain to keep up, "Will you breeze Roman?"

Georgie had to reach out to hold onto something, her hand curling around the edge of the seat.

"What?"

"You heard me."

"It sounded a lot like you want me to ride your colt."

He fiddled with the gear shift, not looking at her.

"Harris."

He shoved the car into first, still not going anywhere. Then he looked over at her.

"I need to know if Dean's right."

"Dean is an idiot," Georgie said, watching the smile that managed to climb its way onto Harris' face before he killed it off. "He ran his mouth to cover his ass, and you know that."

"Maybe," Harris said, "but that doesn't change the fact that we finished out of the money this weekend, finished third before that, and I know this colt has it in him. If we keep going down this path, that means the Florida Derby next and I need someone I . . ."

He stopped himself, looked out at the high beams on the white fences and tapped his fingers repetitively against the steering wheel. *Tap, tap, tap.*

"Someone you can trust," Georgie said.

He pushed back from the wheel, wouldn't look at her. Georgie stared at the side of his head, wondering what was going on in there.

"Do you trust me?" she asked.

Harris let the question hang there in the air between them, working the insides of his cheeks between his teeth like he could gnaw them off before he made a strangled noise. "I trust you on the horses. You on the horses . . . there's a reason you're good at what you do, okay? I want you to bring that out in Roman."

Georgie stared at him, eating away at that nugget of honesty while it was his turn to wait on her answer. Finally, she pointed to Red Gate's main drive.

"Take me the rest of the way."

Harris pulled onto the road, turned with a squeal of rubber onto Red Gate's drive, and down the lane of live oaks, the silver-gray Spanish moss drifting in the night breeze like living tendrils hanging from the thick branches. Ennismore appeared like a ghost in the headlights, all peeling paint and rotting boards. Harris took the path that crept up on the house, its pale white columns casting shadows on the walls and the live oaks clustering against it like protection from the outside world.

Harris parked by the kitchen door around the back, didn't look at her as she pushed the door open and got out. She stood between the door and the car, looking up at the house and trying not to think too hard about what she had to say next.

She ducked down, found Harris watching her with that impatient *tap, tap, tap* on the steering wheel.

"I'll ride him," she said, and then stepped away from the car, slammed the door, before she could watch the reaction on his face, before she could really start considering what it meant to ride Harris' horse at the crack of dawn.

She jogged up the back steps, burst in through the kitchen in such a rush that her mother startled by the counter.

"Georgie!" Claire exclaimed, putting down her glass of wine and pressing a hand to her chest. Behind her, the gas stove hissed, a pot boiling away on the burner. "I wasn't expecting you back so soon. Is that . . . Harris' car?"

She peered through the torn screen door, her mouth dropping open in astonishment. When she turned back to Georgie, she looked almost happy, like maybe this was a good thing. She crossed the kitchen and brought a hand to Georgie's face, nestling her fingertips into her short, flaming red hair.

"I'm glad, sweetie," Claire said, face bright with something Georgie wanted to describe as hope. Deep inside Georgie's chest, her heart trembled, like it had been kicked.

Her mother went back to the stove, picking up the glass of wine on her way. Georgie looked down at her empty hands and realized she'd left the book on the BMW's floorboards. She wondered if Harris would notice that, right when she realized she hadn't finished reading it.

She hardly remembered the story at all.

Two weeks later, Georgie stood in Roman the Great's stall, the big colt pressing his nose against her knee and breathing her in like he could tell all the things he needed to know about her through scent alone.

Probably he could, if his obsessiveness was any indication.

She'd already tacked him up, tightened the girth, gotten it all done with only an impatient stamped hoof on Roman's part. Works had been in full swing for two hours, and the colt was eager, primed. Two weeks of jogging and two-minute licks around the track under a tight hold had that effect, and if Harris wanted Roman in the Florida Derby, today was as good a time as any to see what they had on their hands.

Or, more accurately, for Georgie to see what Harris had on his hands.

"You know," Lynsey said from outside the stall, "I'm going to need the background on this again, because I'm still having a hard time accepting what I'm seeing."

"You're having a hard time?" Georgie asked, pulling the stirrups down and gathering the reins at the base of Roman's neck. "I agreed to it and I'm still not sure what I was thinking."

She swung into the saddle with a bounce and a kicking leap, pushing herself upright. Roman turned a circle, looking for somewhere to go, as Lynsey opened the stall door to give them the outlet they needed. They clattered into the stable aisle, turning toward the training track as Lynsey walked next to them, hands shoved deep in her down vest and scrunching her face up at the cold.

"Moment of insanity?" Lynsey asked. "I would accept that, you know. The Armstrong family can't pass judgment there."

Georgie rolled her eyes, putting her feet in the stirrups and moving with Roman's quick walk. He had places to be, and Lynsey scurried to keep up.

"Moment of . . . déjà vu, I think," Georgie said, shaking her head when Lynsey cast a confused frown up at her. "It was annoying Harris, as usual, and then . . . not. Déjà vu."

"You got hit with phantom Harris," Lynsey nodded, like she'd seen it before, too. Could attest that her brother still had some soft, gummy center that they could still recognize. "At least you know that's not normal," Lynsey continued. "I honestly think he pulls that card to get what he wants, and looks like he got it without much trouble."

Georgie bit her lower lip, nodding. "Played me like a fiddle."

Maybe. Georgie still wasn't sure what to make of this arrangement. He wanted her opinion, and she could give it to him well enough. But anyone could do that. Reece was full of expert opinions, and she knew he'd given them. Any of the farm's riders would have told Harris what they thought, and she knew she would only echo them. For whatever reason, he needed hers and Georgie tried to see some good in that instead of the trap she was prepared to find instead.

The fact of the matter at present? Georgie didn't know what she was sitting on. Maybe Roman was a powder keg, just waiting to blow. Maybe he was only a colt that showed early promise and got pushed up the ranks too soon. She'd been in more than half of his races, and had seen the ride Dean had given him, so it wasn't out of the question that Roman had run right up against human error—foiled from greatness with one bad jerk of the reins.

Lynsey laughed, tilting her head back to look up at Georgie. "Don't be shocked when this turns into something else. It's never just one thing with Harris."

"Never is." Georgie nodded, walking through the gap in the track's outside rail. Lynsey stopped there, her eyes slipping over them as they bounded into a trot up the thick dirt. Roman found Georgie quickly, put his whole body into the trot with a swish of his tail and a kick to his step as Georgie rose up and down in the saddle. She felt him out like she was going on a test drive, gave him room to lengthen his stride and reeled him back in, testing the brakes. The colt snorted and tipped his ears back, like he knew he was being put through the paces.

When she asked for the canter, he leapt into the air like a stag, knees tucked and neck arched. A white ring of excitement showed around his deep brown eyes, and Georgie rode over it, put her heels to his sides and lifted over his withers when he settled and gave her the gait she wanted.

He opened up, lowered his head, found her hands again. They had their orders: a five furlong breeze, working on the inside of a four-year-old gelding. She found him cantering down the middle of the track, his rider nodding over at her.

"New ride?" he asked.

"Very," Georgie replied, tugging the colt down to a jaunty walk toward the outside rail and halting him. They worked the opposite way, bounding into a slow gallop toward the inside rail until they passed the starting pole and Georgie chirped to the colt, felt him respond with a roar of wind in her ears.

The gelding leapt in response, digging in on their outside to keep the pace swift from the outset. They galloped head-to-head into the turn, a blurry set of moving legs and pumping bodies. Roman's ears flicked back, his mane whipping up like a mohawk down to Georgie's hands, which she kept still by his withers, crouching over the center of his back so she appeared stationary even when she was moving so fast her eyes would have teared up if not for the plastic goggles protecting them.

Bursting around the turn, Georgie gave Roman the go ahead to put the gelding in his rearview. The colt shook him off in three lengthening strides, launching down the homestretch with such a powerful drive Georgie had to work to keep up with him. She didn't want to get left behind, jabbing him in the mouth at the peak of his speed. Roman put his head down, unfolding and collecting, sweeping past the finish marker and galloping full tilt into the next furlong with Georgie encouraging him with her fists in his mane.

Once they were well past the finish, she began to ease up on his neck, slowly redistributing her weight and sinking down, down, until the colt broke stride and rocked into a canter beat with a satisfied huff of milky warm air. Georgie kept reeling him back in, tugging back slowly. When Roman walked down the outside rail with his head up, ears pricked at the crowded track, she sank into the saddle and let out a breath.

"Talk to me, Georgie girl." Reece popped into her headset, voice crackling through the connection. Georgie squinted down the outside rail, saw Harris standing there next to Reece with his arms crossed, facing her like he was standing sentry.

Maybe he was bracing for the news.

"I think the Boy King will want to hear what I have to say," Georgie said, listening to the chuckling from the other end. She rode up the outside rail and motioned to Harris to walk with her as she pointed the colt off the track, onto the pathway back to the training barns for a cool out and a bath, the regular routine Roman would have come to expect by now.

"What was the time?" she asked, keeping light contact on the colt's mouth as he jigged up the rise to the barns.

"Fifty-nine flat," Harris said, clearing his throat. "For the five furlongs. The last eighth was eleven and three."

So Roman was a powder keg, then. Georgie had felt that whoosh of speed in her muscles, and knew what it meant. She sent a look down the colt's shoulder. It landed on Harris hard enough for her to watch him duck under the weight of it.

"I know," he sighed, pushing both hands into his hair, making it stick up in wild dark tufts. "It's exceptional. It's what good horses do."

"And you needed me here why?"

"So you could ride him five furlongs in fifty-nine, that's why," Harris said. "Tell me how it felt."

"It felt like what riding an exceptional race horse feels like,

Harris," Georgie replied. "You don't need my opinion. Luna, or any other exercise rider on the farm, could have told you that."

"But they're not you," he bit back at her, stopping as soon as the words left him in a harried rush. Georgie didn't know what to do with a person who wanted her help and didn't want it at the same time. What was she supposed to do? How was she supposed to make sense of any of this?

The breeze picked up, sending the palms clustered near the barn into a rustling frenzy. Roman pricked his ears and stopped so suddenly Georgie hardly had time to think before he whirled on his haunches, bowling over Harris as he took a wild leap off the path and into the grass. His hooves hit the solid ground with a thud, head up and breath blowing in quick snorts. Georgie kept up with him, turning him into a circle on the grass and craning her head around once the colt settled into a high-stepping, happy walk.

Harris climbed to his feet, brushing the dust off his jeans. Georgie put the colt back on the path and swung down, walking Roman up to the mouth of the barn.

"You okay?" she asked, brushing at the back of Harris' shirt without thinking and sending a plume of white dust into the air. She felt his muscles tense, and dropped her hand, pushing her elbow into Roman's shoulder when the colt decided he wanted to inspect too, shoving his nose against Harris' head and breathing loudly.

"Just another day working with this guy," Harris told her, resting his hand on the colt's nose and taking the reins out of her hands.

"Must make for some interesting days." Georgie scrubbed the colt's neck, reaching under his neat mane and rubbing the tips of her gloved fingers against his coat. Roman pawed at the gravel, twisted his head down to check out his miniature dust cloud, and blew a dissipating breath into it.

"Even more interesting when you're riding him," he muttered, like he wanted her to hear, but maybe wasn't so sure. Georgie, of course, heard. Two years' worth of muttering left her an expert at knowing exactly what Harris said to her, however garbled.

"You did ask," Georgie said. "Remember?"

"I did," Harris said simply, to the point. Georgie narrowed her eyes, waiting for the twist. Harris studied the reins in his hands, the smooth leather sliding across his palm as Roman chewed the bit impatiently, waiting on them to make up their mind. *In or out*, he seemed to say. *Let's go, people.*

"Today was Roman's best work," Harris told her, and Georgie tried to keep her expression schooled to indifference, blank and unknowable. Harris searched her face, and she hoped deep down that he knew what it was like to be on the receiving end this time. Just a little bit.

"I want you to ride him again." He said it with a rushed impatience, like the question in it got lost in favor of the demand. Georgie raised an eyebrow.

"He'll have one more timed work before the Florida Derby, and I want you to be his morning rider up to that work."

"That's a big ask, Harris," Georgie replied. He nodded, grinned like he knew and it pained him even to say the words.

"I know," he said, leading the colt into the dim barn, undoing the girth for Georgie to haul the saddle off the colt's back before handing Roman to his groom. The colt needed a cooling walk, a bath, his next meal. There was no time in his routine to stand around talking.

Georgie clutched the saddle against her chest. She still had two more horses to ride before getting to school, and she stood in the middle of the barn aisle like her boots had rooted to the spot as she thought about Harris and Roman, whether or not she could do what he asked of her, whether or not that was something either of them could live through and produce a winning horse.

A winning horse she would be riding against when the gates opened for the Florida Derby.

"What do you say?"

Oh, an actual question this time, like he was letting her have a choice. Georgie let out a breath.

"You know it will all mean nothing if you put Dean on his back for the race," she said as Harris sighed.

"Dean isn't getting back on."

"You say that . . ."

"He's not," Harris told her, a tendon in his jaw ticking.

"Then who will you get?"

"Let me figure that part out," Harris said. "All I want you to do is ride him in the mornings. Can you handle that or not?"

"The way you ask me just makes me want to leap at the chance!" Georgie said, throwing her free hand up. Harris rocked back on his heels, rubbing his thumb between his eyes like all of this hurt his head. Maybe it was too much trouble, Georgie thought. She should say no. She shouldn't even be wasting her time entertaining the option.

"You're right," Harris muttered, and Georgie's inner tirade screeched to a halt.

She was right? Since when had she been right about anything

in Harris Land?

"I'm not doing this correctly." Harris said, shaking his head.

"I don't see how we'd be able to make this work," Georgie said slowly, shifting under his gaze.

"We'd make it work," he said. "It's not about us, Georgie. It's about the horse. We've made it work with Bell, haven't we?"

"And what a fun time that was starting off," Georgie replied, rolling her eyes.

"But we're past that," Harris told her. "And we're already past that now with Roman. Look at us, talking like two normal people."

"I don't know that this is normal."

"Close enough."

Georgie sucked in a breath and held it, letting it out slowly. Harris shrugged like he didn't know what else to say.

"It's about Roman, George."

Oh, damn it all.

"Fine."

He smiled at her. A real smile, like a person who might actually be happy. It made a little part of Georgie jerk awake, come alive like she was standing in a shower of sparks that singed and glowed on her skin. She pushed the saddle firmly against her chest, could feel the leather digging into her breastbone, and shook off the feeling.

That was a feeling that couldn't be allowed, for all sorts of reasons.

"Thanks, Georgie," Harris said, still smiling.

Thanks. Georgie looked at him like he had two heads.

"See you tomorrow morning."

He popped his fist against her shoulder, like she was one of the guys doing him a favor. And she was, really, so she let him follow through. He left her there in the aisle, holding her saddle and trying to remember which horse she needed to ride next when her head was cluttered with Harris and Roman and the decision she'd made.

March

Chapter Nine

THE SKY WAS pink when Georgie rode Roman the Great off the main track, the tall palm trees dark explosions popping against the morning sky. The gray colt walked like a prize fighter underneath her, showing off how well he'd done with his big stride and his eagerness to jump and shy at any tiny opportunity. At the horses headed toward the track. At the groom rinsing out a bucket in the shedrow. At the cat dashing across the drive.

Especially the cat.

Roman stopped and lifted up. Georgie went with him, waited for him to come down with a scrape of hooves on stones and pushed him back into a walk. She couldn't give him time to think about rearing again, especially when anything seemed to set him off.

And anything would. Georgie had Roman the Great memorized, down to the way he liked to keep her waiting just that split second before he did what she asked, like he wanted her to know that he was executing her commands because he'd thought it all through and decided *sure, what the hey?*

Then there was Roman's owner. Georgie couldn't explain what it felt like to ride the colt down to the training oval every morning with Harris watching her every move, his voice in her ear asking if the colt was off on his left fore, wasn't putting enough effort in, could possibly be putting *too much* effort in.

Georgie sighed into the headset and told him he was being a mother hen. That usually won her some peace until she rode the colt off the track to more questions. Working for Harris wasn't so much a ceaseless fight as it was constant attention to detail. Roman, however, kept thriving and showing up, pushing into the bridle and zooming around the track.

Roman snorted and yanked at the reins, skittering at the sight of a lawn chair sitting innocently by the mouth of a barn they passed.

"Dork," Georgie muttered at the colt, who whipped his ears back to listen. She laughed and nudged him into her hands, felt for his mouth, and sank her weight down when they arrived at the receiving barn, where Tupelo's stalls housed their temporary runners at the track.

"You calling my horse names?" Harris asked her, walking up behind her as she bounced out of the saddle and let Roman's groom lead the colt into the shedrow.

"I'm calling him the names he deserves," Georgie said, unbuckling her helmet. "He spooks because he enjoys it."

"He's a sensitive guy," Harris replied, handing her his phone. Roman's time glowed up at her, cutting through the early morning dim. Four furlongs in forty-seven and three. "A sensitive guy who's on the war path."

Georgie handed the phone back. "You've got a good horse on

your hands, Harris. You know that."

"I have a good horse on my hands when you're riding him," Harris said, falling into step with her as she started off for her next ride. Whether Harris knew it or not, she needed to be at the Castellano barn to jump on Little War. Nick's colt had already done his five furlongs, and was set to jog leading up to the Florida Derby.

"I would save that statement for after the race. Who do you have assigned to him?"

He fell silent, walking along next to her like a looming, uncomfortable shadow.

"You do have an idea about that, right?" she asked. "The race is four days away, Harris."

He let out a breath. "I do have an idea, yes."

"Do you feel like sharing?"

"I was going to name you," he said quickly, like if he said it fast enough she might not question him. Georgie slid to a stop, turning toward him.

"And then you realized what a bad idea that was, right?" she asked. "You laughed and laughed and then you found another rider, right?"

Harris screwed up his face, shaking his head. "Why would I do that? You've gotten more out of him than anyone. You should be the person who rides."

"Those are morning works, Harris," she said, voice rising. "Anything could happen on race day, and whether or not I'm in the saddle won't—"

"Will, actually," he argued right back.

"How?" She started walking again, forcing him to keep up with her.

"You've been riding this colt every morning, and I know you've fallen just a little in love with him," he said, jumping in front of Georgie and making her stop short.

"I ride a lot of horses in the morning," Georgie snapped at him. "I don't ride all of them in the afternoons."

"Come on, George," Harris said, sighing. "Little War is a one-gear horse and you know it. I've watched them try to teach that colt how to rate and he won't put up with it. You know Roman won't run off rank if things don't go his way. If you want to win the Florida Derby, I'm offering you the best horse."

"That's remarkably confident coming from a guy who wasn't sure if his horse even had the talent to run with graded company not two weeks ago," Georgie reminded him.

"I'm a quick study," Harris told her.

"Apparently."

"You know I'm right about Nick's colt, and we both know that this race won't set up easy for him. Dean's riding Second Sail, and he's going to go straight to the lead. Little War has a speed duel coming, and Senior knows it."

Georgie had seen Second Sail's races, knew the colt was a ball of speed. She knew exactly what Senior would tell her when she walked into the paddock for the Florida Derby, which would be get to the lead first. When Dean came at them on Second Sail, which he would because he was Dean, *keep the lead*. The race would be over from the start if they couldn't lead.

"I don't want to have this conversation," Georgie said.

"But you're having it, Georgie," he told her. "Right now. Little War or Roman. You have to make a call."

Georgie wanted to tell him to take his offer and go to hell, but the temptation of it kept the words from tumbling out of her mouth. For the first time in a long while she wished she could be anywhere else. She would take the unparalleled awkwardness of sitting through a test where she knew none of the answers to this.

Georgie closed her eyes, forced herself to answer him.

"I'm already riding Little War."

"George."

"No. Don't *George* me right now, Harris. I made that commitment, regardless of his ability to settle off the lead, or however much I like your colt. This isn't a popularity contest. This is my career."

He didn't say anything, so she turned the corner to the Castellano barn and ducked into the shedrow, expecting to find a tacked up Little War and Nick. Only she found the colt still in his stall, ripping at hay and chewing with single-minded purpose.

"Hey, bud, where are your people?" Georgie asked the colt, scrubbing his nose when he came to investigate her for snacks. She pushed away from the stall and continued down the aisle, finding Nick in the feed room going through supplements and muttering to himself.

She paused in the doorway, hedging her bets.

"Do I want to know?" she asked, and he sent her a glowering frown.

"I forgot to text you," Nick sighed, wiping his hands off on his jeans. "Vet found a bone chip in Little War's left ankle that's bothering him, so we'll be scheduling a surgery instead of planning for the Triple Crown."

Georgie's heart stuttered in her chest.

"Is it bad?"

Nick rubbed a hand over one eye like he was wiping at something. "Bad enough to put his training on hold until summer. Right now, he's on stall rest. I'm sorry, Georgie."

"Don't apologize," Georgie insisted, finding her voice and shaking the shock off. "Let me know when you want me back on."

"Let's hope it's sooner rather than later, huh?" Nick shook his head, because they both knew. With horses, there were no guarantees. You worked yourself raw and hoped until your heart hurt just for a little heat in a foreleg to derail everything.

Georgie slumped into the doorjamb, closed her eyes, and steeled herself. Then she stalked out of the Castellano barn. She found Harris where she'd left him.

"You knew."

He shrugged. "Maybe a little."

"You're such an ass," she accused, and he grinned at her wolfishly.

"Yeah, but at least I have a morally upstanding jockey, right?"

"That isn't why you named me to ride."

"No," he said, suddenly serious. "I named you because you're the best I can get. Roman deserves that."

Georgie snorted. "That's a remarkable change of tune, Harris. I seem to remember you loathing every second I was in Bell's saddle."

"This is about Roman, not us," he said. "Maybe it took owning my own horse to figure that out. He likes you. Why screw with something that works?"

Why indeed. She worked her thoughts over that, realizing that not riding Roman would just be another argument. It would be something for him to blame her for later, if he lost. And what if they won? What then? She wished not racing in the Florida Derby were as tantalizing as running it on a horse owned by Harris. Although, she had to admit that she'd ridden Roman for two weeks and they hadn't killed each other.

Yet. She sighed.

"Don't make me regret this."

He winked at her.

"Not planning on it."

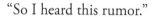

"So I heard this rumor."

Georgie sat cross-legged on the common room sofa before the Florida Derby, gnawing on her pencil's eraser with an Algebra textbook splayed open in her lap. The numbers in it held meaning, mostly in their ability to give her a headache. Outside of that, she had the tiring suspicion she'd slept through too many math classes during night school, because none of the numbers made any sense.

Dean leaned over the back of the sofa, resting his chin on her shoulder and chewing loudly on a piece of gum. The smacking rang in her skull and made her cringe like fingernails on a chalkboard would send showers of needles down her spine.

"Georgie," he said again, bouncing against the back of the sofa to get her attention. "Don't you want to hear the rumor?"

"If this doesn't have anything to do with logarithmic expressions, I don't feel it's pertinent."

Dean scoffed. "Come on, girl. Don't be like that."

"Be like what?" Georgie sighed, slamming her textbook shut. "I can't always make you feel like the center of attention all the damn time."

A chorus of amused agreement echoed through the room. Jockeys waited around for the next race in their white undershirts, thumbed through the day's entries, napped on the sofa when it didn't have Georgie perched on it with a textbook. Someone threw a ball of rolled up socks at Dean's head, and he ducked too late.

"She knows me so well," Dean announced to the room. "One of these days—"

"You're boring me, Dean," Georgie cut in, lifting the Algebra book. "Logarithms are more interesting."

His smile fell.

"You never let me have any fun," he accused.

"Maybe you should try being fun," Georgie said, rising both eyebrows. "Then maybe everything would be different. I might actually like you, for starters."

Dean fell onto the sofa with a thump, throwing an arm across Georgie's shoulders.

"Don't you want to know the rumor?" He rested his head against the cushion, lolling over to look at her too closely. Georgie gritted her teeth, wanting desperately for someone to film this so she could take it back to her teachers and tell them that this is what she put up with every day she was at the track. Then maybe she'd get a passing grade just for suffering Dean Hayes while trying to do her job.

Not killing him had to win her some brownie points, at the very least.

"Not at all, but if it will get you to be quiet even a little bit then sure, knock yourself out."

"There might be some talk about you screwing your way into

riding Roman the Great," Dean said, holding up his hands like it couldn't have been him doing that talk. That would be preposterous. "And damn, Georgie, I said you'd known Harrison Armstrong forever. Practically grew up together and all that, but you know how talk is. You got that ride mighty fast after the Castellano colt dropped out."

Georgie looked up at the ceiling, wondered if there would ever be a time in her life when she didn't have to hear this sort of crap in the jockeys' room. Probably never. Racing was a man's sport, after all. A girl in the common room was bad enough, but a girl that routinely beat the best boys on the track? If Dean couldn't beat her on a horse, he could at least start a rumor. He looked so gleeful he was positively radiant.

"Here I thought the known fact was you lost the ride on Roman the Great because you screwed over Harrison Armstrong." Georgie lifted Dean's arm and dropped it into his lap, standing up. "Maybe focus on the riding instead of the talking. You're not good at it."

The jockeys who were paying attention nudged each other, a few laughing openly. Georgie smiled at a glowering Dean, bowed to their audience, and picked up her Algebra book on the way to the kitchen.

She had homework to do.

Midway into the far turn, Georgie checked to see how much horse she had underneath her. Roman responded like gangbusters, pinning his ears back and surging into the bridle. The colt plowed up the inside rail, dark mane whipping back at Georgie's face and stride lengthening. The horses on their outside fell back in two leaps, Roman taking sight of the colts ahead of them—the struggling Reliance and Second Sail, who was on the lead and just getting started.

Once they were clear of the pack, Georgie stepped on the gas hard, taking up slack in the reins and pointing the speeding Roman to Reliance's outside. The other colt huffed as they flew by, his stride faltering. Ahead of them, Dean saw them coming, already swinging the crop left-handed down onto Second Sail's hind end. The pale gray jumped, cocking his head toward the inside and swinging away from the sting—veering crookedly into Roman's path. Georgie had no time. Second Sail's pearly white hindquarters plowed right into Roman's shoulder.

She felt the jarring right up Roman's front legs, and forced herself to keep her weight low as Roman went down. Second Sail straightened off the impact, and Roman curled toward the dirt. It happened in a split second that felt divided into thousandths for Georgie, who loosened the reins and mentally crossed her fingers with her heart flying up her throat. They were at the height of speed coming into the stretch, with horses behind them. If they fell now there was only the smallest hope she wouldn't be trampled by a half-ton horse after she hit the dirt.

Save it, Roman, she thought, digging her fingers into his wind-tangled mane. *Get up, get up, get up!*

The colt's nose grazed the dirt next to his knee, but instead of the inevitable roll, the sickening thud and crash of bodies, Roman scrambled. For one split second he kneeled down on the ground, and the next he pushed up and moved *faster*.

"Yes! Come on!" Georgie shouted, ducking her head down and letting Roman take the outside path, galloping so fast up Second Sail's side that Georgie didn't bother going for the whip. She pumped her arms up the crest of Roman's neck and the gray colt collected, lifted, ran angry toward the wire.

She didn't look back to see where Second Sail ran behind her. Roman's hooves hit the dirt like staccato strikes and catapulted them by the finish pole a length ahead.

Lifting herself high over the saddle on the gallop out, Roman lowered his head and gratefully took the rein Georgie gave him as he slowed. A flash of white pulled even with them.

"What the hell was that?" she yelled over at Dean, who shook his head.

"My bad, baby," he said. "He ducked out on the turn, left no time to correct him. You okay? Was sure you'd spill."

"Fine so far," Georgie said, easing Roman into a bouncing trot. Dean afforded her a sunny smile over his arm as he kept cantering up the track, Second Sail less eager to slow with his mouth gaping and his tail twitching. Roman, on the other hand, was happy to turn in toward the grandstand. His sides heaved against Georgie's ankles, adrenaline still running high on their way to the winner's circle.

Georgie waved to the crowd, holding her crop hand up in victory to whoops of celebration and camera flashes. Roman's ears swiveled toward the noise, his body shivering. She slapped his dirty shoulder, a grin stretching across her face that didn't die when she looked ahead of them and saw Harris, who stood with his shining leather shoes sunk deep in the dirt. Sunglasses covered his eyes, but a naked grin graced his face, making a certain, older part of Georgie hurt at the sight. He looked so happy he could hardly contain it all inside, so he didn't, letting it pour out around him in beaming waves that lapped over her when she pulled Roman to a halt in front of him.

"Quite the save," Harris said, putting a hand on the colt's forehead as Roman lowered his head and let his ears flop, looking curiously around him.

"All him," she said, pointing to the colt. "I don't know how you got so lucky."

Harris laughed—actually laughed—an infectious kind of joy that made Georgie thrill to the sound. Reece's assistants rushed up with buckets of water. They doused the colt's hindquarters, his chest, handed Georgie a sponge so she could lean forward and squeeze water between the colt's ears. She helped haul the blanket of blue, yellow, and pink orchids over Roman's withers, keeping her knees nestled together and pressing against the flowers.

Harris took the colt's bridle and led him into the winner's circle to applause and beers raised in salute to a winning ticket, a job well done. Roman the Great's ownership contingent surged closer, like they were magnetically attracted to the colt. Lynsey bounced in her heels between Mabel and Samuel, standing front and center. Harris' fleet of friends took up the rest of the circle, all college boy antics.

"Back up, guys," Harris said to the crowd, which collectively edged away as Roman approached, lifting his head and snorting. Georgie ran her fingers through his dark mane, shushing him, and turned to the camera.

The shutter popped and Georgie jumped down, landing lightly on her toes and turning to undo her saddle. She bounced on and off the scale, and when she turned to hand off her saddle to her valet she ran straight into Harris' chest, his spotless shirt and blue tie at eye level. She clutched the saddle against her silks instead of letting it press into the field of perfectly clean clothing stretching across his chest, taking a breath as she looked up at his shaded eyes and the smile that seemed to have taken up permanent residence on his mouth.

Georgie could list all the reasons this put her on alert. Happy Harris, all bushy-tailed and energized from a win she'd supplied on the edge of falling, was a new creature she didn't know how to handle. She also didn't know how to respond other than to let his enthusiasm pull another goofy smile out of her, because this was good, wasn't it? Winning was good. Georgie wanted to kick herself in the shins and tell herself to grow up. Nothing was ever so simple.

Roman walked past them, his coat rinsed dark and dirt still speckling his face. Georgie eased a step back, finding it easier to breathe when she had more than a racing saddle's worth of distance from Harris' chest.

"I think this goes without saying," Harris said, waving off his friends that called for him to join in the fun on their way back to the stands. "But I have to ask if you'll ride Roman in the Derby."

"You *have* to ask?" She watched Harris' horde trail out of the winner's circle, pleading with Lynsey to join them. She shooed them off.

"Do you need me to beg?" Harris asked, pulling Georgie's attention back to him.

She shrugged, like it was all nothing to her. "It couldn't hurt."

"Will you please ride Roman in the Derby? Pretty please." He bent just enough at the knees and laced his fingers together, a mocking supplicant to her will.

She cocked her head to the side, looking at him curiously. Then she reached up, lifted his sunglasses off the bridge of his nose. She folded them into her hand gently and pushed them into his suit pocket, surprised that he stood there impassively and let her. When she finished that task, the smile was still on his lips, only now it was amused, like he knew he'd never figure her out so he wasn't going to try.

And that smile reached his eyes.

The words came out of her mouth before she could call them back, lured there by something she couldn't name. Hope? Optimism?

"You've got me for the Derby."

Harris let out a breath in an audible, relieved whoosh, making that part of her that reacted to him—that old, dusty part of her—spark to life again.

That glowing feeling surged, and she liked it. Georgie had no idea what that meant, but she clung to it, searching for the Harris she used to know glimmering there underneath this new Harris' skin. She wanted that person to appear, so she doubled down. She found his wrist, his hand, and squeezed despite the dirt rubbed into her skin.

Harris glanced down at her fingers wrapped around his wrist, narrowed his eyes like he was trying to figure out why they were there. She let go quickly, told herself that of course this was business first. Harris didn't do sentimentality, and it was silly to think he would.

"I was sure you'd sooner handcuff yourself to Dean than abandon a ride like this," Harris said, like he was that confident in her decision all along. "But I had to ask."

"You got your answer."

Business done, she thought.

Georgie slipped past him, handing her saddle off with an apologetic smile at her valet as she undid her helmet, ready for the first fan to thrust a pen and program into her hands, ready to scribble her name in thick black ink. Then she moved to the waiting cameras and the reporter with a question already halfway out of his mouth. She looked back once, unable to help herself, but only saw Harris' back before he was swallowed up by the crowd.

Chapter Ten

"LADIES AND GENTLEMEN," Mr. Wilcox announced near the end of Georgie's English class. "I have in my hands your graded term papers, which, due to my extreme nefariousness, makes up a third of your grade."

Georgie sat at her desk, barely paying attention at she stared at the calendar on her phone. Race dates filled the weekends in April. Worse, they were all at Oaklawn Park in Arkansas. With Sweet Bells preparing to ship for the Apple Blossom Handicap, Angel was exuberantly saying yes to any trainer at the track who looked interested.

You can't refuse, Angel told her in texts that seemed to arrive every five minutes.

She'd be a journeyman come the end of April, and Angel wanted to fill up her schedule while she still had the bug—a little asterisk next to her name in the post positions that designated her an apprentice jockey. Lining her up in races where she'd have an advantage for easier money in case she fell on her face when that mark disappeared was a good strategy, but she wasn't planning on

"LADIES AND GENTLEMEN," Mr. Wilcox announced near the end of Georgie's English class. "I have in my hands your graded term papers, which, due to my extreme nefariousness, makes up a third of your grade."

Georgie sat at her desk, barely paying attention at she stared at the calendar on her phone. Race dates filled the weekends in April. Worse, they were all at Oaklawn Park in Arkansas. With Sweet Bells preparing to ship for the Apple Blossom Handicap, Angel was exuberantly saying yes to any trainer at the track who looked interested.

You can't refuse, Angel told her in texts that seemed to arrive every five minutes.

She'd be a journeyman come the end of April, and Angel wanted to fill up her schedule while she still had the bug—a little asterisk next to her name in the post positions that designated her an apprentice jockey. Lining her up in races where she'd have an advantage for easier money in case she fell on her face when that mark disappeared was a good strategy, but she wasn't planning on failing once she shed the bug.

She was planning on soaring higher.

Mr. Wilcox put her paper face down on her desk and leaned over her. Georgie jerked upright and let her phone fall into her lap.

"Ms. Quinn," he said in that congenial way he had, "please see me after."

Red hot adrenaline shot through her in a momentary wave while Georgie stared at her paper, knowing without having to look at it that she wouldn't be receiving accolades. She shut down her phone and lifted the paper halfway, just enough to see the F drawn in Mr. Wilcox's fat blue lettering.

So that was it, then. Georgie folded the paper as the bell rang and collected her things, walking down the aisle of desk-chairs toward Mr. Wilcox like she was headed to the gallows.

"I've made an appointment for you at the counselor's office," Mr. Wilcox said as soon as the last student was out the door. It was lunch. Lynsey would be waiting for her. Georgie's stomach growled for its tiny jockey's ration, and she stoically silenced it.

"I honestly don't need an appointment," Georgie said, folding the paper over on itself again, trying to put as many layers of paper between her and the F as possible.

Mr. Wilcox sighed, pushing back his shoulders like he was going into battle. "Georgie, this isn't cutting it."

Heat washed down the back of her neck. "I have an arrangement with administration."

"Does that arrangement involve me giving you a pass when you're getting a failing grade in my class?" he asked. "I know you're busy, Georgie, but when you're here I need your head in the game. Not at the track."

She cringed, absolutely hating that expression. Her head was *always* in the game.

"I'm concerned," Mr. Wilcox said. "I understand from the counseling office that you won't graduate if you fail this class. It's not just me, Georgie. This work isn't up to your standard."

"Right," she said, shoving the paper into her book bag. She couldn't keep the sarcasm from overflowing in her voice. "I should just apply myself more."

Mr. Wilcox shook his head. "I know you apply yourself. What you're applying yourself toward, however, is my question. Go to the counselor's office."

Georgie walked away without another word, storming out of the classroom and down the hallway. By the time she was in and out of the counselor's office, lunch was halfway finished and the words *graduation, application, failure* were zooming around in her head. Words that Georgie did not associate with herself at all. The note she held in her hand for her parents informing them of her course toward not graduating was sticky between her fingers.

Not graduating.

She slumped into her chair next to Lynsey at their usual lunch table, plopping her salad in front of her unceremoniously and shoving the greens into her mouth.

"Where were you?" Lynsey asked, spinning to look at her. "I had to come to the conclusion that you'd abandoned me for something better, but I couldn't come up with what could be better because, you know, I'm me . . ."

Georgie handed over the note, and Lynsey's mouth dropped open.

"Why didn't you say something about your grades?" she asked, mortified, like the idea of Georgie not graduating with her was so preposterous that it couldn't be real.

"I don't know," Georgie sighed, stabbing a tomato and then dropping her fork into the salad, appetite gone. "School and I are not exactly compatible anymore. The homework gets done after the actual *work* gets done, and grades just seem . . . meaningless in comparison."

Lynsey made a face. "But not graduating?"

Georgie pushed the salad away, her stomach roiling. Lynsey stared at the note like she was trying to find something positive about it, and then shook her head.

"I was accepted to the University of Florida last week."

"You didn't tell me that," Georgie said, swinging her attention to Lynsey's good news. It was so much better than hers that a little part of her crumpled further.

"Well, you were busy winning the Florida Derby," Lynsey said, waving her off.

"No, that's great," Georgie insisted. "Your news is so much better than mine."

"It would have to be, considering," Lynsey said, putting the note on the table. "What are your parents going to say? Your mom will flip out."

"My parents have enough to worry about," Georgie said, staring at the parental signature line on the note and pulling a pen from her bag.

"What are you doing?" Lynsey asked slowly, her mouth falling open when Georgie signed her mother's name. "Who are you and what have you done with Georgiana Quinn?"

"My mom doesn't need to know," Georgie said, folding up the note and sticking it in her bag.

"I hate to break it to you, but that's not going to be the school's only attempt to contact your parents," Lynsey said, ever the voice of reason.

"Then she doesn't need to know right this minute," Georgie replied. "I'm not graduating, and I don't have time to fix this. Summer is Belmont and Saratoga. That means no time for summer school."

"So, what?" Lynsey asked, lowering her voice. "That's it? You'll just quit?"

Georgie eyed the cafeteria exit. She didn't want to quit. Not really. But she couldn't help noticing her lack of choice. Now that graduation was off the table, that only meant she'd have to find the time to squeeze in more school later in an already packed schedule. Angel said yes to trainers left and right, the demand already going beyond what her schedule allowed.

"Screw it," she muttered, pulling her bag off the table when the bell rang, kids throwing away their trash and dragging their heels for the next class. "The last I checked riding horses didn't require a degree."

"Georgie!" Lynsey hissed at her, reaching over to grab her wrist. She moved just out of reach, standing.

"What are you going to do, walk home? It's seven miles," Lynsey said, still reaching for her, eyes wide.

Georgie shrugged, mind made up. "I'll have time to think," she said, heading for the door.

She had the presence of mind to stop by her locker, pulling what she wanted out of it and into her overstuffed bag before banging through the front lobby and into the stark Florida sunlight.

So this is what quitting feels like, Georgie thought to herself. She took her first tentative step away from the school, and found she felt the same. Maybe better, like a small portion of the load had lifted off her shoulders.

Georgiana Quinn dropped out of high school, the whispers would say.

This time, Georgie thought as she put another foot forward and walked from the school, the whispers would be right.

Four miles down the road, Georgie's cell phone chimed with a text from Lynsey.

You are such a moron!

Georgie looked at it as she paused in the middle of horse country's sprawling green fields.

I am a high school dropout, she texted back. *Isn't that expected?*

She didn't receive a reply, leaving Georgie to walk in silence until she made it to the back end of Tupelo Stud. She collapsed in the bedding of Bell's stall the second she slipped inside the barn. The filly gave her a thorough inspection, nudging her insistently. Once no treats could be sniffed out, Bell went back to her hay net, ripped out a section of straggly strands, and pressed them against the crown of Georgie's head as she chewed.

"Dork," Georgie sighed up at Bell, even as a bit of her felt so much better. Being with the filly let Georgie shed off so many of her concerns, allowing the world to shrink down to just this—a girl and a horse in a box stall.

Georgie pulled off her shoes and rubbed her feet, stretching her legs out in front of her and resting against her book bag. The barn hummed around her, soft noises of horses milling in their stalls and grooms laughing during the afternoon lull. It lured her into relaxing, cocooning her from the outside world just enough to remind her that this was home. It was her present, her future, and leaving school in a fit of pique was only today. It would have no bearing on tomorrow or a year from now, maybe not ever.

Georgie smiled to herself, looking up at Bell and feeling lighter than she had in months.

It was only as her eyes drifted shut that she heard it. Her mother's voice slipped into the barn's calm like it belonged, but was so distinct and sudden that it drove a bolt of ice into Georgie's chest.

"You understand my reservations," Claire said. "This can't be a favor."

Then there was another voice, and Georgie had to clench her fingers into fists on top of her knees to keep calm.

"I wouldn't dream of offering you anything you didn't want, Claire."

Oliver.

Georgie paid strict attention, her breathing going shallow as the voices moved up the aisle toward Bell. Her mother would want to see Bell. She'd bred Bell, after all. Georgie sipped at the air and scooted into the corner, curling up in the filly's shadow, and then craned her neck around to see if she could get a glimpse of what was happening in the aisle. All she could see were the ceiling's intricate rafters, more suited for a church than a stable. Georgie pressed against the wall and tipped her head back to listen.

"There's already enough blood in the water," Claire said. "This is done professionally or it isn't done at all."

"Says the woman who always seems to have it both ways."

Georgie jerked her head back so quickly she knocked it against the wall, and had to stifle the pained squeak that popped out of her mouth. It wasn't surprise so much as it was in the way Oliver said the words. *Have it both ways.* Like Claire was getting away with something she shouldn't.

"What are you saying, Oliver?"

"You know what I'm willing to offer you. You've always known," Oliver said, his voice low. "I want you here, Claire."

"You have a funny way of showing it."

That was met with a sigh. "I think the question is where do

153

you want to be?"

Claire murmured a response, but Georgie couldn't hear it. She pushed closer to the stall opening, straining for something through the quiet rustle of horses. Balancing on the balls of her feet, Georgie found just enough clearance over the stall door to see Oliver graze the tips of his fingers over the ends of Claire's hair, the look on his face soft, hopeful. Her mother stood like a statue, breath coming quick and quiet.

"Oliver." Claire said it like a plea, and his hand slipped into her hair, finding the back of her neck.

The clop of horse hooves down the aisle pushed them apart hastily, and Georgie crouched back into the bedding, ducking beneath Bell's water bucket as the filly pricked her ears at her and came over to investigate.

Her mother sprang away from the stall, her high heels tapping down the aisle quickly. Oliver's solid, sure footsteps trailed after her.

Georgie slumped against the wall, dropping her forehead into her hands. Of course Harris would want to know what she'd seen. He'd want to hear her regurgitate it all back up, word for word, action for action. He'd want to know just how close they'd come to proving him right.

All at once everything was too much, like a roller coaster ride that simply wouldn't stop plummeting. Bell bumped her nose against Georgie's shoulder, as though she was commiserating. Georgie looked up and lifted a hand to the filly's soft muzzle, running her fingers over Bell's lips.

"What do I do?" she whispered to the filly.

Bell snorted into her hands, giving Georgie a rough rub with her face, and then moved back to her hay net. Such was the wisdom of horses. Georgie wiped her hands on her jeans and stood up, already knowing the answer.

April

Chapter Eleven

SAY SOMETHING. YOU have to say something.

Every time Georgie opened her mouth to let the truth out, it stayed stuck to the roof of her mouth, lodged stubbornly. When she tried to shake it loose, it clung tighter. So she said nothing. She climbed onto her mounts in the mornings, listened to Harris' instructions for Roman while she silently screamed at herself to *say something.*

She had, after all, made a promise. And she let weeks pass, falling into the same routine.

Churchill Downs opened under the pressure of the Kentucky Derby. Horses raced under a sky dotted with hot air balloons as the city began to fill up in anticipation. Hotels turned on no vacancy signs. A parade marched down main streets seemingly every day. The newspapers shouted headlines on favorites, hot trainers, young jockeys with aspirations to get to the wire first. The Derby was coming, and the most common question asked in Louisville was one that couldn't be answered.

Who will win?

Georgie wiped the grime off her skin in the shower, her muscles aching from an unexpected fall that punctuated her final race on the card like a sudden curtain call. No wins for Georgie this week, fate seemed to be saying. Sorry, play again next time.

"Georgie!" One of the girl jocks yelled to her from the changing room. "Your phone won't stop ringing!"

She turned her face into the spray, no urge to jump out of the warm water to tell her mother to stop calling. Stop trying. Just *stop*.

There wasn't anything to talk about. Or, there wasn't anything Georgie wanted to talk about. So she let her phone ring and told herself she'd just deal with it when she came home.

If she came home.

After she'd walked Sweet Bells into the winner's circle at Oaklawn Park without the bug to her name, Georgie realized she didn't ever need to go back. She was a journeyman now, a full-fledged jockey. She had a name everyone recognized, a face that graced magazines. She could pick her tracks, settle into a circuit, find a routine that never involved setting foot in Florida. There wasn't even a need to go back to Tupelo. Sweet Bells could come to her, couldn't she? They were track brats, cycling through races. Who needed the craziness of Tupelo?

Georgie shut off the shower, standing naked and trembling on the grungy tile with her thoughts cascading in circles. No one needed Tupelo except Sweet Bells, and Georgie needed Sweet Bells. She needed the filly in her life, day in and day out, a solid mass of faith made horseflesh. It was the only way she got through this, the only way she got through anything at all.

She dried off and pulled on jeans and old boots, a T-shirt that regrettably bore Red Gate's emblem in worn screen print. The shirt was about as broken down as the farm, but Georgie put it on anyway. Her phone blinked with messages, but Georgie pocketed it, flinching as she moved her shoulder, and headed for the backside. She had to see Sweet Bells before crashing at the hotel. Just a few minutes with the filly would calm her down, sooth her jittery nerves, would make her forget the way her shoulder throbbed for just a little while.

Only by the time she got to the shedrow, Harris stood there, harmlessly feeding Bell bits of carrot while the filly nuzzled his fingers and crunched. Georgie's heart did a little flutter, like it needed a minute to process the severe emotional turmoil Harris stirred up every second he came near enough.

She stopped, fine dust rising up around her boots.

Say something.

"Don't lurk out there on my account." Harris gave her that wry smile, the one that pulled across his mouth.

The first step was the hardest. After that, Sweet Bells pulled her in like a tractor beam. She slipped up against the filly and rested her forehead against her warm neck, ignoring Harris. Bell crunched on her carrot, bobbed her head to lip at Georgie's jeans in moderate criticism that she'd come with nothing to feed her, and the tension in Georgie's aching back untwisted enough for her to take her first deep breath since the fall.

Then her phone started to ring again. Georgie jumped like she'd been burned, and squeezed her eyes shut.

"You going to get that?" Harris asked, raising an eyebrow at her stoic refusal to reach for the phone, not even to turn off the ringer. The call went to voice mail, the shedrow falling into the sound of horses shifting.

"You're right. My mom is working with Oliver," she said instead, like it was the most common thing in the world. She opened her eyes, lifted herself from the filly just enough to look at him. "I saw them in Tupelo's training barn. They looked a little more than professional."

He was quiet for a full minute after the details fell from her mouth.

"The best scenario?" Harris' voice finally broke the stillness. "Your mom is pulling a Hail Mary. My dad is an opportunist, so he's profiting."

"And worse case?"

He looked at her like she was wasting his time. "I don't need to tell you the worst case, Georgie."

"Now you know," she told him. "I upheld my part of the bargain. What's the plan now? What is all of this leading to, Harris?"

"On my part? Nothing."

She stopped short, blinking at him.

"Nothing?"

"What's at stake for me, Georgie? The worst already happened and you know that better than anyone. What do I really care if your mom and my dad are still doing what they've always done?"

He knocked his knuckles together and Georgie screwed up her nose, shaking her head.

"You've badgered me about this for *months*, and now you tell me you've never cared?"

"Georgie, if anything I've always cared too much," Harris said. "This time, it's about you. What are you going to do?"

"That's deeply not fair."

"It's not about what's fair." Harris took a deep breath, looking over at her with a frown of concentration, as though he was having trouble explaining. "It's about doing what's right."

"Tell my dad, you mean."

He nodded. "You closed ranks before because that was the easiest thing to do. Look at it this way: now you've got a second chance. Right the wrong."

Sure, she thought. It was so simple for Harris. Telling her drowning father this would surely be shoving him deeper into dark water. Was that kindness or cruelty? She knew how Harris looked at it, but this time it wasn't his family being dragged across the rocks. His had broken so swiftly, over before either of them could blink. Hers had fallen apart slowly since then, tearing itself apart and disintegrating with each day. Harris hadn't been stuck in the middle of that. He didn't know. There was no way he could possibly be able to tell her what was right.

"This isn't righting a wrong," she told him. "This is my *family*, Harris."

He watched her carefully, dark eyes assessing and giving nothing away. He had become good at that since Lilliana had died, always finding the hidden motives and obsessively sifting through information until he came away with the truth. That was the sort of talent Georgie needed right now, not that she thought it would help.

Harris shook his head, sighing. "They're going to do what they're going to do, Georgie. The question is whether or not you can know and do nothing."

"I don't know what I should do," she told him. There was a half a beat, where he looked down at the dirt between their feet, and then reached out to touch her wrist. When she didn't flinch away, he squeezed lightly.

She looked at his fingers there wonderingly. Was this comfort?

"I know." He said it so quietly she barely heard him, but of course she did.

Georgie nodded haltingly, but what was that worth? What was the meager support of someone who could only halfway stand you, couldn't be convinced to care when there was nothing in it anymore for him? And what did it mean that she'd even searched for support from him?

She was pathetic. Pretty sure.

Before she could think of anything to say, his hand fell away.

"It's a dark day tomorrow," he said, turning for the rental car that sat outside the shedrow, the moment gone. "After a day like yours, I think you'll need it."

"Asshole," Georgie muttered at his back, but it lacked the usual tightness in her chest, the feeling of drowning. He laughed, shot her the middle finger.

The car spun off. Georgie turned her face into the filly's mane and pressed close.

Morning at Churchill Downs painted the twin spires rising over the grandstand red. Georgie trotted Bell away from them, up the outer rail where onlookers were stationed with cameras and notepads, scrutinizing her as she passed. The track teamed with horses at varying stages of speed, their bodies soaking up the sun and reflecting it back in orange and copper, eyes glinting and manes a spray of flame along their necks. Bell huffed and tugged on Georgie's hands, her own coat streaked with sweat from their breeze.

"Bring her back in, Georgie," Reece said, accent clipping neat and sharp through her headset.

"Ten-four," she murmured to herself, patting Bell's damp neck and rising to the filly's beat back to the clocker's stand, where Reece stood with eyes on her.

"Report?" he asked when she got close enough.

"Happy to go and keep going," Georgie said with a shrug. "Does she have any other setting?"

"Not that I've noticed," Reece said, his attention skipping over Bell for a half-beat when a chestnut filly galloped by, so aglow with light that her tail licked behind her like a flamethrower. Her saddlecloth labeled her an entrant for the Kentucky Oaks, the female version of the Kentucky Derby. But it was her name that stuck to Georgie.

"Hero has arrived," Reece said, sounding barely interested when every photographer on the track was eagerly snapping photos.

"How's she liking her first go over a track that isn't in California?" Georgie pulled her gaze away.

"If I was a betting man," Reece said, squinting after the filly, "I'd lay down money that she'll be running with the boys by the time the month is out."

"Seriously?" Georgie asked, surprised. Hero's connections had been adamant about not putting the filly on the Triple Crown trail when she'd blown apart the Breeders' Cup Juvenile Fillies the same day Bell had won the Classic. She craned her head to watch the fireball filly slow into a ground-eating canter, her head low and her rider standing over her withers with a hand in her mane.

"I don't see why not," Reece replied. "She's more impressive than most of the colts entered for the Derby, including Roman."

"Those are fighting words," Georgie chided, but Reece shrugged.

"Guilty as charged," he told her, and motioned her up to the shedrow. "Get that one home; bring Roman down."

She nudged the filly into a bouncing trot, Bell holding her head high and her spirits higher. Georgie tipped her toes out of the stirrups as she went, wrapping her legs around the filly's barrel and crooning to her to calm down. Bell blew into Tupelo's rented stretch of stalls like a tornado, all gusto and energy. Georgie leapt off of her the second Miguel appeared to take her reins, giving Bell two hearty slaps on the shoulder and moving off in search of Harris and Roman.

She caught sight of Roman and his groom walking along the shedrow, his coat, tack, and bandages pristine. The shiny yellow saddlecloth given to all the Derby entrants ruffled along his flank in a soft breeze that kicked up the colt's dark mane in comical flips along his neck. Harris stood in the sun, looking at his phone with a frown of concentration dipping across his lips. In her pocket, Georgie's phone buzzed.

"I'm here," she announced a little breathlessly. "You can call off the search party."

"Well, it wasn't that dire," Harris replied, pocketing the phone and handing her a piece of bright yellow paper. "I was actually sending you a photo of this, racing's most trusted news source."

Georgie groaned, scanning over the cartoons that looked hand drawn by a toddler with a mean streak. Then she got to the headline.

First Female Winner of the Kentucky Derby? Not if Georgie Quinn has anything to say about it. Once unstoppable girl jock hasn't won yet at the Churchill meet. Harrison Armstrong still insists she's his jockey for Roman the Great, leading this dashing reporter to wonder: what unearthly sway does Georgie Quinn have on Armstrong? Donations for the Save Harrison fund have been set up in Barn 25.

"Oh, for Christ's sake," Georgie sighed, shaking her head. "If anything I resent being called *once unstoppable*. I'd like to see him stop my foot from hitting his face."

"Think you can take him?" Harris asked, deadpan. "You're pretty tiny, and last I checked *Uncle Moe* was punching extra holes in his belts."

Georgie glared at him. "Not the point. It's two days from the Kentucky Derby and there are far more important things on my mind than what one man with questionable artistic talent thinks of me."

The corner of Harris' mouth turned up in a sardonic smile, all muted laughter.

"But you are planning on winning a race between now and the Derby, right?" he asked. "That might shut him up in the meantime."

"Nothing shuts up *Uncle Moe*," Georgie replied, dodging the question. Aside from the fact that she was right, there was also no way she wanted to talk about her win percentage, which sat lazily at the bottom of the Churchill jockey colony since the start of the meet. Arkansas had gone well enough for Georgie, but Churchill Downs?

Churchill Downs hated her.

Harris boosted her onto Roman's back, the colt beginning

an excited jig underneath her at the first hint of her weight. She slipped her feet into the stirrups and gathered up the reins, heading toward the track. "What's the plan here?"

"Jog him once around," Harris said, walking with them down to the track chute. "I don't want to mess with his tune up yesterday, and by some miracle Reece agrees."

"I will do so happily," Georgie said, running her hand through the colt's unruly mane. Roman huffed excitedly, lifting his legs animatedly the second he landed a hoof in the deep cushion of Churchill Downs' dirt track. The colt danced sideways, tipping his head toward the outside rail. Georgie moved with him, letting him dance his heart out and chuckling at the throaty whicker he tossed at Hero as she passed by, her chestnut coat still flaming in the morning light, bright white star a luminous spot on the middle of her forehead. Muscles rippled across her chest as she bobbed her head, snorting with each stride and bearing down on the reins.

Overcome, the colt called to the filly, whinnying high and throaty. Hero paid him no mind, rolled past on cruise control. Her long legs folded and stretched, nostrils flared gently to red. Roman pricked his ears at her departing figure, like a boy watching a girl sashay away from him, every line of muscle rigid. Georgie put her heels to his sides, told him to shake himself out of it.

"You have plenty of time for that later," she said, settling the colt into a jog. Roman trotted purposely clockwise up the outside rail, licking his lips and rounding into Georgie's hand. She perched over his withers, standing in the lowered stirrups with her hands nestled neatly at the base of the colt's neck, watching the ground slip by under the churn of his two-beat. Jogs on Roman felt effortless, like gliding on a monorail sliding through the air.

Horses worked on the inside rail, racing toward them and thundering away with a rain of dirt. Roman lifted his head at each one, bursting into a rocking, eager canter. Georgie sat back, let her seat settle in the saddle, brought him to a jaunty trot, and stood again once his head lowered, pushing into the bridle and using the pressure she put on the reins to keep churning.

One two, one two. On and on around the track.

Roman snorted, tipped his ears back to listen. Georgie murmured a litany of *good boy* to him, re-crossed her reins to pat him thoughtlessly on the neck. Ahead on the turn, a bay colt blew across the track, crow hopping twice in a shower of dirt and squeals. In a split second the colt went from middle of the track to the rail, his shoulder banging into the plastic with a reverberating crack. The rider toppled off and landed with a thud on the other side of the rail, leaving the colt to pivot on his haunches, spooking sideways and straight into Hero's path as she blazed off the turn.

The filly skittered mid-stride, her ears pinned back, eyes wide with fright as she struggled to get out of the way and went sideways right toward Georgie. A shudder wracked its way through Roman, the colt lifting her into the air. He leapt sideways, feet tucked neatly under his body like a hunter popping over jumps. Georgie grabbed mane, pushed her weight to the center of the colt's back, and let him carry her clear until he stopped short and spun.

Georgie sailed over the colt's shoulder, landing with a bone-jarring thud in the thick dirt. Instinct made her scramble, push past her desire to contemplate how she'd gotten in this position by Roman's hooves. She still wildly clutched the reins in one hand, Roman taking mincing steps by her head as she pushed herself off the ground and grabbed one dangling stirrup, hauling herself to her feet.

The emergency lights flared to life, a siren filling the air.

Hero charged past, all excited snorts and wild, whipping tail. The problem colt raced after her, a flurry of black mane and clanking tack. Georgie didn't waste time, throwing the reins over Roman's head and leading him up the outside rail. She led the colt off the track, one of dozens coming off all at once.

"Georgie!"

Harris jogged toward her. She swung around, Roman prancing lightly in an arc by her side. The big gray quivered, rolled his eyes at the commotion. Georgie put a hand on his shoulder, blocking him from turning a full circle around her. Harris stopped in front of her, eyes narrowed as he looked her over for injury. It unnerved her, being on the end of Harris' concern rather than his scrutiny for faults.

She shook her head, rolled her already tender shoulder and felt a spasm burn bright along her back.

Harris sighed at her, but didn't argue, moving to check over Roman. The colt stood firmly, tail raised like he wasn't quite sure whether or not he'd need to take off again without a moment's notice. Georgie pulled her dusty helmet off, rested her sweaty forehead against his damp neck, and murmured nonsensically to him while Harris moved hands down each of the colt's legs.

As soon as he was done, he came back up to the colt's head and took the reins out of Georgie's hands. Then he seemed to hover there, maybe caught between caring or not. Georgie didn't know. She looked up at him and couldn't process his expression.

She needed to say something.

"Your jockey is fine, Harris," she said, finally pushing out the words. "Still race ready."

"It's not the race I'm worried about," he told her, his hand tight on Roman's reins. The colt lowered his head, the coiled tension in him shedding off his frame in a heap at their feet. He nudged Georgie's shoulder inquisitively, as though asking what they were doing, just standing around like this.

She flinched, and Harris raised an eyebrow.

"Nothing's broken," she assured him. "Maybe a few bruises."

He nodded toward the shedrows, lines of barns popping out of a gravel sea.

"Then let's take you home."

Harris led Roman back to the barns, leaving Georgie little choice but to follow.

Candles quivered on the tables, an orange glow dancing up to the trellis of wisteria and honeysuckle vine. The Ohio River curled around the city, a lazy streak of dark blue-brown water dotted with boats and birds. The Belle of Louisville churned past, steam pumping into the sky and wheel working through the water. From her roof-top perch, Georgie could see the Galt House's annual Kentucky Derby gala begin its upward swing.

The roof-top bar offered a breeze and a view, even though Georgie was without a drink and had more than enough thoughts to make her wish for one. Her shoulder still ached from the previous day's fall, the painkillers doing little to help. She rotated her shoulder gingerly, stretching the upset tendons as she watched the people packing the roof-top all the way to the railing she leaned against. Tupelo employees, friends of the Armstrongs, business associates, and people with too much money glittering around their throats and at their wrists. Oliver and Mabel drifted between groups, mint juleps at hand, smiles plastered across their mouths.

"Hero is all over *DRF*," Lynsey said, head bent over her phone as she scanned the stories. Georgie glanced over, catching sight of the chestnut filly walking into the infield winner's circle with her pink and white stargazer lilies draped over her neck. She could still feel the rumble of the crowd as she watched the Kentucky Oaks from the sidelines. Hero dominated the news, pushing Georgie's win on Sweet Bells in the La Troienne further down the page.

Hero, Hero, Hero the world seemed to sing. *We want more.*

Sweet Bells felt old hat now.

"Her owners are bemoaning not putting her in the Derby." Lynsey shook her head as she read down through the race notes.

"And so we all sigh in relief," Harris said sarcastically next to them.

"She won on a hand ride," Georgie said. "What makes you think she couldn't demolish colts?"

"There are twenty colts in the Derby, and eight fillies in the Oaks. Hero is the best of a mediocre group of fillies."

Lynsey stood straighter. "Don't get too cocky, brother mine. You haven't won the Derby yet."

"Not suggesting any such thing, sister dear," Harris answered, to which Georgie found herself smiling.

The band struck up a new song, the brassy beat tapping over the patio. Lynsey whirled off, snagging one of Reece's younger assistant trainers by the hand and dragging him to the dance floor. Georgie watched her go, left alone with Harris.

"Talk to me, Georgie," Harris said after a moment of silence.

"Roman," Georgie said, lifting her voice to be heard over the music, "is in good hands, Harris. His gate position is promising and the pace will be decent enough to coast up the backstretch. Twenty horses will be a traffic nightmare, so my main priority is finding the easiest route, most likely on the outside of horses. Given Roman's running style, that shouldn't be a problem at all."

Harris stared at her, dark eyes trained on her face. She smiled up at him.

"Still worried?" she asked.

"You are good at that," he said to her, letting a wave of relaxation ripple over his shoulders, loosening him out enough to smile.

"I know," Georgie said, shrugging her good shoulder. "I'm well-trained when it comes to knowing what to say to the right people."

"So you're playing me," Harris replied.

"Not entirely," she said, watching him lean against the railing next to her. Their arms brushed against each other, her bare skin up against his where he had pushed up his sleeves. Harris had tried to go black tie, but seemed to get bored with it halfway through the night. His sports coat was abandoned on the back of a chair and his dress shirt sleeves were pushed back in sloppy rolls. The tie he wore was loose around his neck.

Georgie, on the other hand, was pristine. Her heels were still strapped onto her aching feet, her silk dress rippled around her knees, and earrings glittered against her neck. Nothing about her outfit was out of place, and she was prepared to Iron Woman it out of this party the same way she'd walked in.

Harris rubbed a hand into his hair and let out a long breath.

"So I should calm down, huh?"

"The gates are going to open up tomorrow," she said, "and then it's just going to be me, Roman, and nineteen other horses who want it just as much. I'd say it's time to let me be nervous and enjoy the party."

Harris made a face. "My jockey shouldn't be nervous."

"Do I look nervous?"

"It's your first Derby," Harris said. "I'm surprised you aren't. What's wrong with you?"

Georgie laughed and pushed away from the railing, fuzzy with reckless energy. She needed to move, needed to think about something else other than her aching shoulder, their chances tomorrow afternoon, Claire, Oliver—all of the problems weighing her down. She turned around and offered him her hand.

"You caught me," she said. "I'm nervous. Now give me something else to think about?"

She remembered Harris being good at that. Maybe he still was, deep down.

He lifted himself off the railing as though he had to seriously consider her first. She crooked her fingers at him, beckoning.

"Come on," she said. "One dance. For luck."

"I don't think that's a thing," he said, taking her hand, letting her drag him into the dancing crowd. As soon as she stopped in the middle of the swaying couples, he turned her into him and she wrapped her arms around his neck.

Because that was the thing. She was nervous. Her pulse thrummed in her throat and her palms were a sweaty, slippery wreck. If Harris noticed, he didn't say anything. It was his silence that Georgie noticed more than his hand on the middle of her back, the way the warmth of him soaked through the silk of her dress and his breath ruffled through her hair because she was close enough so brush her nose against his chest. But then maybe she noticed that, too.

Georgie could feel eyes on them. They swirled through rumors, kicking them up and twisting them into fantastic stories she scarcely believed until she noticed the kernel of truth at their cores.

What was she thinking bringing him out here?

"The *Uncle Moe* story," Harris said, so suddenly she gave a startled jump, looking up at him. "I brushed that off yesterday, but I want you to know it's bullshit."

"What is bullshit?" she asked, forcing herself to go back over it, picking the pathetic four sentences apart to find the truth in the lies.

"The assumption that you can't win now that you're a journeyman, and that you're going to drag me down with you," Harris said. "*Uncle Moe* can screw off."

Georgie looked down, studying the loose tie and swallowing the thickness in her throat. It was a weighty statement, his declaration of support, despite her recent inability to hit the winner's circle. Praise in racing was flighty, a routine of what-have-you-done-for-me-lately. What Harris offered wasn't a small thing.

It was exactly what she wanted, and Georgie didn't know how to respond.

"You're remarkably 'go team' today. You seriously don't mind where I drag you?" she asked, looking up and finding him *there*. So close that a part of her felt flung back to that spot in time where this felt possible. The weight of Harris' hands on her and the feeling that spiraled through her before it all went to hell.

"Seeing as how we wound up here," Harris said, "I'm happy to go anywhere you lead."

Georgie sucked in a breath. Held it. The tips of his fingers found the dip of her back.

Then the song ended, and she loosened her grip on him while her heart beat a staccato rhythm within the cage of her ribs.

May

Chapter Twelve

BY MIDMORNING, CHURCHILL Downs transformed from empty house to thundering spectacle. Women sipped drinks while shaded by extravagant, feathered hats. Men roamed the grandstand in suits and fine leather shoes. The infield was a wave of people; drunk, muddy, and stumbling before the gates opened for the first race. The air was dense with energy that shredded the nerves of horses, and it only became more oppressive as the day spiraled on, the crowds growing, becoming more eager for those tense two minutes they'd all come to see.

"Three more races to go," Lynsey sang after Georgie jumped off the scale after a dismal last-place finish in the sixth race. Despite the dirt, Lynsey threw an arm over Georgie's shoulders, shading her from the sun with the wide brim of her hat.

"Please don't remind me," Georgie said, pausing to sign programs and photos, chattering to fans about the prospect of a Hero and Sweet Bells match race. "That's three stakes races from now, and I'm riding in each one. One race at a time, Lyn."

Lynsey trotted after her in glittering heels as she scowled at her marked up program.

"You'll bounce back," she said. "Hopefully like my ability to pick a winning horse. Give me some pointers on who I should bet."

Georgie shook her head. "Oh, no. If you ask me I'll go by who has the best name."

Lynsey looked up at her, eyes wide. "But you are a *jockey*. At least tell me to bet your horses!"

"Then bet my horses." Georgie started to run up the escalators to the jockeys' room. "Of course, I haven't hit the board all day, but more power to you!"

The jockeys' room at Churchill looked like a hurricane struck mid-way through the day. Georgie cycled between the common room and the women's lockers, stopping off in the kitchen for a snack somewhere between an epic loss in the Churchill Downs Stakes and the Woodford Reserve Turf Classic, snarfing down half a sandwich in five bites before running out the door.

In the hour of downtime before the Kentucky Derby, she managed to clean up, shake off the nerves of nine fresh losses, and put on clean Tupelo silks before passing out cold on the common room sofa. It was the crack of a crop next to her ear that jerked her back into the land of the living.

Dean Hayes stood in front of her, wearing Second Sail's green and black silks and a shit-eating grin that Georgie wanted desperately to smack off his face. She rubbed the heel of one hand across her eyes and uncurled herself while the echo of jockey laughter rang in her ears.

"Do you not have anything better to do with yourself?" she asked.

"Hey, I'm being helpful," he said, motioning to the line of

jockeys moving out. "It's picture time. I thought maybe you'd like to do something about the dark circles under your eyes before we go."

"What, do you have concealer I can borrow?" she asked, standing up and picking up her helmet, shoving it on her head and tucking in the escapee hairs that threatened to poke out from under the brim. "Move your ass, Hayes."

"Always so pushy," Dean complained, dodging her swipes as television cameras followed their every move down to the paddock.

In the paddock, Georgie wound through the crush of people and horses until she got to stall nine and saw Roman the Great giving everyone the side eye while Reece adjusted his girth. An electric current ran through the saddling paddock, but then Georgie figured that could just be her nerves. Her blood thrummed in her veins, adrenaline zipping along every nerve ending until she felt fizzy with excitement. Roman tossed his head, dragging his groom in a semi-circle around his stall.

"What did I miss?" she asked, buckling her helmet.

"Everything?" Harris asked with a smirk, then nodded to the colt. "He's golden. How are you?"

"Nerves of steel," she replied. The paddock judge called for riders up and, like a cascade, horses began to move. Jockeys bounced from the ground onto their backs, the crowd surging like a wave against the paddock in anticipation. Harris walked along with Georgie, grabbing her boot when she kicked up, and lifted her smoothly onto Roman's back. From here, she could see across the paddock, across the sea of people that lapped against the sides of the grandstands.

The gray colt arched his neck and danced his hindquarters

around toward the crowd. Georgie gathered the reins and put her feet in the stirrups, glancing down at Harris. He nodded to her once, and she nodded back. Wordless.

Then she was on her own. The colt's groom led them toward the track, murmuring Spanish into Roman's ear as *My Old Kentucky Home* drifted down through the tunnel under the grandstand, the crowd rumbling the lyrics in unison for longer than the race itself would last. Roman snorted in the dim light, and then startled a fraction when they burst out into the brilliant afternoon, skittering across the tilled dirt and bounding into the hands of a pony rider, who grasped the colt and gave Georgie a hard smile.

"Sometimes they get spooked at the sight," he told her, and Georgie had to nod, looking *up, up, up* at the towering twin spires and the rippling mass of people cascading all the way back down to the track, pressing up against the outer rail with no room to spare. It looked claustrophobic, like the grandstand was made entirely of people.

"Who wouldn't get spooked by this many people singing off key?" she asked. The pony rider laughed.

The post parade snaked its way past the grandstand. Before they reached the gate at the quarter-mile pole, Georgie cued the colt into a gentle gallop, his pony working harder to keep up with Roman's ground-eating stride. They curled around the far turn, slowing and stepping back into line with the horses heading to the post.

When the first horses entered the gate, Georgie sat back on Roman's saddle and took a deep breath while pulling her goggles down. When the starter took hold of Roman and led him without fanfare into the nine stall, her heart was in her throat. The metal gates closed behind them. Georgie had just enough time to dig her fingers into Roman's mane and keep herself from leaning over the colt's shoulder to throw up, a sudden onset of spiking nerves. The colt shivered under her, ears pricked. Georgie dug her fingers into his mane and listened to the other horses clang in the gate, their jockeys talking, tack jangling, the crowd drowning it all out even as their noise grew softer in anticipation.

Then the gates exploded forward, releasing twenty heaving horses onto the track.

Georgie jumped as the colt leapt out, the sound of hooves canceling out the crowd's roar. A chaotic churn of legs and whipping manes swept around Roman like a roaring river. Jockeys shouted at mounts, at each other, their voices lost to the wind and the thundering drone. Threading Roman through the charge of horses, Georgie aimed for a spot behind the leaders just as Demon King and Reliance closed the hole. She lifted herself off Roman's neck, checking him hard. All that energy cycled back in on itself. The colt's head jerked back, his stride shortening automatically so he wouldn't run up Reliance's bandaged heels. Midway through a curse, Georgie didn't have time to react when Mediator slammed into her outside, knocking Roman toward the rail.

Roman stuttered, scrambling to sort himself out with Mediator breathing down his neck.

"Get off!" she screamed at the other jockey, who grimaced and held the course, making no move to give her room. Horses pressed into Mediator's outside, shoving them further into the rail, so close Georgie's boot glanced against it with each pulsing shove of Roman's hindquarters. The bubble of space they had to run in was small—too small. Georgie glanced at the outside and found a wall of four horses. To the front, another five vied for the lead. Dirt rained from their hooves, a constant pelting that beat against Roman's chest as they galloped head on into the clubhouse turn.

Stay, she thought, collecting the colt and settling him. This was as good as they were going to get. Conserve energy and wait was their best strategy now as they turned into the backstretch. Georgie counted out the furlongs in her head as the field went dashing down the track. When they hit the beginning of the far turn, the pace quickened. Horses heaved, their breath coming quick through blown nostrils.

It was time to start running.

On her outside, Mediator's jockey scrubbed at his neck.

Go.

Georgie gritted her teeth, felt Roman want to go with all the rest and only running up against the horses in front of them. The grandstand unfurled around the corner, that wall of people roaring, and just when Georgie was ready to scream at Mediator's jock to *move goddamnit*, a hole opened. The Wily Fox fell back, hindquarters brushing against Roman's shoulder. Georgie pulled the colt's head toward the hole and chirped as Roman rolled through, the horses racing so fast into the homestretch that the force of their speed sent them wide off the turn.

Plowing past horses, Georgie could finally see what was happening on the lead when they hit the quarter-mile pole. Second Sail was in front, a stream of clean white from his easy trip around the track. Watching the seat of Dean's pants in front of her was enraging, so she put Roman on a course to run past Second Sail on his outside and pushed the button.

Roman flattened, pouring on speed. The rail slid into a hazy line of white. Noise—from the crowd and the horses breathing down her neck—rang in her ears. She flicked the crop past Roman's eye and brought it down on his shoulder, feeling a surge of power that gave her hope for a split second until a flagging horse knocked into her tiredly, pushing Roman off course and forcing her to recollect.

She pushed her hands into Roman's mane with a determined grunt, pulling on the right rein and shoving free of the crowd of horses, gaining on Second Sail. They were first and second, Roman the Great racing up on Second Sail's flank until Reliance, like a pulsing blur, thundered by them both and blew across the finish with energy Georgie knew Roman had expended during the first turn just to stay on his feet.

They slipped under the wire in third. Roman evened out with Second Sail, Reliance reluctantly slowing down in front of them as they galloped into the clubhouse turn standing in their irons and their horses pushing their noses toward the dirt.

"Shit, man," Dean groaned, "where the hell did he come from?"

"Got the perfect trip."

Dean shook his head, lips curling into a bittersweet smile. "Well, here's to the runners up."

He held out his right fist to her, nodding his head in invitation. Georgie glanced at it, and sighed.

"Screw it," she said, and bumped her knuckles against his.

Dean laughed uproariously, patted Second Sail on his sweat-streaked shoulder and slowed him into a bouncing trot. Georgie did the same with Roman, slowing him down to a heaving halt so she could lean against his neck and scrub her fingers over his shoulders, patting him and crooning into his pricked, curious ears that he was amazing and beautiful and they were going to *kick ass* in the Preakness.

Chapter Thirteen

"RELIANCE CONJURES IMAGES of champions from great eras past, when racehorses were work horses and took on all we could throw at them. A glutton for work is Reliance, who gallops most mornings like a colt on fire."

Georgie dropped her copy of the *Daily Racing Form* into Harris' lap and said, "I don't think I can read this anymore."

"Why?" Harris asked, tossing the paper onto the empty seat next to him. "Don't think we can compete with a horse on fire?"

"Actually, I think we can," she said, looking out the window of the charter plane as it taxied toward the airport. Soon they would head to Pimlico, where Roman the Great had arrived the day before. Sweet Bells had gone on to Belmont Park in New York with a smattering of other Tupelo horses, meeting up with the new two-year-olds the farm had sent to New York to train for the summer meet.

Since they'd gone wheels up, the flight was remarkably mild. Mabel filed her nails for the majority of the trip, perfecting each half moon. Oliver nursed a glass of whiskey while consulting with

Samuel on Tupelo related business matters that Georgie drowned out in the off chance that someone mentioned her mother and the upcoming yearling sales. Lynsey played on her cell phone, tuning the rest of the world out, which left Georgie with Harris in the back of the plane, each taking up two seats and throwing bits of conversation across the aisle that separated them.

"Reliance got a lucky trip," Georgie said, cuing up the Derby replay on her phone and skipping to the end, watching the red colt go skipping past her in the middle of the track. "He's also a closer who got up at the last possible second, and the Preakness doesn't have that added distance. He's not a lock. Besides, Roman will be there."

"Hey, Georgie," Harris said, leaning across the aisle, almost into her space as he looked at her.

"What?" she asked, distractedly analyzing Roman's stride as they crossed the finish line.

"Your obsession about this is a remarkable turn on," he said with a straight face. She reached over the aisle and smacked his arm as the plane jerked to a halt in the hangar. Harris laughed, falling back into his seat.

After winding through the airport, Georgie packed herself into the rental car bound for the track. At the last second, Oliver slipped into the backseat, landing next to Georgie in a whiff of fine whiskey and cologne. Panic must have crossed her face in a myriad of ways, because Lynsey mouthed *I'm so sorry* at her as she climbed into the hotel-bound rental with Mabel. Harris, from his perch in the driver's seat, glanced into the rearview mirror and shook his head.

Georgie pressed her lips into a thin smile, forcing herself to acknowledge Oliver when he sharply patted her jean-clad knee. She moved out from under his hand, slumping into the door and crossing her legs away from him as every inch of her flesh started to crawl.

"Let's get this show on the road," Oliver declared after Samuel had situated himself in the passenger seat. "Go on, Harris. You know the way."

With a flash of rolled eyes in the rearview, Harris cranked the engine and pulled away from the airport. The drive to the track was peppered with conversation between Samuel and Oliver, their business meeting on the plane spilling into the car. Oliver tapped at his phone, shaking his head and muttering about the progress of the yearlings, putting Georgie on high alert.

"I'll speak with Claire concerning the Reflections filly," Oliver said, tossing around her mother's name like Georgie wasn't finely attuned to the words coming out of his mouth. Georgie found Harris' eyes again in the rearview. "It's possible we still have time to add her to the roster going to the August sale."

Georgie sucked in a small breath, staring intently out the window as the landscape shifted from speeding highways to dilapidated row houses, green yards a mixture of the maintained and the wild. Empty lots, boarded houses, and shuttered businesses were peppered with the occasional stray cat darting between dumpsters. Turning toward the racetrack wasn't much of a relief. Pimlico was a rectangular, glassed-in hulk looming over its oval tracks and flanked by weed-ridden parking lots and scrubby barns. Gold horses leapt across the building's side over the words *Home of the Preakness*, the race that would see Pimlico gussied up with enough yellow flowers to distract from its age-worn grounds.

Harris parked the car and jumped out faster than she could, heading toward the stakes barn with purpose that forced Georgie into a jog so she could keep up. She called after him, diving into the dim barn and finding him outside of Roman's stall. The gray colt pricked his ears at her, chewing on hay that stuck comically out of his mouth. Harris rubbed a hand up the colt's nose and let out a long-suffering breath.

"Too much time in close confines with dear old Dad," Harris said, a sardonic smile twisting over his mouth.

Roman stuck his head out of his stall, nickering low in his throat and shoving his face into Georgie's hands. For one pure moment, Georgie felt like her heart might burst. The colt had perfect timing, always there when he was needed. She bent over and pressed a kiss onto Roman's forehead, her tinted lip balm getting on his coat.

She rubbed at it until it smeared into a light pink blob.

"Good going," Harris said, breaking into a genuine smile. "You just had to make a mess."

"It looks good on him," Georgie defended.

Harris snorted, and cleaned it off with water from the colt's bucket. "There. Like new."

"He liked it," she said as the colt went back to his hay net. "I'm his jockey, Harris. I know these things."

"About that," Harris said, resting against the colt's stall and making Georgie's heart speed up. For an illogical second she was sure he was going to deliver bad news along the lines of *it's great that you love my colt, but your win percentage has sucked for a full month and I'm putting another jock on him for the Preakness.*

She didn't give the colt the best trip in the Derby, so Georgie would understand. But then the colt came back over to the stall door and plopped his nose back into her hands and her heart seized all over again, love pouring out of her and into the colt like a torrent she couldn't suppress.

"I want to be honest," Harris said, and Georgie tried to follow him as she looked down at the colt, telling herself that it was all going to be okay, really it would.

"You could have said no, Georgie. You had every right to say no to Roman and me, but you haven't and I don't get it. I've been a shitty person to you."

Georgie looked up at him, blinking and trying not to stumble all over herself in order to say the words that came haltingly up her throat. "Stop," she said, and he just nodded, looking down at his feet. His hands, Georgie noticed, where clenched into fists. She reached out, enveloping one with her much smaller hand.

"It wasn't about Roman. Not really," she admitted, sucking in a breath when he looked up at her. "I wanted *you* back. For a second, when you asked me to ride him, it felt like I saw you again. So I said yes."

He opened his mouth, but she shook her head. "No, just . . . let me say this. I know it's stupid, and you're not that person anymore, but I guess I wanted you to trust something, and maybe I thought that could be me. I wanted to see you again. Maybe you just wanted a win for Roman, but I took the opportunity you gave me with my admittedly limited skill set. It was never about Roman, at least not at the beginning."

Harris looked at her like she was a particularly complicated painting there was no hope of comprehending.

"You don't have a limited skill set," he finally said, and she scoffed.

"I ride horses in a circle," she replied.

"It's death defying," he came back.

"Fine," she said. "It's a death defying, singular skill set."

They smiled at each other. She offered him her hand. "Friends?"

"Are we?" he asked, eyes narrowing.

Georgie sucked in a breath. "I certainly hope so."

"I guess I should keep my award-winning jockey happy," Harris said.

She arched an eyebrow.

"Friends," he amended, and took her hand.

Midway through the turn, Georgie was down to her last set of goggles. The colt underneath her churned as she scrubbed at his neck, leaning into the turn while Roman flew around horses on their way past the quarter-mile pole.

The homestretch unspooled in a gauntlet of noise, crowds on both sides of the rail, the infield a mess of bodies and the grandstand filled with camera flashes she had no time to consider as she guided Roman onto a straight path to the wire and pulled the trigger. Just like that he lowered his head and burst forward, overtaking the leader and pinning back his ears when a flash of chestnut appeared at their inside.

Reliance.

The chestnut pushed ahead by a length, his copper tail slapping in the wind as he went. Georgie flicked her crop into her right hand, tapped it against Roman's shoulder, demanded that he switch to his right lead. The colt surged back alongside Reliance as they raced down a tunnel of roars.

Seconds ticked on the clock as they sped past the tote board, Georgie pushing her body so she could shove Roman past Reliance, reaching her crop hand to flick the leather past his eye and then back to tap him again, again. Faster, Roman, *faster*.

The gray colt lunged, gathered himself, and lunged again until he was just there, in the right spot at the right time when they blew past the finish line a head bob in front and leaving a whole grandstand sucking in their breath.

Georgie stood in the irons, lifting her crop hand with a wild whoop as Roman plowed into the clubhouse turn a Preakness champion, going fast enough to frustrate the outrider pony sent to catch him. Georgie sat back in the saddle, managing to slow the colt with the outrider's help, slapping Roman on the neck and running her fingers through his mane as they turned back for the grandstand.

It was a wild mass of flashbulbs sparking.

The on-track reporter arrived, microphone in hand and her questions breathless. Georgie didn't remember how she answered them, her heart thumping too fast and her voice cracking. People shouted across the track at her, everything from congratulations to drunken slurs. War whoops and groans. Tickets fell from hands or were eagerly taken to the betting windows. The grandstand was alive, and Georgie had won the Preakness Stakes.

The colt blew out of red-rimmed nostrils and walked like a prince onto the turf track, approaching the winner's circle at the infield cupola, where Tupelo's people were gathering in a flood of smiles. Roman's groom helped lift the blanket of Black-Eyed

Susans across the colt's withers, people scurrying around the colt like harried personal assistants giving him a quick manicure so he'd look perfect for his photo. Georgie helped place the flowers and re-arranged the reins as she was handed a giant bouquet, flowers pouring down the colt's neck. They were bedecked in flowers, showers of yellow petals trailing after them in the grass as they stopped in front of the cupola so Roman could put his nose in Harris' hands.

After the win photo, Georgie jumped off the colt, landing in thick green grass. She pulled off her helmet, pushed a wayward clump of hair back under her bandana. Reece shoved a ball cap with Roman's name embroidered across the front onto her head, pulling the brim over her eyes as Lynsey wiped at the mud on her face, admonishing her about how she couldn't look this dirty on national television.

"So that was unexpected, huh?" Harris asked her on their way up the cupola steps, where a hulking silver trophy gleamed in the sun, miniatures lined up next to it. The miniatures would be their take-home prizes, and one of them was specially made for Georgie.

"Unexpected?" Georgie laughed, shoving Harris' arm as they shouldered their way toward a beaming sports anchor, microphone ready and waiting for them to address the rumbling crowd, the millions watching on television. "I worked my butt off for that win. That was deserved."

Harris grinned down at her, flushed and bouncing on his toes as Reece and Samuel talked with the anchor, their voices booming through the grandstand rafters and echoing back across the track.

"Okay, maybe not too unexpected," Harris said, shooting her a look as Reece grabbed his arm, pulling him toward the micro-phone. Harris snagged her hand, pulling her along with him. She laughed into the microphone when the anchor asked her how un-expected this was—a girl winning one of the biggest races in the country.

"Not to me," she said. Simple enough.

They huddled in the mass of people crowding the cupola while the track busily set to work painting over the weather vane with the Tupelo colors, wasting no time. Harris handed her the silver trophy, its weight solid and warm. He smiled, the stretch of it sending sparks racing up her fingers, fizzing in her heart.

"This is surreal," he told her, the noise cocooning them against the cupola. Georgie ducked her head, cuddled the trophy close. She looked up at him underneath her eyelashes, underneath the ridiculous baseball cap's brim that shadowed her face.

"Are you ready for more of it at the Belmont?" she asked, watching him reach out, slide his hand underneath the trophy's handle where she held it. Their fingers brushed, and she definitely needed her glowing nerves to calm down. She needed to take a breath, ride out the wave of exhilaration that lapped all around her, except Harris was only ever the person who pushed her to new heights. Of course he would only be ready for more.

He shook his head at her, leaning into her so she could hear him in the noise.

"Is there any world in which I wouldn't be?"

They were so close, so pressed together, so in each other's space that in the end it was easy. It was just a tip of his head, a slight move upward of her traitorous toes, a brush of lips as her eyes shuttered closed. It was even easy to want to let it keep going, and Georgie wanted major bonus points for pulling away, plummeting back down to earth in the space it took for her heels to meet the ground.

When she opened her eyes all she could see was Harris. They stared at each other long enough for her to wonder why people weren't asking her what was going on, why no one was noticing. Then she realized that she was only experiencing split seconds, that people hadn't seen, that the vase was lifted to Oliver, to Samuel, to Reece.

No one noticed, she told herself. Her heart jackhammered at her ribs. Her lips parted, mouth dry. She knew she looked stunned. She *was* stunned.

Harris cast her a look over his shoulder as he was dragged away for interviews, the crowd breaking up. Another race had to be run and it was time to take the celebration off the track, where hopefully everyone would still not have noticed Harris kissing Georgie like it was the easiest thing in the world.

Georgie wiped her hand across her mouth, swallowed hard, and stepped off the cupola.

Part Three:
Full Out

Chapter Fourteen

SUNDAY MORNING DAWNED lazily, the sun rolling into the cloudless sky and casting red rays onto Pimlico. Only a smattering of horses dotted the track. Most walked the shedrow, their coats glittering and stud chains jangling. Roman's blanket of flowers stretched over the railing at the stakes barn, providing the media with a focal point as the colt did his rounds with the photographers, standing with his ears pricked for the photo op with Harris while Georgie's life wildly spiraled out of control.

Lynsey showed her the photo in the local paper, innocently sitting there on the fourth page of the sports section after the jump from Roman's first page story. Harris and Georgie, lips touching for eternity in print.

Georgie wanted to die.

Harris, of course, stood next to his colt and basked in the adulation.

"Where else is this?" she asked, her voice shaking as much as her fingers as she held the paper. Lynsey looked at her piteously.

"Georgie," Lynsey said, holding out her phone. "It's everywhere."

On YouTube, video of the kiss pulled from the live broadcast. Georgie tried to swallow down the lump in her throat, but instead the lump seemed to be trying to kill her because she couldn't get a good breath. She sucked at the air, nearly dropping the phone. Lynsey caught it and pushed Georgie down into a lawn chair.

"Breathe, Georgie," Lynsey commanded. "It's not the end of the world. Granted, it burned my eyes to see it replayed this many times and the word *why* keeps spinning through my head, but otherwise it's not the end of the world."

"Oh my god," Georgie groaned, putting her face in her hands and looking up at her. "I have an interview in thirty minutes with HTV and this is out there. First female jockey to win the Preakness I can talk about, but this? I can't talk about this."

"Why not?" Lynsey asked, looking at the photo critically. "Say it's nothing. People do silly things when you're caught up in the moment."

"I think I'm going to be sick," Georgie announced, pressing a hand against her belly and not complaining when Lynsey hauled her into the barn office's tiny bathroom.

"You have to calm down," Lynsey ordered, shoving her down on the closed toilet seat and wetting paper towels, depositing them in Georgie's limp hands before wiping at Georgie's face herself. "You cannot go on television looking like this. Are you breathing?"

Georgie let out a breath and nodded.

"Listen," Lynsey said, wetting another towel and pressing it against Georgie's neck, bringing the bright pink flush there under control. "You won the Preakness yesterday. Do you remember that feeling?"

Georgie nodded.

"Think you can grab onto that?" Lynsey asked.

Georgie nodded again, crumpling the paper towel in her hands.

"The kiss is none of their business," Lynsey said. "If they ask about it you can tell them that. Or, if you want, you can tell them my brother is an idiot and he did everything wrong because he's an idiot."

Lynsey paused, pursing her lips, and then made Georgie look at her. "You're Georgiana Quinn, damn it."

A laugh bubbled out of Georgie's throat, and she wiped at her eyes again. "Yeah," she said, nodding. "I'm Georgiana Quinn. I'm amazing."

"Damn straight. You can do this," Lynsey said sternly. Georgie nodded haltingly and stood up, throwing away the towels and looking at herself in the mirror. Slightly pink, definitely damp. But she could work with that. Besides, who walked onto HTV looking glamorous?

No one, that's who. They were going to talk about Roman and the Preakness, not Harris. Never Harris. Georgie pushed her hair into place and turned to hug Lynsey.

"Thanks," she murmured, and Lynsey squeezed her tight.

⌒

They asked about the kiss, showed it on television again for good measure. Georgie smiled and said, "Is 'no comment' an appropriate response?"

The interviewers watched her unblinkingly, and so she plunged onward.

"Heat of the moment," Georgie said, waving a hand. "Harris and I have known each other forever."

She winced inwardly at the ridiculous words coming out of her mouth. They were shadows of truth, murky around the edges, and Georgie told herself that people could read into them what they liked. Hadn't they always? Nothing had stopped them from doing just that in the days after Lilliana died, when nothing felt right except working with Sweet Bells.

Staying at Red Gate felt impossible in the windfall of Lilliana. Georgie couldn't look her parents in the eye, couldn't form words for her mother, couldn't stay in her bedroom at night without thinking too much about the things she hadn't wanted to see and the way Harris looked at her when she couldn't tell the truth.

Tupelo was an easy walk across the road, and Sweet Bells was the perfect excuse.

I have to help with Sweet Bells was her go-to answer for any question from her parents about her whereabouts, and they let her go because they were falling apart. Georgie didn't need to see it happen in front of her eyes, not like Harris and Lynsey had with Lilliana, who hadn't been able to help it in the end.

So she went to Tupelo, and she helped train Sweet Bells. She stayed in the filly's stall, did her homework there, nodded off instead of going home, where things would never stop falling. She was always with Sweet Bells, so it became easy for Harris to find her.

She heard the BMW pull up outside the barn, heard his shoes on the concrete, knew she should skip out when she had the chance. Only she couldn't seem to make herself leave the stall, couldn't stop thinking about the possibility that maybe things could be different. Maybe there was still some hope that he would forgive her, and it was powerful enough for her to wish that he'd smile at her when he showed up at the stall.

"What are you doing here?" he asked her, leaning against the stall door. His voice slurred, making the hairs on the back of her neck stand on end.

"I'm always here," she said, running the brush over Bell's side. "You know that."

He sighed. "Yeah, and why is that?"

Georgie stopped brushing the filly, arm falling to her side. Bell swung her head around, bumping her nose insistently against the brush, asking for more.

"You know why, Harris. It's not a mystery."

"Why is it that you never say what happened?" he asked, looking at her with brutally open eyes. She felt like he was seeing right through her. "You always dance around it and act like it's not there, but you're always here. Not at Red Gate, I notice—here."

"Why do you think talking about it will help?" Georgie demanded, feeling absurd for arguing with a drunk person, and Harris was quite drunk. He looked at her challengingly, stepping into the stall and making Bell back toward the middle of the stall.

"Because life was pretty damn good before, and now it sucks," he said, staring at her like she had something to give him. "Because it's all falling apart and it isn't fair to us. Because our parents are selfish assholes and you act okay with that when I know you're not because you're *fucking here*."

Georgie's temper flared as she spat back her retort. "How about you stop criticizing me for trying to keep it together when you're drinking yourself into oblivion. I can't act like you, okay?"

"I'm not drinking myself into oblivion," he said, like that was news to him.

"Oh, no," Georgie replied sarcastically. "You only smell like a distillery because that's the trendy cologne these days. Sober up, Harris."

"Don't tell me what to do," he said so petulantly she laughed right in his face.

"Don't tell *me* what to do," she parroted back. Then she went on the offensive, because she was sick of the attitude, and someone needed to say it. "What is it to you how I act? My mom made a mistake, and believe me, my days are probably right about par with yours in the suck category."

"It's not her mistake, it's *yours*," he said. "How can you keep staying there like she didn't ruin everything?"

Georgie stared at him, stunned.

"Because she's my mom," she said quietly.

He stepped closer, backing her into Bell's side. The filly danced away, snorting. Georgie decided then to stand her ground, looking up at him when he grabbed her arms and told her carefully, "Did it ever occur to you that's not good enough?"

Her mouth opened as she realized what he was saying, that he was disowning his father, and he was expecting her to do the same. But for what? She wanted to yell at him, force him to take it back, but the words were stuck in her throat. The way he was looking at her made a finger of heat slide up her spine, adrenaline hitting her bloodstream like showers of sparks raining down to her fingertips.

Run, said every fiber of her being, just before he kissed her.

By instinct, she lifted her hands, wanting to frame them

around his jaw until she realized that he wasn't trying to be nice. This wasn't a kiss about her, or even about them. It was about Harris, searching for something that didn't exist anymore, and he knew it.

He'd punish her for that, too.

She pushed him away, gasping, and brought her hand up to her mouth.

"I thought that was what you wanted," he said, his voice just shy of snide. Georgie blinked back tears, thinking that she *had* wanted it, but in another life, with another Harris who was not this boy standing in front of her now.

"Not anymore," she said, and pushed past him, breaking into a run the second she hit the night air.

Afterward, she wondered how it had been so easy, to simply fall into him like it was meant to happen despite everything. After the Preakness, she found herself wondering the same exact thing. It had felt so easy to tip into Harris. It was instinct to let it happen, an easy fall into an abyss that always jolted her back into the land of the sane. She wondered how the axis had shifted again. How did they make it back to this spot? Was it really this easy? More importantly, did she want to stay there, hovering over that void she couldn't name?

She stared at the HTV interviewers, looked hard at their striped ties and their cat-caught-the-canary expressions.

"You know what I think?" she asked them, tilting her head sweetly. They blinked at her, unsure smiles answering back.

"I think it's now my policy not to answer questions about my personal life."

They guffawed, straightened the papers on their desk, and she leaned back in her chair, waiting for the next question.

The cameras kept rolling.

Chapter Fifteen

HERO TO TAKE on Boys in Belmont.

It was the top news story, images of the golden filly racing across the face of Georgie's phone. She shoved it into the back pocket of her jeans and said to Reece, "Well, that's happening."

"To be fair," Reece said, "that's been the rumor since she set foot on Belmont's backside."

Georgie nodded, fiddling with her crop as they stood in the barn's yard. Roman stepped high, arching his neck into his groom's arm like he was trying to piaffe his way to Georgie, all exaggerated movements and swishing tail.

"You don't seem ruffled," said Luna, who was up from Tupelo to exercise ride while the farm's big horses raced at Belmont. She stood waiting on Roman's workmate, twirling her crop in her fingers and chewing loudly on a piece of gum.

"Reece is never ruffled," Georgie said. "It's the British stiff upper lip in him. If he ruffles, it's time to panic."

"Thank you for that dissection of my character, Georgie," Reece said, while Luna stifled a smile. "Please get on the horse now and do your job."

Georgie swung into the light exercise saddle, her jeans sliding against the smooth leather, and set off toward the training track that curled between Belmont's barns. Horses crisscrossed the dirt, arriving in groups of chattering exercise riders. Georgie caught a flash of chestnut jogging around the far turn and half expected it to be Hero, appearing like a wraith through the mist. Looking closer, she found Little War instead, Nick in the irons. Nick had a fuming colt underneath him, all bottled energy boiling to the surface in fits that he kept bringing back to a methodical jog. It was little wonder the colt was ready to go. Two months off the track and he looked offended by the prospect of light work.

"Now that one looks good." Luna craned her neck, watching Little War disappear into the glancing morning sun. Georgie smiled to herself, and nudged Roman toward the track. With Little War back on the work tab, she knew who she'd be visiting soon. Just as she thought it, Roman yanked his head down, pulling on her arms like a jarring reminder that she was riding *him*, thank you very much.

"Okay," she whispered to him, leaning over his crested neck. "You caught me. I'm all yours today, boy."

She straightened, glanced over at the onlookers gathered at the outside rail, some with cameras, some with cups of coffee steaming in the early morning mist. It didn't take much work to notice that one of those cups of coffee belonged to her mother. Harris stood next to her, leaning against the rail with that careful expression trained on his face, hiding any true feelings he might have about that. For her mother's part, she smiled. Wide and white, like nothing was wrong.

Sometimes there were moments in life where nothing seemed fair, and this moment qualified.

A little part of Georgie snapped, and Roman felt it, rising up on his hind legs and beating at the air with his hooves in wild imitation of a performing circus horse. She grabbed mane, kept herself in the saddle, and exhaled a big breath when Reece appeared at the colt's head before he could rise back up again and make a real show out of it.

"Get on the track, Georgie," Reece commanded, throwing a glance at their onlookers. Harris shifted uncomfortably, but her mother waved, still not getting it.

Georgie rode past them, kept herself moving forward while feeling everyone's eyes trained on her safety vest.

"You okay?" Luna called to her once they'd made it to the training gate, the beaten up contraption clanking as the gate crew opened the back doors.

"Stranger things have happened," Georgie muttered, and quickly smiled when that did nothing to shake Luna's concern. "I'm fine."

Roman loaded into the training gate, bumped his hindquarters against the sides as if testing the metal. Georgie shifted her weight in the stirrups, combing her fingers through Roman's mane. Next to her, Luna loaded with fanfare, her colt banging into the metal, throwing his head back and screaming hoarsely. Roman jumped, snorting as the gate groaned around the colt.

"Calm, boy," Georgie murmured, watching Roman's ears tentatively flick back toward her voice. Georgie's thoughts drifted, falling back into Florida's dark hole and her mother's strangely shiny presence on the rail. She watched Claire, wondering just why she was here. Why wasn't she at Red Gate?

The doors slammed open.

Georgie had a plan. Break out of the gate, then continue around the training track in a five furlong breeze. Except that went all to hell when Georgie's reins slipped, giving Roman the go ahead. The colt barreled onto the track, sideswiping Luna on his way. The other colt leapt to the outside and stumbled, tossing Luna and jumping clear before taking off after Roman in a crazed urge to catch up.

Georgie stood in the stirrups, bridged the reins and pressed them into the colt's withers, forcing him round and deep. Luna's colt blew by on their outside, a streak of ruddy brown with reins flapping wildly around his head. Roman huffed huge breaths, his body quivering with excitement that Georgie pushed in on itself, refusing to let him run off with her any more than he already had as they galloped into the turn.

Ahead of them, an outrider caught the brown colt and trotted back the way they came with the colt's head over the pony's withers and his mane askew.

"Bring him back in," Reece's voice spoke tinny in her ear. "Second try will be the charm."

Georgie let her weight sink into the stirrups, pushing the colt's speed down until they cantered along the backside of the track. Roman complied, rocking his body out into the middle of the track until Georgie eased him to an ambling walk up the outside rail to where Reece stood with Harris, a rumpled Luna brushing dirt off her jeans nearby. Her mother helped, dusting the dirt off Luna's shoulder and holding her coffee well out of the way.

"You okay, Luna?" Georgie called, guiding Roman to the

rail and halting him. The colt peered around curiously, taking big breaths like he'd just come back from the best thing in the world and couldn't wait to get back out there and do it again.

"Nothing that won't come out in the wash," Luna reported, lifting her chin just enough to show that she wasn't affected. Still fearless in the face of another fall, this one only a mere knock to her ribs and maybe her pride. Georgie knew that resolute feeling well.

"Sorry about that," she said, patting the colt's neck. "He clearly knows how to break, maybe better than I do."

"If that's how you feel, no wonder he ran out on you," Harris said, clearly past the point of keeping his opinions to himself. That wasn't the way of things in the racing business. "What the hell was that?"

"A mistake," Georgie snapped at him, pinning him with a look. "I've made one every so often."

He stared at her, infuriatingly silent, and Georgie pushed her calves into Roman's sides, riding back down the track to the starting gate before Reece could remind them to get back to the work.

Once Roman went in the gate and came out of it a victorious if trembling success, Georgie breezed him around the track as ordered, Luna keeping her colt close to Roman's shoulder. They came back to the outside rail on horses that felt like clouds, floating on long legs.

Harris wasn't there, but her mother still stood watching her hopefully. Georgie pointed the colt past her, kept Roman to a jigging walk that forced Claire to scurry alongside.

"Georgie," Claire said breathlessly.

"I'm working, Mom," Georgie said over her shoulder, tapping Roman's sides when he stilled to yell his fool head off at a passing filly. The colt grunted and bounded back into his ground-eating walk, all fussy tail thrashing and head bobbing.

"Georgie," Claire said again when they got to the shedrow, her voice moving well past inquiring and into demanding. The I-am-your-mother voice that made Georgie twitch.

"What are you doing here?" Georgie asked.

She dismounted, pulling the saddle off Roman's back and letting his groom take the colt to the hose.

"If you checked your messages or ever answered my calls you might know," Claire snapped at her. "I came to see my daughter, who apparently isn't interested in being involved with her parents anymore."

Georgie bit down on the inside of her cheeks, telling herself to stay calm. The backside had ears, and most importantly it had a mouth. There were no secrets on the backside, especially after you were done emptying them right on its lawn. She could only imagine *Uncle Moe*'s next headline. Maybe something like *Quinn Family Fight Nights, Tickets $2!* The accompanying cartoon could be Georgie and Claire, armed with boxing gloves.

"I cannot talk to you here," Georgie hissed at her. "You know that."

"I'm past the point of caring where we have this conversation, Georgie," Claire told her, face red as her hair. "You cannot leave school, leave home, and not talk to us for two months without a hell of a lot of blow back. We need to talk, and it's happening now."

A sick slip of nausea trailed up Georgie's throat, bile bitter on the back of her tongue.

"You've got to be kidding me."

"Do I look like I'm kidding?" Claire asked. "Your father and

I flew up here with money we don't have, because you can't be bothered to pick up a goddamned phone. What are you thinking, Georgie? What the hell goes through your head? You realize the amount of chaos that you've rained down on us? The farm is a mess, and the school is—"

"How is any of that my problem?" Georgie cut her off. "I quit. I quit all of it."

Claire sputtered. "You can't quit!"

Georgie clutched the saddle to her chest and waved an arm at the backside. "Do you see this, Mom? This is what I do. I'm doing what I need to do, just like you, apparently."

"What are you talking about?" Claire asked.

"Working for Oliver, Mom," Georgie said. "How did you think I wouldn't find out about that?"

Claire pressed her lips together, like she was forcing herself to keep the words she wanted to say inside. Then she squared her shoulders, lifting her chin.

"Red Gate isn't going to save itself."

The acknowledgment of it stunned Georgie, mainly because it was the first time anyone had finally put a voice to their fears. There was no saving Red Gate. It would keep slipping and they would all slowly abandon it for something else. Something like Tupelo.

They'd both already done it. Georgie felt the sharp spike of tears wet her eyelashes.

"So this is your great contribution? Taking Oliver's money?" she asked, her voice breaking. Claire tilted her head at her, watching her like she was looking in a mirror.

"How is that so wrong?"

The question was simple, but the weight of it blew into Geor-

213

gie and knocked the breath out of her lungs.

"Because it's *Oliver*. This is what you call helping?"

Claire's face was all darkening storm clouds. Georgie could feel the astonished stares of riders as they passed. The backside had gone silent, soaking in every word of their conversation, and there was nothing she could do about it. It was already done.

"I don't need a lecture from my daughter about this, Georgie," Claire said. "As you said, you quit."

"Because of you," Georgie yelled at her. "You went back to Oliver after I insisted you hadn't done any of the things everyone already knew you'd done. I stood up for you, like an *idiot*, and got nothing for it in return, so don't tell me I haven't fought. I did, and I failed. Don't tell me I didn't try."

Georgie let out a shaky breath, adrenaline still pumping red hot through her heart that beat wildly in her chest. Her mother opened her mouth, and shut it again, shaking her head. *Loss of words,* Georgie thought. Fitting. Claire never did have much to say about that day in the kitchen—or all the days after it—like if she couldn't make the words come then nothing had happened.

But it had, and Georgie was done pretending that it hadn't.

Turning on her heel, Georgie stalked away from her mother, hackles still raised for a fight that didn't come. Claire didn't follow her as she wound her way into the tack room, throwing the saddle into its empty spot with enough force to make the beam rattle. She stood there, staring down at it, and wanted to pick it back up, throw it against the wall to excise some of the guilt out of her. Just so she could breathe again.

So she did it. She picked the saddle up and threw it as hard as she could, satisfaction bolting through her veins at the sound of stirrup irons clanking, a whole shelf of ointment and medications toppling to roll at her feet.

"Feel better?"

Harris stood in the doorway, resting a shoulder there like he had all the time in the world. Georgie afforded him a glance, and then looked down at her mess.

"No," she said, clenching her fists.

Silence greeted her, and she felt the awful urge to scratch herself into another fight. Push until she got a response, because she hadn't done that before. Maybe she was past due.

"You have to love this," she said. She wanted him to say something terrible, something that would wrench them back into the place where they hated each other and everything made sense.

There was a pause.

"Georgie," he started, like he wanted to be the rational one when all he'd ever done was push her past the brink.

"That kiss at the Preakness? That won't happen again," she said, reaching for something that would hurt. The kiss sat there, all soft in her memory, a moment she gave a wide berth. She didn't want to think about what it meant to her, not when she could throw it in his face to watch the flicker in his eyes before nothingness settled there like a shroud she knew so well.

"That so?"

"How could you possibly think it would?"

Harris sighed, like he really didn't want to have to be the one to tell her this. He lifted himself off the doorjamb with the heel of his hand. "Because it wasn't just me up there on the cupola. And it wasn't just you. The whole country was there, and you still met me halfway."

The retort she'd prepared in the face of what she was sure would be a blistering comment died, withered up in her throat for her to choke on. Shaking his head, Harris pushed away from the doorway and disappeared down the shedrow, leaving her there with a whole new round of thoughts doing merry-go-round whirls in her head.

It wasn't like she could argue with any of that. Facts sucked that way, and Georgie was trying so hard not to live in denial anymore. She clenched her fists tighter, felt her blunt nails bite at her palms, before unfurling her fingers with a blood-rushing tingle.

Then she settled on her knees in the dust, and began picking everything up.

June

Chapter Sixteen

GEORGIE FELT HER mother's eyes on her back. It itched, knowing how watched she was, and her fingers shook against the reins with the knowing. Bell tilted her head against the pony's neck, pressed her muzzle against the smaller horse's mane in an insistent kiss. Georgie wiped one hand against her stark white pants, feeling the sweaty warmth bleed into her thigh.

Not good. So many worlds of not good.

She looked up at the rain falling from the sky in shiny silver drops, coming down so fast and exploding wetly across Bell's coat, Georgie's silks, sinking into the sloppy-wet track that had been sealed into an impenetrable thick blanket only hours before. The Ogden Phipps Handicap was full of fillies and mares they'd beaten before, save one. Blue Arrow, a giant gray mare, was new. Shipped off the West Coast and walking along like she owned the place.

Georgie took a deep breath as they went into the gate, pulled her goggles down over her eyes and listened to the preparation of jockeys around her. The shifting of horses. The clang of gate doors shutting. The sound of rain plinking on metal. She hooked her fingers into the filly's damp mane, felt her mouth only lightly through the reins.

The bell rattled across the metal starting gate, and the gates burst open with ten Thoroughbreds bunching muscle all at once to get out. Sweet Bells, ears back, leapt and dug in. The track slipped beneath her feet, and Georgie pushed her out of it, gave her the rein she needed to dig her hooves in and jump through. Her strides left a splatter of mud in her wake as Georgie sent her up the inside of the pack past the grandstand.

Fillies pressed against them on all sides, their hooves a thunder under the wind that tore up Bell's mane. Georgie watched the wall of hindquarters rise and fall in front of them through the backstretch. Sweet Bells lifted her head to avoid the spray, mud smacking her chest and sluicing down Georgie's cheeks. The ground continued its slippery slide underneath them, churned up by the frontrunners before they could get a chance to really run. She could feel the filly struggling to hold it together just as well as she could feel the sting of her mane on her skin followed by the cool rain dripping off her goggles, trickling down her nose.

In the homestretch the field bunched, began to push for more speed. Georgie shook her reins out, let the filly know it was time to find a hole. Somewhere, there needed to be a hole so they could get through. The fillies in front of them stretched out, ate up the ground in explosive bursts, but Georgie knew somewhere deep down that they would flag underneath Sweet Bells. They had to. That was always the way of it.

But there was no room to run on the outside and Blue Arrow was a streak of gunmetal gray wrapping around horses. A blink and she was there. A blink and she was already gone.

Fear flooded Georgie's throat. There had to be an opening. There wasn't.

Sweet Bells ran with her jaw locked on the bit. Georgie felt the frustration pent up behind the horses that wouldn't break and wanted to scream at their backs that they needed to *move*.

A sliver of an opening winked along the rail, maybe room for half a horse if they were lucky. They could barge their way through, bump along the rail to the front. Before she could think, Georgie turned the filly's nose to the opening and simply hoped it would be enough.

Sweet Bells dived for it, shouldering her way into the hole and glancing off the rail. It grazed up her shoulder, bounced once, twice off her hindquarters with each stride she took. To their outside, Edward Suarez on the 30-1 long shot took one look at her and brought out the crop, showing it to his filly and pushing for more speed. The long shot filly pinned back her ears, looking wildly over at Sweet Bells.

Then the hole closed.

Sweet Bells threw on the brakes so hard Georgie grabbed mane, had to push herself up in the stirrups to stay balanced on the filly's faltered stride.

The long shot cruised ahead of them, opening up on the rail.

Curses rained out of Georgie's mouth, got caught in Sweet Bells' flying mane as she pulled the filly's head to the outside and pushed her hands up Bell's neck. They had to get back online, had to burn it all to get to the front, because Blue Arrow had too much of a head start and they had lost so much time. She made herself as small as she could, flicked the crop up and felt like a wild person as she swung it. Sweet Bells dashed forward, the ground still slipping underneath her and the field still never falling back.

It never fell back.

Blue Arrow hit the wire first, and Sweet Bells hit seconds later, a lone dot caught on the outside of the mass of horses stretching for second.

Georgie pushed herself up, resting her knuckles on Bell's neck and bowing her head against the onslaught of rain. It slid like cold fingers down her neck, dripped off her lips and slipped muddy into her mouth. With trembling fingers, Georgie pulled the willing filly back down to a trot in the turn and wished she could take it all back when she saw that tote board glowing through the silvery haze.

Sweet Bells in fourth.

Bile rose up her throat as she rode the filly back to the grandstand. It filled the back of her mouth and she had to swallow it back down to boos littering the crowd upon her arrival. She kept her eyes forward, her head bent, slipping off the filly as soon as Bell was safe and heaving in Miguel's arms. Her heels sank into the track as she turned, going through the motions to pull off the slippery saddle and pat the filly tiredly on the neck.

Bell craned her head up, ears pricked at the winner's circle, confusion sketched across her face at the break in her routine. Racing meant wild applause. It meant a winner's circle, sometimes with a blanket of flowers framing her neck. Not a quick trip back to the shedrow. Georgie watched Miguel lead her back down the outer rail and slunk to the scales, handed her saddle to her valet, and wiped at the mud crusted around her eyes.

Mud on the soles of her featherweight boots slipped along the concrete as she walked back to the jocks' room. She stopped to scrape them off, glad she had time leading up to the Belmont Stakes. Roman the Great was no doubt already prepared, his coat gleaming and his people polished, primped. She would look like an urchin next to them if she didn't clean up.

"Georgie."

The word echoed down the hallway, and every nerve ending came alight like fireflies going aglow in the dark. Soft, obvious, tender little things.

She turned around to face Harris.

"I couldn't get past," she whispered, almost to herself. That was the truth. She couldn't get past. She'd tried and she couldn't.

"No kidding," Harris told her. "That wasn't an opening you tried to push her through, it was a pinhole. You could have gone around."

"It was five wide," Georgie defended, her hackles going up. Nothing like a good argument with Harris to get her motivated all over again. In the back of her head, she thought *good*. This would get her back on track for the Belmont. It would set her straight for Roman. Because as much as she didn't want to admit it, she was shaken. "I couldn't have taken her five wide around the turn, not with the way Bell was slipping in that mud. It would have killed her off faster."

"But it was your only option."

"Blue Arrow was there half the . . ."

"Stop making excuses," Harris cut over her. "You let her sit behind a wall of horses the entire race like you were on autopilot, expecting her to do all the running."

"I know!" Georgie pushed off the wall, the red hot feeling rolling up her throat. "I know, okay? I didn't make the right moves."

"You didn't make *any* moves."

"What do you want me to do, Harris?" Georgie asked, hating that she sounded pleading. "I can't go back."

He looked down at her, unimpressed with her answer. She didn't blame him, not when she was so unimpressed with herself.

"It took way too much shouting to dissuade my grandpa from coming down here and sharing his outrage with you," he said, blowing out a breath.

"Samuel has every right to be pissed with me."

"This is more than pissed. This is pulling you off Sweet Bells and never letting you on her again."

"That's not going to happen," she said quietly as a stream of jockeys walked by for the next race, their pristine silks hiding the grime from the track.

"Isn't it?" Harris asked, watching her like he expected answers to illuminate off her forehead. "You didn't win a race at Churchill. You've barely hit the winner's circle here. Sweet Bells just ran off the board and we're putting you on my colt in two hours. What assurance do I have that your head is in the game at all?"

Georgie couldn't breathe anymore; the suggestion that she would be abandoned for one bad ride and a streak of losses knocked the wind out of her. She gaped up at him, her mouth falling open and her throat working, wanting air so badly she sucked it in audible sips.

"You can't . . ."

She couldn't finish the sentence. He only looked at her like she was lying to herself, lying to him. It was a look she'd seen so often, and was so sick of seeing it. They had Roman now, they had tenuous baby steps back to something kinder than what they'd been.

They had that moment in front of the world in Baltimore.

"Give me something here, Georgie," Harris said, voice gravelly with something Georgie couldn't recognize. She looked at his lips, told herself to stop before she took that dangerous leap. She couldn't lie to him. There were no assurances in her life anymore, so what would a lie be worth?

"Give me . . ."

She pushed up on her toes before she could think about it anymore, her lips catching against his. This was the only promise she could give him, that down deep he was right all along. That she did still think about them in a way that made her skin flush pink.

It was only when he pulled back, both of them stumbling, that she dared look up at him. Mud peppered across his slack mouth, beckoned for her to wipe it away. She didn't, not when he looked ready to burst out of his skin.

"Damn it, George," he said as he slid a hand up her neck, all of those fireflies glowing on her nerves burning bright.

He crossed the space he'd put between them in one quick rush, mouth meeting hers again in a crush. Georgie pushed her dirty hands against his pristine sports coat, smearing mud along the lapels as she grabbed for something to hold. His fingers met the bandana tied over her hair, loosening it enough for red wisps to peak out.

Her eyes popped open as her back met the wall, his hand cushioning her head from the cinder blocks. Harris pressed his free hand against the wall, pushed back from her just enough to look at her questioningly, as if wondering if they were really doing this.

Georgie pulled him back down with shaking fingers, her whole body thrumming and shivering as she let him past her lips in full view in the hallway. She didn't care who saw. Let people see. Let *Uncle Moe* write a drooling headline. What was there to lose anymore?

She kissed him until her lips were raw with it. Until she'd transferred enough mud to his clothes that surely he would need to change before making their grand entrance onto national television. It was nothing, though. She licked into his mouth, arched into him until he hissed and pulled back, hands on her hips like a vise.

Georgie couldn't help the smile, caught as they were in this pocket of time between races, where nothing could touch her except Harris.

"You're a wreck." She tugged on his destroyed silk tie.

He took her hand in his, and there it was again. That bloom of warmth.

"Yeah, well, so are you," he pointed out. "More."

"Guess we're even," she murmured, resting against the wall.

"What are we doing, Georgie?" he asked her, the question hanging there between them. She didn't know, not really, and she couldn't very well say that she wanted to remove herself from reality for a moment, however tenuous and uncertain her actions. The unshakable super filly was defeated, and it was all her fault. She needed to hold on to something. She needed to stop denying herself, lying to herself. She needed to do something true.

"I," she started, stopped to lick her swollen lips. "I can't promise anything, Harris. Not for Roman. Not for you."

He only nodded, like he'd expected that all the while.

"What will you tell Samuel?" she asked.

Harris stiffened at the mention of his grandfather, the force of sheer will that could take her off Sweet Bells. As much as Samuel liked her, there were home fires to tend. Tupelo and its horses came first, their money-making potential second, and people like Georgie a distant, hazy third.

"That Bell wasn't handling the surface," he said. "She's never run in the mud at Belmont."

Georgie hated that her filly would be blamed for what was her fault. Then, down deep, she realized that it was only an excuse to buy her time until the Belmont Stakes. It wouldn't stand on replay. It would barely stand at all, not when the entire world could see her ride.

Harris squeezed her hand, his fingers warm and sure around hers, and for a second she believed it would be okay.

"I've got to go calm the troops," he said. "See you in the paddock?"

She nodded, let his hand fall away from hers when she wanted to keep grasping it tight. He walked back the way he'd come, glanced at her once over his shoulder, and then disappeared out of sight.

It took so many minutes to calm down. Georgie stood in the hallway by herself until the jockeys came back mud-covered and soaked from the last race, eyed her up and down like they knew why she was out there pretending the whole world didn't exist. Even Dean walked by her with silent eyes, never saying a word.

She slipped into the women's changing room to shower, shrug into fresh silks. With no other girl jocks on the rest of the card, she finally had the room to herself. Georgie could sit and replay the race over and over. She could replay the kiss over and over. She could imagine all the best and worse scenarios that could unfurl ahead of her in the Belmont Stakes.

Her mother called, and she ignored it. Her father called, and she hovered her fingers over the face of the phone as it vibrated insistently on the bench. She couldn't convince herself to pick up. Couldn't bear the thought of having that conversation she knew she needed to have. The phone went dark.

Laughter from the common room seeped through the wall, and Georgie felt it like pinpricks on her skin. There were so many reasons to hold her head high, walk in and take the heat they threw at her. She could take it, and she could dish it back. It was all part of living in such close quarters with the competition.

But today she couldn't, so she swallowed down the nerves and waited for the rap at the door. When it finally came she pushed her shoulders back and joined the small herd of jockeys in the hallway, heading up to the paddock and its curtain of rain.

Each horse could be found tucked in their open-air stall, avoiding the wet until they couldn't. The giant oaks in the paddock dripped. Fans that braved the rain hunkered under umbrellas, pressing against the rails to get a good look with post positions rolled up in their hands. Those who'd had one too many stood in the rain, laughing, beer dripping from their fingertips.

Georgie had no choice but to walk in it, get soaked again early. The rainwater sunk into the silks, dangled off her helmet in shiny dollops. Her breath fluttered in her lungs when she found the Tupelo crowd milling under umbrellas. Oliver and Samuel talked with heads bent in the stall. Reece and Harris stood with the colt, hardly noticing her arrival. No one looked for her except Lynsey, who stood on the fringes. Lynsey's lavender umbrella stood out in stark contrast to the sea of black behind her.

Lynsey waved, hopping on her heels and splashing rainwater up her ankles. Georgie dove under Lynsey's umbrella, eager for a safe refuge from having to approach the men clustered around Roman's stall.

"You would not believe the talk," Lynsey muttered, flicking a hand in Oliver's direction. "They haven't shut up."

"I think I can guess."

"Oh, it's been colorful," Lynsey went on. "I should have recorded some of it for my own nefarious purposes."

"As much as I appreciate your nefarious purposes, I don't think I want to hear what they said." Georgie shuddered to think about what had been so bad that Harris had gone looking for her. Then she couldn't help thinking about Harris. His hands, his arms, his mouth.

She whispered at herself to stop it.

"What was that?" Lynsey asked, and Georgie shook her head.

"Nothing." No, nothing at all. She had only attached herself to Harris' face, and who knows if that was a good decision? Georgie felt like she was beginning to unravel at the seams, like her life had gotten away from her somehow.

Then she saw her parents through the crowd, her mother watching her balefully from under an umbrella as her father stepped into the rain, making his way to Georgie. Lynsey reached down and grabbed Georgie's hand, keeping her anchored there as Tom stopped in front of them with a sigh, like he was operating under the worst circumstances.

229

"I'm sorry about Sweet Bells," Tom said, and Georgie wondered what he was sorrier about. How the loss affected Georgie or the purse money that came with owning half of a horse that finished fourth.

She suspected it was a bit of both.

"So am I," Georgie replied simply.

"You know where we're staying," he said. "After the race, we can look at our options, see what we can work out with Tupelo to keep you on."

Harris hadn't been exaggerating, then. Samuel had been that loud, that insistent about making someone pay—making Georgie pay—for a loss that was never supposed to happen. She nodded, wordlessly agreeing although she wasn't sure what her parents could possibly do for her now. There was no fixing the past, and it wasn't like her parents had any say on who got to ride Sweet Bells when their investment was so silent. This was Georgie's fight.

"Thanks, Dad."

Tom nodded, grasped her damp shoulder in one hand and squeezed softly.

"I have to . . ." She motioned to Roman, the team that unfortunately surrounded him.

"Keep your chin up," he advised. "Good luck."

Georgie slipped up to Roman's stall quietly, felt the burning stares on her as she avoided Samuel and Oliver in favor of Reece and Harris. That move, she knew, was a mistake. Any jockey confident in their ability would have plenty to say, plenty of ways to spin the story in their favor. And if there were no ways to spin it, they'd just man up and stick themselves out there anyway.

Harris nodded to her wordlessly, which did little to soothe her nerves. The mud she'd pressed into his clothes was dabbed away, leaving hazy impressions on his damp shirt and suit. With the rain, the horses, it was easy enough for these things to go unnoticed, but Georgie focused on it, her skin flushing quick.

Roman shifted his weight and obsessively chewed on the bit as Reece pulled out his legs. On the other side of the paddock, Hero's people seemed to say *damn it all* and let her circle in the rain like a shark. Her gold body was lithe, all muscle lines. Her mane was done up in show horse braids like she was about to go out there and perform half-passes instead of run blisteringly fast on a soaked track.

A roll of thunder rumbled through the underbelly of the clouds. Roman squealed and danced sideways, right into the wall. The resounding thud sent reverberations up Georgie's spine as the colt's groom shouldered him back into line. Silently, like a watchful nanny, an outrider walked his horse down to their stall in hopes that the track pony would calm Roman's mounting nerves.

"How's his head?" Georgie asked, as Roman shook out his mane and continued to chew, froth building up around the bit.

"Probably not in the best of places," Harris admitted, watching the colt yank his head down petulantly, kicking a hind leg at open air and nearly catching the track pony in the throat.

"Great," Georgie muttered. Hero cruised by behind them, a cool cucumber blinking at the goings on. The paddock judge called riders up to a chorus of applause, a smattering of cheers. Roman announced how he felt about that by rearing halfway up and trying to bolt out of the stall.

Georgie leapt back, found Harris' hand on her arm as Roman's groom dug in his heels, kept the colt from a full-blown tour of the paddock. A Spanish curse, and well-timed yank on the lead, and Roman rounded, dancing airily in a nervous circle with eyes rolling at the sky.

The outrider nudged closer.

Georgie touched the colt's neck as she gathered the reins, feeling the damp of rain or maybe sweat. As soon as Georgie's seat touched the saddle the colt popped his head up and snapped his tail, tension coiling over his back and up to his locked jaw.

"Shush," Georgie whispered, leaning forward and stroking the gray's neck. "It's just me."

She didn't hazard a glance back on their way to the track, but by the time they were in the gate the colt was tight as a drum. He stepped nervously, flicked water off his ears, shook his mane to a spray of rain. Georgie pulled her goggles down, got an eyeful of the track under the layers of plastic, and combed her fingers into Roman's mane before the gates burst open.

The colt took them straight to the front, dragging Georgie unwillingly to the lead. Leaning her weight back to keep the time under control didn't help. The colt shook off all of her attempts to reassert herself and dug in, establishing a four-length lead before they even hit the backstretch.

Who knew where the other horses were. Somewhere behind them, a group of sane riders all probably wondered why she let a half-mad colt go sprinting away from the field. At least, she figured solemnly, there wasn't any mud to hit them on the way home.

"Fine," Georgie muttered, easing off the colt. If Roman wanted to run, he'd run whether or not Georgie had any say in it. He'd either be tired from running at the end or exhausted from fighting her the whole way.

Better to just run.

They hit the far turn still in front, Georgie sitting cool in the saddle as Roman's passenger. The colt's stride was sure, perfect on the turn. It occurred to her that maybe he just wanted to be done with it, go back to a warm stall and a dry bed as quickly as possible. He kept himself glued to the rail, breaths coming in even huffs while Georgie watched the next pole come shooting toward them. Soon it would be time to see how much they had left. She chirped to the colt, letting him know she was about to throw the hammer down. She looked under her arm, saw Hero breaking loose, gunning for them. Georgie sat patiently, waiting for her.

Roman switched leads the second they left the turn, and Georgie threw the first cross.

The colt took off, mane whipping against Georgie's face as she blended into his neck, tucking herself in and pulling out her crop at the sound of Hero pulling up on their outside.

With the touch of the crop, Roman jumped ahead and was met head on with Hero. The filly pinned her ears back, her jockey pushing harder. The horses slid in the slop, hooves digging into thick mud. The rain fell like a silver curtain, so heavy it was impossible to see.

Georgie yanked down her fogged goggles, let them hang around her neck as she pumped her arms against the colt, telling him to keep his head in front. The horses nudged against each other, Georgie's boot knocking against Hero's stirrup. The filly stayed put, locked with Roman until the wire went flashing by with both horses stretching for it at the finish.

Georgie stood in the stirrups, the sound of the crowd mere noise under Roman's blowing breath.

Pulling Roman down was easy. The colt wanted to walk, slowing into an ambling, tired shuffle on their way back to the grandstand, where Georgie found Hero's number on top.

Hero to win, Roman to place.

Georgie ran her hand down the colt's strong neck and leaned into his mane, whispering her apologies, and walked the rest of the way to the grandstand.

⇌

Filly Takes Belmont Stakes!

Georgie chewed on her fingernails as she scrolled through the news on her phone, reading the plentiful articles screaming about the filly champion, and the filly champion that had fallen short. All of them questioned her somehow.

What was she thinking? What was she doing? Sweet Bells never had a chance to run. Roman the Great on the lead wasn't a strategy, it was a death wish.

Pages and pages of comments spewed down her phone, all of them asking just what she thought she was doing riding Roman the Great on the lead and acting like she was a sack of potatoes stuck to Bell's saddle.

"Stop it," Lynsey said. "Give yourself a second before you go on a media blitzkrieg."

"It was my fault," Georgie muttered, picking at her salad and feeling no urge to eat any of it. The hotel restaurant seemed like a holding cell, where she was stuck awaiting judgment as Oliver and Samuel talked somewhere behind closed doors.

"Roman went to the lead," Nick said from his side of the ta-

234

ble, frowning when Lynsey reached over to steal a fry off his plate. "Anyone with eyes could see he wanted to do it. You tried to stop him and he wouldn't have it. You know that better than anyone."

"And yet it's still my fault," Georgie said. Reece would be asked to find a replacement for her because wasn't that the way of it? Harris hadn't spoken to her after the race besides a promise to talk about it later, his attention on the colt and reporters latching onto her like lampreys, all asking *why*.

Was it the track? Was it the rain? Was it you?

Georgie shouldered through the questions like a linebacker, not stopping to answer when her throat had already closed up. It was a crappy thing to do, but she still did it. She regretted it now that the stories were up, her shiny, press-ready image tainted.

Through the restaurant, Georgie saw Harris walking through the hotel lobby in all his post-race glory of jeans and ubiquitous T-shirt. He was freshly showered, all traces of mud wiped clean. As Lynsey and Nick bickered over his fries, Georgie swallowed the lump in her throat and got up, startling them into silence with their hands locked mid-fight, fries scattered between them.

Georgie slipped past them without a word about where she was headed, but the sighs she felt at her back gave her more than enough indication that they knew. They also knew better than to follow. Walking up to Harris felt a little like going to the gallows. Only the fireflies flickered to life in her belly at the sight of him, burning a flush up onto her skin.

Still, she felt like she wanted to throw up.

"What's the news?"

She hurled the question into the air between them, watching him rock on his heels and hunch inward, like he was trying to protect himself already from the fallout. Georgie knew the second he motioned to the doors, offering her the privacy of the whole world when he told her what she already knew.

"Just say it, Harris," Georgie muttered, pushing out the revolving doors and walking into the streets still wet from rain. The air felt heavy with it. He followed slowly, watching her like he was waiting for her to crack.

"They're going to replace you on Sweet Bells."

A laugh popped out of her in a sharp cackle, and she tipped her head back to aim it at the sky. She had to cover her mouth to keep it together. Sweet Bells with anyone except her in the saddle was unthinkable. Georgie felt set adrift and spinning.

She wanted to double over. Wanted to curl up somewhere and not think, but that was all she could do. Think until she was sick of running over all the details.

"There's more," Harris said, watching her fall apart and shoving his hands in his pockets. Georgie wiped her thumbs across her eyes, and nodded.

"Okay, let's keep it coming."

"It's a hard split," Harris said with that face Georgie recognized, the iron curtain he hid behind. "They feel that with your win percentage being what it is, with the fact that no Tupelo horse has won with you since the Preakness, that they'll be finding other riders for those horses as well."

Georgie stared at him, her chest tightening. A flood of adrenaline hit her bloodstream in a fizzy hum, heat flushing through her body in waves.

"What about Roman?"

She had to ask, even though she already knew the answer.

"Including Roman," he said, the curtain lifting just enough for her to see how much it hurt for him to say it. Not that it mattered. She felt the decision like a punch to the gut.

"But *you* own Roman," she pointed out with a hiss.

"Tupelo owns Roman." Harris shook his head. "He's mine in name only, Georgie."

"Oh," she laughed in disbelief. "So Samuel is just going to give you a horse *in name only*, and you get to call all the shots until the decisions suddenly become too hard like, I don't know, deciding whether or not to kick me to the curb. Is that what you're saying?"

"Georgie." He took a step forward, and she stepped back. He stopped, and she shook her head.

"And just like that," she whispered. "I lose the wrong race and boom. Done. Right?"

"No," he said. "I . . ."

"What, you fought for me?" Georgie asked, hardly able to breathe with the crushing weight on her lungs. "No. You knew walking in what they were going to do. We *both* knew, Harris. You've micromanaged every facet of Roman, and still you're trying to convince me that they kicked me off of him. It wasn't them, it was you. At least own it."

"Tell me what I was supposed to do," Harris said. "My grandfather and Oliver had both decided when I got there, and I'm supposed to go up against that? Take a horse my grandfather gave me money to buy and not do what they say is the best goddamn decision for the colt?"

"I know this is a hard concept to grasp, but *yes*." Georgie stepped back up to him, poking a finger into his chest. "You were supposed to do exactly that."

Harris pressed forward, letting her finger dig harder into his breastbone, like he knew he deserved it. For a minute she got it. She did. Harris had no hope in hell against Samuel and Oliver when they were thick as thieves. It came down to Tupelo or her. He'd chosen Tupelo. He'd chosen *Oliver*, and Georgie couldn't formulate words to express how wrong that was, especially now.

She thought about being pressed against him, the warmth of it, and her skin crawled.

"It's not that easy," he said, voice thick.

It began to rain, a gentle mist settling over them like a shroud.

"No," Georgie said, pushing away from him. "It was never going to be easy."

She turned and walked back to the hotel, leaving Harris to the rain.

Georgie pushed the elevator button again and again, whispering curses at the metal doors. She needed to escape, needed to not be near Harris, needed some sort of privacy so she could fall apart without *Uncle Moe* splashing her tears across every track in the country.

The doors slid open with a robotic, unconcerned chime. *Going up*.

Georgie felt like she was falling, falling, never hitting bottom. She crossed her arms over her ribcage as she watched the numbers light up, one after the other. When the doors opened, she headed blindly toward her parents' room and knocked, not knowing what she'd find inside.

She only hoped. That seemed to be all that was available to

her now.

Tom opened the door, surprise crossing his face. Georgie pushed past him into the room, stopping short when the suite proved empty. Paperwork exploded over half the bed, a half-empty bottle of amber whiskey sitting on the desk in the corner.

"Where's Mom?" Georgie spun around. Her father shut the door, taking his glasses off and rubbing his thumb against the bridge of his nose.

"Out," he said, waving a hand at the air. "Business."

"Sure." Georgie laughed. "Tupelo business, you mean."

Tom blinked at her. "I realize you and your mother have been at odds lately, Georgie, but what she does with her business is not up to us."

"That is such a crock of shit," Georgie spat, being met with a glare. "Do you not care?"

Tom poured himself another whiskey, taking a healthy swallow. Georgie waited for some sort of answer, crossing her arms and trying to be patient even when she was very well near bursting. This was not what she needed right now. Not at all.

"I don't tell your mother what to do," he said, which wasn't much of an answer. Georgie was about to protest when he continued, licking whiskey off his lips. "That's why she married me. Maybe she found out that was a mistake in the long run. I certainly can't blame her there."

"Are you kidding me?" Georgie growled. "You start drinking with your morning coffee. If you don't stop, you're not going to be around to see the end of Red Gate, much less save it."

He laughed, reaching for the whiskey bottle. "Oh, I've thought of that. Believe me."

"Then why aren't you doing something?" Georgie asked plaintively, grabbing the bottle out of his hand and slamming it down on the desk.

"Why aren't you—"

"Georgie," he interrupted, snagging her hand and squeezing. His skin was clammy, not what she remembered about her father, who was always working with those hands.

"What would you like me to do? We keep Red Gate going on borrowed time and try not to let the numbers crush us. We all know they will, so we do what we have to in order to keep ourselves sane. You ride your horses, be death defying. Your mother has Oliver, and she always has. Me?"

He lifted the empty glass.

"Always have," he continued. "We do what we have to do to get by, Georgie. That's what we're doing."

She stared at him, awe-struck.

"She always has?"

The words were ragged around the edges.

"I thought you didn't know," she said, her fingers trembling. "That day, I didn't tell you. I thought I was protecting you, and you've always known?"

Tom looked at her, glassy-eyed. She wanted to claw at him, rip the truth out of him with her fingers until she was satisfied. But it wouldn't mean anything, not now.

Not if he'd always known.

"Ah, Georgie." He sank onto the edge of the bed, staring at the space between his knees, at the pieces of paper he'd dropped on the floor. Pieces of paper that no doubt held bad numbers. He sighed, and she gripped at the edge of the desk, tried to anchor herself.

She remembered walking into Ennismore after Harris dropped her off that day, leaving a dust cloud in his wake as he sped home. The dust got in her eyes, found its way onto her tongue, and she swallowed it thickly as she walked into the barn's dim aisle and found her father tipped back in his chair, feet on the desk, phone cradled against his ear.

He lifted a hand to tell her to wait a minute, and she sank into the chair opposite the desk, perched at the edge like she couldn't quite convince herself to sit. Georgie watched her father talk, his words drowned out by the debate raging in her head.

Tell him. *Don't tell him.* He needed to know what she saw. *He never needed to know.* She could forget it happened, couldn't she? She could fix this by never saying a word.

But there was Harris. Georgie bit her lip, could still feel his dark eyes on her with expectations in his gaze. She could still feel the burn of it on her skin, clinging to her.

"Okay, Georgie." The phone clattered back into its hook, the sound startling her. "What's your news?"

She flinched, but nothing came out of her mouth.

Nothing could ever come out of her mouth.

In the hotel room, Georgie squeezed the edge of the desk until it bit into her hands. Tom wouldn't look at her, and she was so tired. Her legs burned, demanding that she sit down before she crumpled to the floor. Georgie pushed off from the desk, sinking onto the bed next to her father, staring unseeingly at the beige hotel walls, the bland artwork that covered them. All she could think was *it doesn't matter.*

It never did.

"They took me off Bell," Georgie whispered, tears welling and her fingertips cold. "All of the horses, actually. And Harris took me off Roman because apparently Oliver has replaced him with a pod person."

Tom cast a glance at her. "I know. Your mother gave me all the details."

Georgie laughed. "Of course."

"I'm sorry." Tom stroked a hand over Georgie's hair, fingers light as they rested on the back of her head. Georgie shut her eyes and pretended for a moment that this was what she needed, that her father didn't make her equally sad.

"I can't figure it out." Georgie curled inward, crossing her arms against her chest. "I get on each horse feeling great and then the gates open and it's like I can't see it anymore. I can't anticipate the race, I can't make the right moves, I can't give the horse what it needs, and we lose. *Magnificently.*"

"You've won," Tom said quietly. "I have the records to prove it."

"Not with my help. The horse lucks out, finds the right path, gets the win. It's nothing that I did."

Tom shook his head. "You're running yourself ragged, Georgie. People burn out in this business all the time."

"I lost my bug in April," Georgie pointed out. "I can't be burned out from day one."

"I mean all the months before that," Tom argued. "Campaigning Sweet Bells last year and riding all of those horses in every spare moment you had made you the best apprentice in the country, but it doesn't come without a cost. You're tired. It's obvious."

"So I should come home," Georgie said, sitting up, shaking off her father's warm hand. "I should give up and come home, is what you're saying."

Tom stared at her for a beat. "No."

"Then what?"

"Tupelo isn't the only owner of racehorses," Tom said, so vehemently that Georgie raised an eyebrow. "Yes, you've ridden the biggest races on their horses. You'll probably never have another horse like Sweet Bells—"

"This is not the pep talk I was expecting," Georgie interrupted, getting a narrowed glare from Tom.

"There are more trainers out there willing to give you rides than I think you realize," Tom told her. "Losing streaks happen, and I know better than anyone how hard they are to pull out of, but they will end. You'll push past this, and you'll do it without Tupelo's help."

Georgie swallowed, her throat thick with unshed tears and raw with arguing. She felt so ragged around the edges that picking herself up and beating up new rides from new trainers felt like an exercise in exhaustion just to think it.

But that was what she'd been yearning for, a chance to tear free of Ocala. Only she'd thought of it in terms of freeing herself from Red Gate's continual spiral, not Tupelo's ever-ready string of horses.

Welcome, she thought, *to the real world.*

She pulled her cell phone out of her pocket, saw the texts piled there from Lynsey and Nick, asking her what was wrong. There was Harris insisting it wasn't his fault. It wasn't his doing.

Georgie swiped them away.

"Screw Tupelo," Georgie said, looking at her father as she hovered her thumb over Angel's number. Angel her agent, her savior. He would have plenty of awful words about the news she was about to bring him. "That's what you mean."

"Yes," Tom replied simply. "Screw them. Screw Oliver, and Samuel. Even Harris, for that matter."

Even Harris. Yes. She could do this without them, even Harris.

Georgie hit the call button, and waited for Angel to pick up.

July

Chapter Seventeen

"CAN'T SAY I wasn't looking forward to this," Nick said from the back of Brave, his track pony. The buckskin Quarter Horse flicked his ears, walking dutifully next to Little War. The colt swished his tail contentedly, taking big strides under Georgie as they ambled to the training track through Saratoga's backside. Potted plants hung along the eaves of each barn, tall trees dappling the horses with shifting shade.

"Looking forward to what?" Georgie asked, smoothing a hand down the colt's bright red neck.

"You on Little War," Nick said, looking down at the colt. "The Fountain of Youth feels like an eon ago."

"It kind of was." Georgie straightened, forcing herself to think all the way back to that race, which only led to that conversation with Harris that put her in Roman's saddle. She pushed the memory away, not wanting to think about Harris and Roman, because that was a hazardous path back to Tupelo, back to Sweet Bells.

Whenever Georgie thought about Sweet Bells, her throat closed up. Her eyes burned. It had been six long weeks since she'd last ridden for Tupelo, closing the Belmont meet riding other horses for other owners. Instead of showing up at Tupelo's barn in the morning, she showed up at Nick's. Instead of riding Tupelo's horses in the afternoons, she rode whatever Angel scrounged up and felt off the whole time. It would have to, with everything feeling like a favor cashed in. She still blushed when she remembered Nick arguing to put her on Little War, Senior grunting a flat *no* until Nick shouted, "She made Little War a graded stakes winner. You're going to say no to that?"

Then there was a string of Spanish that Georgie couldn't hope to follow as she stood in the Castellano shedrow, watching father and son argue until Senior pointed at her and said, *"Mala suerte."*

That? Georgie understood that.

"I really hope not," Georgie grumbled, looking away from Senior, down at her boots.

"Graded stakes," Nick said. "Put her on Little War and we'll get a grade one. The colt likes her, Dad."

Senior snorted, looked between the two of them for a half-beat like he couldn't believe this was something he had to decide. "Be here in the morning," he said to Georgie. "Trial basis. If you put a foot wrong you're out."

"Yes, sir," Georgie said so quickly she nearly fell over herself to shake Senior's hand.

Nick grinned.

That had been six weeks ago. Now Saratoga towered in green trees above her, smelling fresh and new, like a beginning. Georgie needed the shift in scenery just as much as she'd needed the Belmont meet to end. Here she wiped the slate clean, starting back at zero with every other jockey who had left her in their rearview at

Belmont. Breathing a gulp of the cool morning air, Georgie felt pounds lighter, the weight on her back slipping off her shoulders.

And she was still with the Castellano barn, happy to have Nick's company on the track. It helped buffer the attention she got riding Little War through the shedrows when she was expected on a Tupelo horse, although Georgie knew people were already adjusting to the change. Saratoga, despite its elegance and history, its Disney World of horse racing quality she couldn't quite explain, still had *Uncle Moe* drifting through its backside, collecting in dusty corners and piling up outside of the local haunts.

Fog blanketed Saratoga's Oklahoma Training Track, a milky swath enveloping the infield turf and curling tendrils over the dirt. Horses snorted plumes of misty dragon breath, the morning light catching on their bodies as they entered the track in clumps. Whole strings arrived together from separate barns, their saddle-cloths stamping them for particular trainers. The horses glowed gold, silver, ruby red as they galloped into the morning sunrise.

Nick let go of the colt, cuing Brave into a canter as Little War rounded into Georgie's hands, picked up a trot and settled into his work beating out a gentle rhythm on the outside rail. They headed the opposite direction as the fast works, intending to keep Little War to a jog the entire way around as Nick kept up on Brave, serving as escort.

Horses cantered down the middle of the track, galloped flat out on the inside rail. Every time a horse blew past, Little War launched into a yearning canter that Georgie brought back down to a trot with her seat firm in the saddle. The colt settled with a huff, and she lifted out of his saddle, listening to Nick's chatter the entire time.

"We're thinking the Jim Dandy," he said. "Which, yes, I realize is a big ask for a comeback . . ."

A flash of sun on a bay coat, a flicker of a blue saddle pad, and Georgie's mind left the conversation. Luna rode Sweet Bells around the turn. The filly held her head low, charging past the quarter-mile pole and switching leads with professional ease. Luna curled over her back, a pair of soft hands giving solid encouragement as the filly plunged down the track, leaving Georgie and Little War in their wake.

She could still feel Bell underneath her, the rise and fall of her back, the rumble of her hooves. Those weren't even the things she missed the most. Above all, she just wanted to walk into the Tupelo shedrow and fold her arms around the filly's neck, press her face into her mane, and let the world melt away. One day, she promised herself, she would do it. No matter the stares.

No matter the people she'd find along the way.

Little War threw his head up, lifted into a jaunty canter that she had to bring back down to the ground again, pushing him into a trot and lifting herself out of the saddle.

"Georgie?" Nick brought Brave even with them, the little gelding snorting with effort to get closer to Little War's head. Nick reached, snagging the bridle with his lead.

Georgie tugged the colt down to a bouncing walk, both eager for something more than a mile jog. Still, she felt like she was on autopilot, her attention on Luna taking Bell off the track, heading back into the maze of barns to the Tupelo shedrow.

"You still with me?" Nick poked her in the shoulder, startling Georgie out of her trance.

She nodded. "Of course."

"Right," Nick replied, finding Luna and Bell in the stream of horses heading off the track. "Now I'm glad I came out here with you."

"I would take offense to that," Georgie said, and sighed, because what was it worth, fighting the truth? "But you're right. It's distracting, watching someone else ride her."

"Eyes forward," Nick ordered. Instead of following the command, Georgie swung her attention down to the rail, where Harris stood watching Roman enter the track. He looked up at her briefly, his expression perfectly schooled.

It didn't fool Georgie at all.

She turned away, swallowed her heart back down where it belonged, and put her heels to Little War's sides. Kept riding.

Rain dripped off the eaves of The Graveyard Pub, making for a larger-than-normal Saturday crowd clogging the bar. Georgie sat at one of the tables with her back against the wall so she could watch the televisions lining the bar, every one replaying the Jim Dandy Stakes.

She watched Roman and Little War battle it out down to the wire. Watched herself throw crosses, tucked into the colt's mane with the rain driving into their eyes. Roman stretched just as Little War collected, a matter of an inch separating them at the wire, the win decided by one stride.

Despite the rain, The Graveyard was warm. A fire crackled in picturesque fashion, casting flickering shadows up the walls. Georgie propped her boots on Lynsey's chair, watched her thumb wrestle Nick and win with a shriek of victory when she pinned him.

"Winner and still champion!" she shouted, getting a few looks from the bar. Georgie laughed, pulling her eyes away from Roman in the winner's circle, Harris at his head.

"You realize he lets you beat him, right?" Georgie leaned forward, snagging one of the fries from the basket sitting on the middle of the table.

"He does not," Lynsey replied. "I am a naturally gifted thumb war extraordinaire and I will not tolerate such talk."

"Whatever helps you sleep at night," Nick replied, winking at Lynsey's frown as he headed back to the bar for another pitcher, courtesy of his fake I.D. and lax oversight. The Graveyard Pub was good at that, looking the other way for certain people. Senior happened to be a certain person, and so they all benefited.

Georgie looked up at the television again, at Harris and Roman, the gray splattered with a sheen of pale brown dirt. Raphael Ortiz leaned over the colt's withers, a wide grin showing off pearly white teeth and one hand posed on Roman's neck. Deep down, Georgie thought they were all lucky Hero had gone home to California, leaving the colts she'd demolished for West Coast competition.

"Harris doesn't like using Raphael, you know." Lynsey caught Georgie in a rushed attempt to turn her attention to studying her hands.

"Well, that's his issue, not mine."

"Georgie."

"It was his decision."

Lynsey stared at her flatly, then set her jaw.

"Okay, do I have to be the person to point out that this is

more than Roman? My brother, simpleton though he is, has never once, even for a second, gotten over you. And I don't think you ever got over him, despite how horrible you've been to each other."

Georgie scoffed. "Please. We were never a thing, and he seemed pretty content with his girl of the week scenario up until . . ."

"Up until you become a *thing* again," Lynsey argued. "Yes."

"No," Georgie pushed back. "Nothing happened before the Preakness."

"Right," Lynsey said. "Maybe not on your end. But on his? Like I said, Georgie, Harris is emotionally stunted and I don't blame you for his many faults. But he's been working on this way longer than you have."

"Then he can work on it some more."

"I'm just saying."

"Fine."

"Fine."

"What are you two arguing about?"

They turned to look at Harris, who arrived slightly damp and appraised the goings on with mild amusement. Georgie had to stamp down on the urge to start laughing, the part of her that was still so fundamentally angry, down to her bones, trapped the impulse and made her swallow it.

Nick reached the table with the full pitcher, eyes wide.

"What did I miss?" he asked, putting the beer down between them.

Lynsey glared at them and sighed, grabbing Nick and hauling him across the bar, leaving Georgie and Harris staring at each other in awkward silence. Finally, Georgie just motioned to the beer and said, "I can't drink this by myself."

He poured a cup for himself and sat down across from her, watching her with prickling intensity. Georgie didn't look away, not even when the Jim Dandy played over again, the talking heads on HTV picking apart the race and analyzing it from all sides.

"This is a colt that hasn't run since February. He's coming off a surgery, off of two months' rest, and ran up against a motivated colt in Roman the Great. Little War can only improve from this race, folks."

"Now, will Georgie Quinn improve?"

"That's what everyone's asking at Saratoga. The little lady got herself a good start today."

"Okay," Georgie said, finally breaking down after Harris sat in silence long enough to drink half his beer and listen to the commentary. "Do you have something to say or was your plan to stare me to death?"

"We haven't spoken for two months," he told her. "I'm trying to organize my thoughts."

"Oh my god." Georgie stared at him. "You didn't have a plan when you came in here?"

"Not really," Harris shrugged. "I just got sick of the avoidance and showed up."

"Forethought," Georgie said, slapping a hand on the table by her beer. "Who needs it, right?"

"I know I disappointed you."

"That is so far off the mark."

"Fine," he said. "Maybe it was betrayal, cowardice, some part of me that didn't believe you'd just throw yourself at me without an ulterior motive."

"I don't know what's more offensive. That you think I threw myself at you, or that I had an ulterior motive."

"You did throw yourself at me," Harris pointed out. "I was there."

Georgie pushed her chair back from the table, threatening to leave.

"I've had two months to think about it," he said in a rush.

She took a shuddering breath.

"You thought I'd just give *Uncle Moe* more gossip to circulate? Because that would be super fun?"

"You knew what I wanted," he said simply.

"And I thought you knew me better." Georgie had to fight to keep her voice down, her whole body shaking with the effort. He shifted, leaned into the table and looked her in the eye.

"You're right, okay?"

"Please inform me, Harris. Which part am I so right about in your mind?"

He downed the rest of the beer, pushed the cup across the table.

"All of it," Harris told her, resting his forearms against the table and pushing his knuckles into the wood. Georgie followed the blue veins up the back of his hands, swallowed hastily. "I've hated Oliver for two years, and I let him convince me to take you off my horse. I let him do it, and no part of me feels good about that because I've been questioning myself for so long I don't know how to stop. So I questioned you, too. And I don't know how to stop that. I let myself ruin something that could have been good, because I'm pretty damn sure you're not going to get on Roman again."

"I'm riding Little War," Georgie told him. Nick had fought Senior too hard for her to abandon them for Roman, and no amount of Harris' pleading would change that. Especially now, weeks too late. "There's no amount of asking nicely that will stop me from riding Little War."

"Figured."

"How could you even let Oliver in like that? You hate him. Words out of your own mouth."

He stared at her for a long beat and shook his head like he couldn't answer to her satisfaction. "He's my dad. For all the good that does."

Georgie laughed, a short huff of disbelief slipping through her teeth. What had he told her when she'd said such similar things?

That's not good enough.

"You realize how hypocritical that is."

His lips lifted in a crooked smile. "Oh, I realize it perfectly."

"Good," Georgie said. "I wouldn't want that to go over your head."

They sat, staring at each other in the firelight, both slumped in their seats like the world had become too heavy to bear. So much had changed, and so much was still changing. Georgie felt like an obstinate horse before the starting gate with a towel thrown over its eyes, led blindly toward some unknown destination. The only thing she was sure of was that Harris would be there.

Harris was always there.

"So where do we go from here, Georgie?" Harris lifted his hands up, like the world was theirs for the taking.

"We're going to sit here and try to be nice to each other. In the meantime, we can practice by drinking more beer and not getting into a fight. Think you can do that?"

He looked at her like she was crazy, letting him keep sitting there at her table. Georgie picked up the pitcher, hovered it over his cup with eyebrow raised. He didn't answer straight away.

"My mother liked to say that nobody's perfect, so why practice?"

Georgie stared at him.

"I don't have all night, Harris, and this pitcher is heavy."

"It just means yes, Georgie. Pour the damn beer."

She poured.

August

Chapter Eighteen

HOVERING OVER THE saddle, her hands fisted in the reins and nestled in whipping copper mane, Georgie gave Little War the go ahead with a chirp, a shift of her weight. It was an opening the colt took, transforming from easy gallop to racing full speed with the wind howling in Georgie's ears. Next to them, the colt's workmate shifted into high gear, head low and mind set on business. She kept Little War close to his workmate, head even with the other rider's stirrup, and felt the hiss of bodies passing when she asked him to open his stride. A clock ticked in Georgie's head, a trembling second hand counting the seconds as Little War put each distance marker behind him. He inched past the other horse's body. Georgie chirped, re-crossed the reins, and asked for more.

They surged free, snapping up the lead and driving alone toward the finish line. Georgie lifted herself off the colt's withers well past the finish. Little War dropped his nose closer to his chest, galloping out the last two furlongs to their starting point. Patting his neck as she brought him down to a canter, Georgie hardly noticed Roman beginning his work ahead, his silver ombre tail cracking behind him.

"Good." Senior's voice crackled into Georgie's ear through the radio connecting her to his observation point on the Whitney Viewing Stand, binoculars most likely trained on her like a bird of prey might watch breakfast. "Reel him in, Georgie."

"Ten-four," she announced, hearing the audible sigh in response just as the radio crackled off. She couldn't help the grin, not after she sat boneless with joy at feeling Little War's honed edge. In the spring, Little War couldn't handle coming off the pace. If this work was any indication, being held back hadn't even remotely concerned him.

Score one for maturity and training, she thought, combing her fingers through the colt's mane at the base of his neck.

She pulled the colt back to a trot, turned him toward the outside rail, and headed back to the gap, the colt trying out his best cavalry on parade impression. At the rail, Nick held his phone with the splits still glowing off the surface. Harris stood next to him, a cool presence next to Nick's visible excitement, as it usually had been in the days before.

Also, weird.

Georgie glanced down the rail, found Reece standing with Oliver and Samuel like a pair of country club members at his back. They appraised the string of Tupelo horses dancing past, talking in voices she couldn't hear. At the back of the pack, Sweet Bells appeared under Luna, all focus and attention in the girl's hands.

Her stomach rolled over, rose up her throat. She had to swallow, tear her gaze away and keep her eyes forward as the filly jogged past with one ear tipped her way. Georgie made herself focus down, on Little War. The chestnut arched his neck into her hold on the reins and huffed out a gentle breath as she pulled him up by Nick and Harris.

Nick held up the phone, showed her the fractions with glittering eyes. Georgie took one look and leaned over the colt's shoulder, patting him heartily.

"Good boy," she crooned.

"For the record, Nick didn't cry from joy," Harris reported, eyes on Roman as he passed on Sweet Bells' inside. "If he wanted to, he repressed it, like a man."

Nick hit him on the shoulder, still beaming and not at all crying. Georgie felt like she'd slipped further down the rabbit hole. Why was it that guys seemed to patch up friendships so quickly? Was a nod and a beer all it took? That gnawed at her, the thought that Harris could literally come in from the rain and be welcomed back without thought. Open arms. But she pushed the thought aside. She could let Harris simply be now that she wasn't riding for him and Tupelo, didn't need him to be satisfied in order to get through the day.

It would work, even in this alternate universe world.

She put Little War on a bearing back to the shedrows, the colt huffing and snorting at anything that moved the whole way. With a pat on Little War's shoulder, she pulled her saddle off the colt's back and stowed it away in the Castellano barn. She came back out of the tack room to find the Tupelo horses trailing by, taking excited steps like they were just barely held together at the seams by their hunched riders. Roman walked with his head arched, shaded mane lifting off his neck with each trembling step. Harris held his lead, his attention on the rider as they talked about the colt's work that Georgie hadn't seen.

Behind them, Sweet Bells.

The filly walked sideways, Luna talking to her soothingly. Her sides were dark with sweat, black mane askew along her neck. Georgie wanted to run her hands over it, wanted to be the one perched on the filly's back with such an intensity that it hurt to look at her.

She slipped back into the shedrow, edging into the shadow to find some relief so she didn't have to watch her filly under someone else. The last time she'd touched Sweet Bells, her hands were full of mud in her wet mane, her heart in her throat just before she'd pushed herself at Harris. It felt like an ancient memory, but so close she could still feel the coarse strands of hair between her fingertips like she could feel Harris' silk tie when she pressed her palms against his chest.

The filly passed, digging lightly at the dirt with the tip of one hoof like she did when she felt good, like when she knew she'd done well and wanted to do more.

That was the dance they'd always done, and now she did it with Luna.

"Georgie," Harris said, finding her ducking behind the wall, pressing her back into the cement so she could feel something besides the pain of her lungs on fire.

"I can't do this right now," she said before he could say anything else. Harris watched her steadily, and she shut her eyes so she didn't have to see how well he looked into her and found all of her problems laid bare.

"She's still yours, you know."

"She's Tupelo's," Georgie shook her head. "She's Red Gate's. She's not mine."

Harris eased up next to her, rested his shoulder blades against the cement.

"You know that's not true."

She laughed, shaking her head and looking up at the rafters. In only days, Bell would run without her, would set foot on Saratoga's track with a different jockey on her back. Would it make any difference to the filly? That Georgie wouldn't be the one piloting her home? Georgie thought about that and her skin flushed with heat, an eager reaction to make her do something, make her change something, to make a difference in this hand she'd been dealt.

But there was nothing she could do. It was already done, and she would stand on the sidelines watching.

"I miss her."

"I know."

Georgie swallowed and let herself tip her head to look at him. Harris pulled his hand from his pocket, offered it to her without a word. She took it and held on tight as she waited for the feeling to pass, to stop hurting so much.

They looked out at Saratoga under the eaves, and were silent.

Saratoga shivered with activity for the Travers Stakes. People pressed against the tall white fences, gathered close to watch the horses. They formed long lines at the betting windows. The grandstand and clubhouse crawled with crowds elbowing their way through the throng to see the track. Women wore feathery hats and walked carefully in heels. Cigar smoke hung in puffy clouds above heads. They'd been there since the gates opened, cracked open their beers, gotten drunk before noon.

Georgie pushed her way through it after every race, walked the painted lines with track security blazing a path all the way to the jockeys' room. She changed into Little War's silks and sat in the common room with her eyes glued to the television, ignoring the clatter from the pool table to watch Sweet Bells walk casually into the starting gate under Raphael Ortiz, recently Saratoga's leading rider, for the Personal Ensign Invitational.

"Must suck, huh?" Dean asked, twirling his crop in his hands and waiting, just like her.

"Not as much as it does having to listen to your commentary." Georgie turned up the volume as he laughed.

The horses broke from the gate, Sweet Bells off like a shot. Raphael guided the filly up into fourth around the first turn, a few skips, a few jumps away from overtaking Maghreb on the rail. Georgie sat on the edge of the sofa, remote clutched in her hands, as Sweet Bells took off right on time to cruise around the field on the turn. She hit the straightaway at full run, Raphael sitting icy in the saddle. Didn't even shake his reins to get Bell's attention.

She just took off on her own, galloping across the wire four lengths in front.

"Won it under wraps!" Dean crowed, thumping Georgie on the back. "Did she ever do that with you?"

"She did lots of things with me." Georgie let go of the remote, the plastic clattering to the abused coffee table that had seen dirty boots on its surface one too many times, and tried not to listen to the commentators chattering excitedly about possibilities. Would Sweet Bells run in the Distaff this year after so many races against fillies? Would she meet Hero in the Classic after the golden filly had torn apart older colts at Del Mar, making it look so easy? On the television, Raphael waved to the crowd, and Georgie slumped into the sofa.

It was like watching someone else live her life. The pressure on her chest drove her to her feet. Pushing into the women's changing room, she sat down with a thump on the bench and buried her head in her hands, wishing there had been a better outcome than this. She couldn't keep silently watching Bell in the mornings, keeping just far enough away, and feel this way when good things happened to her horse and she wasn't involved. This was a feeling that would drive her crazy.

She *needed* Bell, and she needed to be with her.

How that would happen, she hadn't yet figured out.

A thump on the door startled Georgie, sent her scurrying. Ten minutes until riders up in the Travers, and she would be late if she didn't leave now. Georgie picked up her crop, pushed her helmet over the bandana she hastily tied over her hair, and met the sunshine.

In the paddock, horses Georgie hadn't seen since the Triple Crown were saddled under a watchful fleet of photographers. Roman circled on one end of the paddock, Little War on the other. The summer sun beat down unmercifully, giving Little War's coat a ruby sheen. Reliance shimmered copper penny bright nearby, rested and ready to go. Second Sail took quick steps, head craned high with impatience and nerves, waiting for Dean to launch aboard. The rest of the field were also-rans in the Triple Crown who had done well enough since, wanting to take a crack at the big names one more time before the fall meets started leading up to the Breeders' Cup.

Owners and their friends milled under the paddock trees, clumping in the shade and watching the horses appraisingly. Watching *her* appraisingly. Georgie walked across the lawn, her boots sinking into the soft green grass. She passed Roman as the colt did another turn around his pathway, his whole body springing with each high-action step.

Harris stood separate from Samuel and Oliver, from Mabel and her group of twittering friends. His eyes slid from the colt to Georgie, his studious expression breaking for a slight nod in her direction. She waved the end of her crop at him.

"You okay?" he asked, turning his head to watch her walk behind him en route to Little War.

"Dandy." She said it straight-faced.

He spun, caught up to her sure strides. "You sure about that?"

"No psychoanalysis on race days," Georgie said, twirling her crop, still walking. "I think I need to set that ground rule."

"Seriously, George."

"Seriously, Harris," she echoed, stopping and putting a hand on his chest to stop him short. "I am fine. If you need physical evidence of my fineness, you can go up to the stands and witness me beating your horse with my horse in about seven minutes."

Harris narrowed his eyes at her, caught between possible comebacks.

"Could you maybe settle for second? That would really help Roman's chances going into the Breeders' Cup."

Georgie laughed, long and enthusiastically. She pushed Harris in the direction of his horse, back to his people, where he belonged whether he liked it or not. She arrived at Little War's ownership posse just as her valet finished tightening the girth on her saddle, the colt walking calmly in a circle all the while, chewing the bit thoughtfully and watching the goings on with soft brown eyes.

The crowd hummed along the paddock rail, sun-drunk and impatient for the race. When she got a leg up onto Little War, Georgie felt electric with it. The colt arched his neck and stalked by the massive crowd with merely an ear flick, and when he went into the gate like a solid mass of eager muscle Georgie knew she had something in her hands.

The gates banged open, the bell clattering through her thoughts. Georgie rushed the colt out of the gate, pushed him up, up, as far as they could go before Second Sail flew from the outside and snagged the lead away going past the grandstand. Cursing, Georgie lifted in the saddle, steadying Little War in second.

"Guess we get to see if you really can rate," she called into the colt's ears, her words whipped away in the wind. They raced into the first turn, letting the rest of the field find running room into the backstretch. Roman was on her outside, the gray colt running easy. Georgie sat still, body moving with the colt, and listened to Little War, kept an eye on Roman. She waited for Second Sail to show some indication of faltering. Midway through the second turn, there wasn't time to wait on Second Sail to fall back, so she chirped just once and let the colt move.

Little War geared up, launching into a larger stride. Dean took a quick glance at them under his shoulder and started to work on Second Sail. Little War had them in their sights, lengthened his stride, blew past them on the inside with so much ease it made Georgie smile into his mane. Roman slipped through the outside, overtaking Second Sail as he ran down the middle of the track. Georgie took one look at him out there, racing like he had no one else to beat, and put Little War on a track down the homestretch. She threw her crossed reins at him, pushing him even with Roman and then asked him again.

It was time to go.

Little War hooked up with Roman, digging in and pushing off with giant leaps that forced Roman to scramble in order to keep up. The two battled to the wire, a Jim Dandy redux, leaving the rest of the field in their wake and surfing on the roar of the crowd. The only thing Georgie heard was the huffs of horses and the thunder of their hooves under the effort she put into pumping her hands up Little War's neck, pushing him, pushing him, until he was just that sliver of a nose in front.

The wire slipped overhead and Georgie stood, wind beating at her face as Little War galloped out, leaving the grandstand gasping for breath behind him.

Walking through the backside, calls of congratulations peppered Georgie from all sides. The beaming smiles and waves sat awkwardly on her shoulders, like the months of hacking through the trials of summer had made accepting adulation difficult.

How lucky was she? *Yes,* Georgie thought, *so lucky.* Horse racing was, as always, all about what she had done for them lately. She lifted the corners of her lips, waved back, kept going. There was something she needed, and the attention only pushed a rushed skip into her step.

The Tupelo shedrow appeared around the corner, still buzzing from the knock-down-drag-out Travers. A slip of gray appeared around the shedrow bend—Roman, head down by his knees, still cooling out from the race with his hotwalker. This wasn't the perfect time to come barging into enemy territory, but Georgie pushed off anyway, walking with back straight, shoulders squared, like she was going into battle because she needed to see her horse.

She needed to see Sweet Bells.

Few people looked up when she entered the dim barn, but those who did nodded to her. Smiled. Not so much enemy territory, Georgie reminded herself. Just a home she could never really return to, especially now.

The tightness in her chest constricted, strangling at her throat. She shifted, suddenly aware that she didn't know where Sweet Bells was stabled. She would have to search for her, going stall to stall until . . .

There.

Bell popped her head over her stall guard, looking straight at Georgie as though she'd been expecting her. Georgie folded her arms around the filly's neck, pulling against Bell's strong, corded muscles. The filly nuzzled her pockets, her hair, huffing great breaths against her ear. Georgie closed her eyes and leaned into the filly, breathing deep.

The weight on her chest lifted, presenting Georgie with air tinged with the smell of horses, of dust, of fresh hay and liniment. She melted against Sweet Bells and the filly stood patiently for it, pressing into the stall guard as far as she could to wrap her neck around Georgie's side. With a lift of her ribs, the filly sighed out a loud exhale, and Georgie laughed softly into her mane.

This. This was everything.

"Congratulations," Harris said behind her, making Georgie's

skin sing all the way down to her fingertips.

"Didn't think you'd be okay with this outcome," Georgie said, watching him from over the filly's neck as he shifted, rested a shoulder against the wall. Harris looked down at the dirt floor, kicking at a loose strand of hay. It looked wrong on him, his race day clothes still smooth and perfectly in place.

"You'd be right," he finally allowed, looking up at her. "I'm not particularly okay. You should have been riding Roman."

Georgie rested her forehead against Bell's neck. Harris put a hand on the filly's mane, letting Bell serve as the barrier between them.

"I wanted to ride Roman," Georgie said, her voice muffled in Bell's mane. "Remember?"

Harris bit his lower lip, nodded.

"I do seem to have some memory of that."

"What can I say, Harris?" Georgie asked, grinning up at him. "Coming in second looks good on you."

"And winning looks good on you," he shot back, throwing her for a loop. This was not how their conversations normally went. Tit for tat, not tit for sudden compliment. Georgie pressed her lips into Bell's mane, twisting her fingers in it. Had she missed something? Some coded message in all of their brief conversations since The Graveyard?

"I'm glad you've finally come to accept that." She rested her chin on the filly's neck. Bell shifted under the weight, nuzzling Georgie's jeans and nipping at the material. "Although, since I'll be racing against you, I don't think that little opinion will survive for long."

"I love you," he blurted out, and she had to dig her fingers into Bell's mane to keep from startling.

"What?"

Harris looked at her like he was falling apart and genuinely surprised, as if the words had popped out and he hadn't been able to stop them. He sucked in a breath, chest rising.

"You heard me."

Doubled down. A rush of adrenaline slipped through her blood, a tell-tale sign to do something, to open her mouth, to *run*. Of course, she couldn't do that. She couldn't hide from Harris, couldn't run from Harris, and never could.

Time for all or nothing.

"You can't tell me that," Georgie told him, sputtering it out as she tried to wrap her brain around his confession. "You spent all summer watching me flail around and not doing anything about it, so try again."

"I fell in love with you years ago." Harris rounded Bell, and just like that Georgie was cornered against the filly. "Then I managed to talk myself out of it, because I couldn't separate you from what happened. I am an amazing fuck up, Georgie. The one right decision I ever made was putting you on that colt, but I talked myself out of that, too."

"Harris," Georgie tried to break in, but he shook his head.

"I love you. I don't think I ever really stopped."

"You don't love me," Georgie stammered, her heart beating chaotically as she untangled her fingers from Bell's mane. "You can't."

She had to get some distance, but her feet refused to move, planting her there for more of Harris' declarations.

"No." Harris shifted, his fingers twitching at his sides like he was holding himself back from touching her. Georgie was glad, because she wasn't sure she could handle it if he did. "You told me you were trying to find me when you rode Roman. Maybe you did. Nothing has felt the same since the Preakness, and I've been trying to figure this out all summer while you've ridden everyone else's horses but mine. I couldn't make the pieces fit until you told me to go to hell when I tried to give Roman back to you. I realized it was because of you. Of my . . . needing you, as more than a rider on my horse."

Tears sprung into the corners of her eyes, and Georgie made a move to wipe at them, taking a shuddering breath.

"I took you off of Roman," Harris said softly, inching closer to her, shifting to touch her. His fingers hovered by her wrist, unsure. Georgie stared at them, not sure what she wanted him to do. "I let that happen, and it's my fault. I'm sorry, George."

She looked up at him, words escaping her like a flood. There was so much that she wanted to ask, because years spread like a gulf between them. Georgie had shoved so many of them away, curled herself up in thick skin, developed an ability to be with Harris and not feel that shower of sharp sparks that told her under no uncertain terms that this one was different, was hers for always.

His fingers tentatively landed on the underside of her wrist, making her suck in a breath. Then they slid up her arm, toward her elbow, going somewhere higher as he stepped in and she looked up, tried to center herself.

"Georgie."

Reece.

They froze. Georgie bent her head, lifting her fingers to wipe her eyes when Harris slowly eased away. Reece looked between them, a simple skip of the eyes, and held his cell out to Georgie with a wordless gesture to take it.

"What is it?"

He just shook his head and she put the phone to her ear. Her mother whispered her name on the other end of the line.

"Mom," she said, listening to the ragged breathing turn softer, evening out.

"Georgie," Claire cleared her throat, her voice scratchy with something Georgie couldn't quite place. "I need you to come home."

"What? Why?"

Her mother sucked in a breath, like she was closing her mouth around a sob. "Don't fight me on this. Not today. I need you here *now*."

"You need to tell me what happened," Georgie insisted, her hackles rising. "Or I'm not coming."

A pause filled the phone, the background noise becoming so much more pronounced in Claire's silence. The beep of a monitor, a measured voice that Claire muffled. It took a few seconds before Georgie realized Claire hadn't heard her, had been somewhere else entirely, and she'd made sure to cover the receiver.

"Mom." Georgie's voice lifted, louder, needing an explanation. "Tell me what's happening."

There was a pause.

"Your father," Claire started, like she was casting for the right thing to say. She sucked in a breath so loud that Georgie winced. "There's been an accident."

The phone slipped from Georgie's hand.

275

Part Four:
Turn For Home

September

Chapter Nineteen

FLOWERS MOUNDED OVER the casket in a white and green heap, their velvety petals brushing against the polished wood where Georgie could almost see her reflection staring back at her. She pressed her hand against the glossy surface, covering up her face so she didn't have to see herself standing there, didn't have to see the cluster of people at her back, watching.

Music drifted through the funeral home, wove through conversations, clung to Georgie's shoulders like a mantle that was impossible to ignore. Her head ached, pain splitting to the back of her eyes, which felt more sore and dry as she wiped at them. Scrubbing at her running nose, she winced at the scrape of raw skin and told herself this would end.

It had to end.

But right now she felt like she was falling apart. Pieces of her fell away, lost somewhere in the crowd as she rested her hand on the casket and tried not to think about the words tumbling out of people's mouths.

What was he thinking?

Drove right through the fence.

She didn't know how her mother stood it, just standing in the middle of it with damp eyes and a fake smile, pretending like she was getting through this like a champ when whispers filled Georgie's ears like a dull roar.

I just feel for the family in a time like this.

Georgie pressed her knuckles into the wood and pushed her shoulders back, a wave of rage swelling up in her chest, threatening to engulf her whole as she fought the impulse to tell off the entire Ocala horse community. Georgie sorted through the people that milled around the room. Mabel was in attendance, blowing from group to group like a leaf caught in a light breeze, but Harris and Oliver hadn't shown yet.

She looked up at her father's photograph resting tastefully in an easel, surrounded by flowers he might have jokingly said were a waste of money better donated to keep the farm out of the red. In the nearest arrangement was a card from Tupelo, signed with sympathy. Oliver and Mabel.

Georgie pulled the card off the clear plastic stick, held it in her hands and tried to remember what her mother had sent when Lilliana died. She stared down at the card and had a faint memory of red roses, the card nestled in them like they were meant for a lover. Georgie remembered digging the card out, finding her parents' names there in curving ink. The card had still been in her hand when she found Harris there by the open casket, looking at his mother like none of this was registering.

Lilliana with her hair swept up, wearing something Oliver had picked out, her hands pale pink and folded just so. Harris looked disgusted, and when he made his way over to her, shaking his head and swiping at his eyes, Georgie shoved the card into her purse, too embarrassed by it to let him see.

"She never wore that," Harris told her, but Georgie hadn't noticed, couldn't make herself look down at Lilliana's face. Harris glanced past her, eyes bouncing through the crowd in their dour colors. Blacks, grays, beiges, frosty shades of color meant for job interviews and death. Georgie shifted in her sensible black flats and followed his gaze back to Oliver.

Oliver and Tom. The two men talked, nodding through a discussion Georgie couldn't hear. Claire stood on the other side of the room, watching them with such rapt attention that George had to look away. Finding Harris' hand, she tried tugging him toward the doors.

"You should take a break," she said, getting him into the cavernous lobby that echoed up a curling marble staircase. Only the best for Lilliana, someone must have said. Someone, probably Oliver. Harris sat down on the cold steps, shrugging his suit coat off like it was trying to cling to him and he wouldn't have it.

"I can't figure it out," he grumbled, discarding the coat in a heap at this feet.

"Can't figure what out?" Georgie asked, standing in front of him.

"The way everyone acts so unbearably normal all the time, like this was just expected and we'll be sad for a while, but ultimately everything will keep going on as it was before. She's been gone four days, Georgie. Four."

Georgie blinked at him. "Maybe because that's how people cope," she said. "They just go on like they did."

"No it isn't," Harris told her flatly, then cast another glare toward the chapel. "They're in there talking like they don't get what happened. Like they don't even know—"

Georgie's breath caught in her throat, and Harris stiffened so suddenly that an icy wash of fear flooded every inch of her before she could tell herself to breathe.

"Your dad doesn't know, does he." Harris said it simply, fastening a look to her that seemed dangerously bland, almost bored. Like it was possible for her to save this if she kept lying convincingly enough. The problem was Georgie didn't know how to do that. She'd barely gotten this far, barely been able to keep it together this long. She'd spent a week covering up what she could, and it had seemed like an eternity stretching out in front of her.

Of course she was lying.

"Harris," she said, so quietly she barely heard herself.

"Fuck, Georgie," he said, laughing in such disbelief that she fell silent. "You never told him."

She couldn't say anything. What could she say?

He nodded as he stood up, avoiding her as she tried to step up the stairs to him, tried to get him to stay still. Harris pulled away, his dress shoes scuffling and echoing on the marble.

"Harris," she said, his name popping out of her mouth with nothing for her to say after that. He ignored her, walked away from her, leaving her in the lobby as he walked stiffly back into the chapel.

Georgie stayed uncertainly in the lobby, wanting to follow but unable to convince her feet to move. The chapel fell silent in a shuttering whoosh. Georgie could hear her panicked breathing, the rush of blood in her ears, and she jumped when Harris banged back through the chapel doors.

He immediately stopped at the sight of her, looking over her like he couldn't quite believe she was still there.

"Let me explain," she said, the words tacky in her mouth. She had to swallow down the bile that threatened to rise up her throat. Harris only smiled grimly at her, walking up to her and stopping so close she could feel the warmth coming off of him like radiation, like she'd burn from it.

"Don't," he told her. "You don't have to explain. You just have to know that we're done here. You and me. There's nothing to talk about."

"What do you mean?" she asked, her voice crackling, another wave of nausea rushing warm up her throat.

"Do I need to explain this?" Harris asked, looking at her like this was such a waste of his time. He shook his head, brushed past her roughly to retrieve the suit coat, and shrugged it on, headed for the door.

"You aren't leaving," she asked, aghast. "It's . . ."

He swung around. "I *know* what it is, Georgie."

"I didn't know what to do," she stammered, tears pricking at the back of her eyelids, gathering in the corners of her eyes, threatening to spill over.

"Here I thought it was pretty damn clear."

He turned on his heel, and she rushed after him, falling into the brilliant afternoon light and squinting as she dashed into the parking lot.

"Harris!" she yelled after him as he stalked to his car.

"Don't follow me, Georgie," he yelled over his shoulder. As if she could. She stumbled to a halt in the parking lot, watched the sleek black BMW roar to life, and couldn't do a thing as he sped away from her.

Now, surrounded by flowers for her father, Georgie blinked back the tears that rushed to fill her eyes anew as she looked at the card.

Oliver and Mabel, with sympathy.

She crumpled it into a ball, squeezed her fingers around it so tightly her knuckles cracked.

Her hand fell off the casket, the tension in her snapping like a brittle twig. She shoved her way into the crowd, pushed through clumps of people with eyes that wandered after her, skirted her mother talking in hushed tones with Mabel like that was the most normal thing in the world, and burst into the sweltering parking lot.

The hearse sat in front of her, back door wide open in wait. She stumbled to a stop in front of it, staring into the dark interior. When a hand landed on her shoulder, she startled.

"Whoa," Lynsey said, letting go of her briefly before jumping forward and pulling Georgie into a hard hug. Georgie let Lynsey envelope her, arms wrapped around her back like firm bars that kept her together, kept the pieces from falling. She pressed her mouth into Lynsey's shoulder to keep the scream from slipping out.

"I called for you, and I swear you didn't hear," Lynsey babbled. "You looked so determined to get out of there."

Georgie trembled, hardly able to form words. How was she supposed to answer? Yes, she was determined to get out. Yes, she hadn't heard. Yes, she just wanted to jump back in time a few months or maybe a few years so she could make different decisions that wouldn't have led them here. Couldn't she do that?

"I'm so sorry, Georgie," Lynsey kept chattering, her voice

soothing the fight out of her, smoothing over the raw spots. "No one could have known this would happen."

She shook her head, because platitudes didn't make it any better. Her father had still veered off the road, driven through Red Gate's fence, and Georgie didn't want to think about the rest. "We all knew what could happen."

Lynsey pushed back, looking at her with concern wrinkling around her eyes. "What do you mean?"

"He had his DUI," Georgie said shakily. "That wasn't just some *Uncle Moe* fabrication. Dad could barely function without a fifth of whiskey at his side and then we all . . ." She gasped, sobs rising up through her words. "We left him, Lynsey."

Lynsey cast a quick glance around, finally settling on leading Georgie over to a sedate bench inside the portico. It had a plaque that read *peace* across the back, and Georgie wanted to rip it off with her bare hands, fling it into the parking lot.

Georgie sat, pushed her head in her hands. Tears leaked onto her fingers. Lynsey put a hand on her back and rubbed absently, making soft sounds that might comfort children, a nervous horse, but did nothing to erase the guilt that Georgie felt because she'd left him.

She hadn't even wanted to come back. She'd wanted to speed away into a life that had to be better than waiting for a failing farm to shift into oblivion. So she'd let her father face that alone.

Lynsey made a little noise, and Georgie realized she was saying it all out loud, pouring it out onto the ground at their feet.

"Your mom was there," Lynsey said.

"My mom," Georgie laughed, lifting her face out of her hands and turning red-streaked eyes on Lynsey. "My mom would have been at Tupelo half the time."

Lynsey's mouth opened and closed like a fish, and she pulled her hand off of Georgie's back so she could rub at the compass tattoo inked into the inside of her wrist.

"How do you know that?" she finally asked, pressing a fingernail into the little N that dipped between tendons.

Georgie told her, more secrets gushed out between them. Lynsey stared at her blankly, absorbing until she stood and waved her hands for Georgie to stop. She sputtered to silence, curling her hands around the bench seat as Lynsey took several deep breaths in front of her.

"Why did no one think about telling me?"

Shame licked down Georgie's spine, overcoming the grief for a split second before it was swallowed up in the mire. "You always seemed so . . . okay."

Lynsey scoffed. "Since when is anyone okay, Georgie? None of this is okay."

"I know," Georgie sighed, closing her eyes and feeling overwhelmingly grateful when Lynsey sat back down next to her.

"My father is a moron and I am going to kill him," Lynsey growled.

Georgie reached out, found Lynsey's hand. "Can we settle on maybe going back in there for the eulogy?"

"Fine," Lynsey said, waving a hand in the air like it would just have to do. She grabbed Georgie's hand harder, and led the way back into the clammy air conditioning. They found chairs near the front, near the casket, the smell of fresh cut flowers and sickly sweet perfume clinging to the air.

Georgie closed her eyes, tried not to think as the words began like a quiet hum over the people who looked on. She kept her eyes closed the entire time, even when Harris fell into the chair next to her, bringing with him the smell of sunshine and horses. His warm hand found hers and he tipped into her just enough to whisper into her ear.

"I'm here."

Georgie wanted to know what sadist decided funerals should come with a meal. She crossed and re-crossed her legs under the table, poked at her salad without managing to bring any of it to her mouth, and watched the restaurant hum with a careful cheer while she soldiered through a litany of questions and advice.

How are you managing?

Certainly you're not dealing with the farm at a time like this.

Let me give you the name of my lawyer . . .

The murmurs droned around her like a low-pitched whine she couldn't escape without making a scene. So she placed herself between Nick and Harris, let their constant badgering shield her from conversations people wanted to drag her into regardless of her kicking and screaming.

"I don't know about the Pennsylvania Derby," Nick said to Harris over Georgie's head while she prodded a tomato across the bed of lettuce lining her plate. "It's only two weeks out. Roman must have come out of the Travers like a goddamned champ."

"It's either that or the Gold Cup against older horses," Harris replied, stretching an arm across the back of Georgie's chair and settling back in his seat, empty plate sitting in front of him. "I like the idea, but I don't want him too worn out before the Breeders' Cup."

"If Sweet Bells isn't going in the Gold Cup, we could come back there," Nick said, nodding his head and then stopping, looking over at Georgie. "She's not, right?"

Georgie made herself smile. "I'm not the one to ask about Sweet Bells, remember?"

She swung a look over at Harris, who sat staring at his water glass like it held all the mysteries to the universe.

"No," he said, after she nudged his side. Harris pulled his arm off the back of her chair. "She's not going in the Gold Cup."

Georgie wrinkled her nose at his tense back, deciding this would have to be something to ask him about later, when they weren't surrounded by all the gossips of Marion County. Sweet Bells still stood in her stable at Saratoga, and if she wasn't going back to Belmont for the fall meet, that meant she might as well come home.

She put her fork down, suddenly even less interested in eating. "Is she shipping back to Tupelo?"

Across the table, Mabel perked up, brightening like she was happy to have something to say.

"If Harris ships her home we'll have to throw a little party to celebrate," she said, and sent a questioning look to Lynsey. "What do you think, Lyn? You're ever the party planner."

Lynsey tilted forward, leaning on Nick to cast querying glances at both Georgie and Harris while narrowing her eyes. "Have I not been told something?"

"Why would Harris be shipping her anywhere?" Georgie asked. Harris shifted uncomfortably under the weight of her question, his mouth opening and shutting, face screwing up like he wanted to say something but couldn't figure out how to say it.

Nick cursed under his breath.

"And what do you know?" Georgie asked him.

"Hey," he raised his hands. "It's all Harris."

"I thought everyone knew," Mabel said, lowering her voice and sinking down in her chair, like her balloon had just been viciously popped. "Oliver was just so generous, and I thought—"

"Oliver was what?" Georgie asked, gritting the words out between her teeth.

"When he gave Harris the half-interest in Bell—"

"He *what?*"

Georgie's mouth dropped open, her heels digging into the floorboards. She swung back to Harris, expecting some sort of response as she watched him push away from the table. She pushed away automatically in response, her chair shrieking over the wood and standing up so quickly she almost tripped in her haste to follow him out the door.

"Harris!" she yelled at him, bursting out of the restaurant. He kept walking, spine straight and stride long enough to force her into a jog in heels in catch up.

She rounded his car as he opened the passenger door, rummaging through something on the seat.

"What the hell is she talking about?" Georgie asked, her thoughts in a wild tumult.

Harris straightened, pulling a small stack of papers from a manila envelope and handing it all to her silently. Georgie grappled with the papers, nearly dropping them between her feet as she struggled to comprehend the words written in black legalese.

Words like *transfer* and *ownership* popped up at her, and she pushed the papers back into his chest before she could read the rest.

"Just tell me, Harris."

He shifted on his feet.

"Oliver transferred half-ownership to me," he said. "That's why we were late to the funeral. We were with the lawyer."

Georgie shook her head. "Why would he do that? Giving you his share in Bell would be—"

"He didn't give me his share," Harris interrupted, and Georgie ground to a halt. She stared at him, caught mid-sentence, her whole train of thought in the process of derailing and falling off such a sharp cliff that Georgie felt her knees go weak.

"Finish the thought, Harris," she said, so softly she barely heard herself. She wasn't sure she wanted to hear it, but she needed to know. Harris looked at her like he'd rather not, like the whole thing was something he was uncomfortable with and had still entered into because how could he refuse?

It was Sweet Bells, after all.

Georgie braced herself as Harris sighed.

"He gave me the share he bought from Red Gate."

Chapter Twenty

THE RIDE HOME was silent. Just the hum of rolling tires on blacktop and the sound of the turn signal ticking on and off with Claire's careful driving. City crumbled into pastures as they drove into the heart of horse country, fences lining the roads. Tupelo's black planks ran along Claire's side of the car; Red Gate's white cross-hatched across the green grass by Georgie.

"Why did you do it?"

The words tumbled out of Georgie, through her clenched jaw, her hand wrapped around the car's door handle like she needed something to root onto to keep herself sane.

Claire wiped a shaking hand against her eyes, and it was only then that Georgie realized her mother was crying. She wasn't entirely sure that she cared. Claire pulled into the farm's main drive, crunching past the weather-worn sign and down the famous live oak-lined drive to Ennismore.

The barn loomed out of the dusk, all peeling paint and shadow.

"There was no way we could afford her anymore," Claire said

quietly, passing by the great broodmare barn and heading up the drive to the old plantation house.

"You couldn't afford her? Bell funded this place!" Georgie cried, her voice breaking.

Claire stared through the windshield, wiped the back of her hand against her running nose. "I know she did, but the insurance to keep her running this year was more than we could afford. Running the farm, running Bell . . . it's all more than we could afford."

"Running the farm?" Georgie asked.

Claire gripped the steering wheel tightly, her knuckles paling. "Sweet Bells was part of a package deal. Georgie, we sold the farm to Tupelo. Oliver bought it all."

Laughter filled Georgie's throat. Hysterical, consuming laughter that had her doubled over her thighs and clutching at the dashboard. Claire slowed the car, putting a hand on Georgie's back. The warmth of her mother's fingers fluttering over her spine—still trembling from admission or grief or both—did nothing to stop the flow from Georgie's mouth. It was too ridiculous. Oliver buying Red Gate, just swooping it up and tucking it away, could never happen because Tom wouldn't have allowed it. The farm meant too much, even as it circled the drain. Selling the farm in order to save it?

Never.

"You weren't supposed to find out this soon," Claire said. "After your father . . . Oliver promised to break the news well after the funeral. Mabel was just being Mabel, of course."

Georgie stared at the side of her mother's head, watched the faraway look in her eyes and felt like it was harder to draw breath. The oxygen left her lungs, and she couldn't bring enough back in.

She gasped for it, and somehow found all the air had fled.

"Stop the car."

Claire startled at the demand, slamming her foot on the brake when Georgie opened the door and dashed into the ditch on the side of the road, throwing up her meager dinner, feeling like she was purging to make weight. Her stomach heaved, and she bent over in the cool grass, pressed her palms into it and kept heaving until nothing was left but an exhausting, dull ache.

She coughed and spit, wiping her mouth with the back of her hand.

Then her mother was there, leaving the car running with the doors wide open.

"I'm so sorry," Claire said, pushing the short hair off Georgie's clammy forehead.

"When?" Georgie swallowed, the sick taste slowly clearing off the back of her tongue.

"Travers day." Claire sat on the grass next to her and put her hand on the back of Georgie's neck. "Everything happened on Travers day."

"I should have known then," Georgie said, pushing herself up and huddling by her mother. Grass stains rubbed green across her knees, the palms of her hands. She wanted to get up, walk away, but she was too tired to get to her feet. Claire pulled her close, and Georgie let herself sink into her mother.

Then the reality dawned on her. Red Gate was no longer theirs. The horses, the weathered barns, the falling apart mansion with its crumbling columns, the grass she sat on, weren't theirs anymore. How long did they have left to stay?

She pushed herself to her feet, knees wobbly and her stomach protesting. Her head swam, her vision flickering to darkness and then clearing just as quickly when she reached out and found the car door warm under her hands.

"I want to go home," she said softly, not looking at her mother as she climbed back into the car and closed the door. The dome lights dimmed, and Claire slowly accelerated up the rise to the house. Georgie closed her eyes and rested her temple against the warm glass, feeling absolutely no relief from her roiling stomach and the knowledge that her home wasn't home anymore.

It was Tupelo.

Sunlight streamed in through the sheer curtains, which billowed out from the tall windows and sucked back in with each breath the morning breeze took. Georgie curled up under the covers, watching the tug of war numbly. Her head still felt foggy from nausea, from hardly sleeping the night before.

Her eyes felt bloodshot and dry, irritated from her constant wiping. Georgie wanted to get out of bed, but couldn't figure out a reason to move. So she stayed put, drifting between the day and the slow pull of sleep, where her dreams would routinely kick her back into the land of the living.

Stop it, she breathed to herself, like she wanted to convincingly tell her nightmares.

With a groan of surrender, she pushed the covers off and sat up, Red Gate becoming visible through the curtains. The farm was awash in light, its green paddocks dotted with pregnant mares. Ennismore sat in the middle of activity, grooms bustling in and out with full wheelbarrows of soiled bedding.

There was work to be done. Horse farms didn't wait for people to get their act together. They didn't wait for vacations, or school, or funerals. The horses needed them now and Claire had left Georgie to sleep through it, knowing she needed the rest and knowing at the same time that Georgie wouldn't have wanted it.

She would have wanted to work, and still Claire let her try to sleep. Swinging her legs off the bed, toes brushing the ancient hardwood, Georgie sat for a moment and let herself stare at the farm. She tried to poke at the edge of her thoughts, let herself fall into what Oliver owning Red Gate would really mean. She imagined him insisting they stay on the farm, like kept women. Oliver at the controls, with Georgie and Claire at his disposal.

Her stomach tipped, and Georgie covered her mouth, dashing for the hallway bathroom, where she dry heaved against the toilet. When she couldn't cough on air anymore, she rested against the porcelain bowl, trying not to think. From her room, she heard her phone chime. Georgie pushed to her feet and stared at herself in the mirror. She looked sallow, sickly, like she needed to put on ten pounds and invest in a good liquid foundation. Turning on the shower, she pulled off her pajamas and stepped into the spray, the hot water rushing down her back and soothing her eyes.

She stood there until she felt waterlogged. Only when the water turned tepid did she turn off the tap and dry off, wandering back to her room in a damp towel and stopping by her phone. She touched it, hesitating only slightly.

Come by Tupelo. Harris' text floated there across the face. *I have a surprise.*

Georgie gulped at the thought of one more surprise. There

was no doubt Harris had known about Red Gate. He was Sweet Bells' co-owner now, turning her filly into some bastardized father-son project.

Pulling on old jeans and a tank top, Georgie pocketed the phone and set out across the farm. Red Gate unfurled under her feet like a green carpet, the live oaks rustling in the breeze. She reached up, the soft Spanish moss catching in her fingers until she came away with a handful of it, and let it fall to the ground on her way to Ennismore.

The barn sat with its wooden planks rotting out at the bottom, like it was melting into the dirt. Georgie walked through the dim aisle, stopped when she saw the light on in her father's office, and found her mother sitting at the desk. The sight jarred Georgie, although she wasn't sure what she expected to see. Her father, whiskey glass in hand, dark smudges under his eyes?

Although to be fair, her mother didn't look much better. Claire chewed on a fingernail, Tom's laptop glowing on the paper-cluttered desk. Stacks of files towered around the room like a miniature city, one that Georgie didn't want to disturb by trying to navigate to the desk.

"I'm going to Tupelo," she said into the room, startling Claire out of her concentration. "I won't do anything rash," she added before Claire could open her mouth. Her mother heaved a sigh, falling back into the chair.

Claire nodded. "You know where I'll be."

Georgie pushed away from the door, put some space between herself and the office before another round of tears could overflow down her cheeks. She was sick of crying, and sick of thinking. Jogging across the street, she hiked onto Tupelo's property and tried not to think too hard about how there was no more divide. There wasn't even a line in the sand. Oliver wiped all of that away, and her parents had let him.

Hell, it had been their idea.

Georgie kicked at the gravel as she walked up to the training barn, hardly recognizing her name when Harris called to her from across the parking lot. She stopped at the barn's mouth, squinting into the high noon sun.

In the shade of the palm trees, Harris stood with Bell's lead in his hand. The filly grazed energetically, ripping at the grass with such focus that the boy holding her was a passive afterthought to her process. A swell of need flooded Georgie, and she dashed across the parking lot to throw herself around Bell's neck.

The filly nudged her knee, blew out a breath, and then went back to the grass. Relief flashed through Georgie, the crush of Red Gate lifting momentarily for her filly who barely gave her the time of day.

"When did she come home?" Georgie asked, taking the lead rope Harris handed her. He shoved his hands in his pockets, shrugging.

"Flew her down this morning," he said. "We want to take it easy leading up to the Classic, and what does she have to prove?"

Nothing. Bell had nothing to prove.

"You seem okay," he said.

"My mom told me everything," Georgie said, forcing herself to look up at him. "So no, I'm not."

Harris sucked in a breath and nodded, his turn to look down at the filly that grazed intently at their boots. "I know I owe you an explanation."

"Yes, actually, you do," she said, coiling the lead rope in her hands and feeling too exhausted to follow it through with demands like why and when and how. Harris wasn't an idiot. Of course he would say yes when offered a share in a filly like Sweet Bells. If Georgie was being honest, she wouldn't have forgiven him if Harris turned down Sweet Bells. Then Oliver would have owned everything she'd ever cared about.

At least Harris had saved her from that fate.

"I just don't want to hear it now," she told him when he took a breath to answer her, like he'd need so much air to explain. He exhaled, looked at her curiously like he couldn't figure out how to approach her. Didn't know what to say. And she didn't know what he could say that wouldn't make her explode.

"I feel like I can't sit still," she blurted. "Like I have to move. I've been grounded for too long, and I wish that Reece would give me something to ride, but he won't because like hell I'm riding a Tupelo horse, right? I'm . . ."

"Stir crazy," Harris finished for her, and then nodded to the barn. "Come with me."

He set off for the barn before she could ask. Georgie looked after him, confused until he called over his shoulder.

"You want to ride, right?"

That got her moving. She followed him inside the training barn and put Bell back in her stall, then walked further down the aisle to find Harris tacking up two of the farm's ponies—Quarter Horse geldings with no-nonsense attitudes and useful speed.

"You can take Rebel," he said, motioning to the chestnut and handing her a bridle. He ducked into the next stall, where a dark bay gelding stood ready and willing for anything.

"This is great idea and all," Georgie said, as she put the bit in Rebel's mouth. "But when I said ride, I meant—"

"I know what you meant," Harris said, leading his gelding out of the stall. "This is the best I can do under the circumstances."

He tossed her a helmet and swung into the gelding's saddle. Georgie blinked at him, wondering how long it had been since she'd seen him on a horse, because the basic part of her—the lizard brain that operated on basic need and want—liked what it saw. Harris turned the gelding easily, making him sidestep away from his leg.

"You forget how to mount without a boost?"

"Ha," Georgie said, gathering the reins in one hand and leaping onto Rebel's back from the ground. "How's that for a boost?"

They walked between paddocks in silence, Harris pushing the bay into a trot, a canter, with Georgie easing Rebel into the transitions to keep up, putting her brain on autopilot as she felt the gelding's smooth muscles work underneath her. The galloping fields spread out beyond the paddocks, acres of green hills where Georgie had spent plenty of time with Sweet Bells when they were learning the basics. Rebel huffed at the sight of them, and Georgie smiled, her fingers itching on the reins.

"Hey, Georgie," Harris said, breaking her out of her trance. "Catch me if you can."

The bay plunged past them, wind catching at Harris' shirt and tearing at the gelding's mane. Georgie gaped after him. It took her a split second of watching the bay's tail trail away from them before she gave Rebel rein, pushing him into a gallop. The second she made it to the fields, Georgie leaned into Rebel's neck and pointed him at the bay's tail, chirped and pushed.

Rebel gained, sprinting up alongside Harris with a few quick bursts of speed. Georgie kept her eyes ahead, watching the ground slope down, toward the creek that ran across the property. There was a shallow spot, easy enough to cross and keep going, so she aimed for it, feeling lighter than air and eager to drive all the way through.

The chestnut huffed, pricked his ears. Georgie turned his head toward the shallow end, expecting the water to come rocketing up from Rebel's feet, smacking her like a thousand hard slaps.

Rebel stopped with a sudden yank of the reins, digging in and rearing around, lunging back for the bank and leaving Georgie with nothing but air between her and the stream. She landed with a warm splash, only inches of water to break her fall on the smooth rocks beneath. Her helmet bounced off the stream bed, her elbows, her hip, her ribs following in a parade of shooting pain. Something scraped hot and red down Georgie's arm, burning all the way to her wrist.

For a moment, Georgie stayed in the water, listening to it trickle past her ear. The sky was blue, beautiful and big above her. The chestnut was nowhere nearby, gone as far from the water as he could get and leaving Georgie to her fate of scrapes and bruises and broken pride.

That was when the tears welled up, and Georgie lifted her wet hands to her face, covering her eyes and shutting out that big sky so it didn't seem so overwhelming. So everything stopped seeming so overwhelming.

Hooves sloshed into the wet river bank, and Georgie saw glimpses of bay and chestnut legs. Harris, with both geldings watching balefully from the bank, splashed into the creek. His hands felt over her, cupping an elbow and then sliding down her neck.

"Can you stand?"

"I think I just need to sit here and wallow," Georgie muttered behind her hands, taking sips of breath to keep herself from falling apart. It wasn't working. She could feel herself spiraling down, no safety net there to catch her when she fell. There were only rocks, a trickle of water, the whinny of a horse somewhere in the distance calling out for reassurance.

Georgie's careful breaths became heaving gasps of air, and she ripped her hands away from her face to suck in more of it. Harris crouched next to her, a hand on her knee. She batted it away and pushed herself up, climbing to unsteady legs on slippery rocks.

Creek water soaked her to the bone. She covered her mouth.

"Georgie," Harris said, standing up, facing her.

"You always see me like this," she said, trying to turn away.

He reached out and stopped her, ducked to look her in the eye.

"That's not true, George," he said, cradling her jaw in his hands. Her tears ran into his fingertips. "Sometimes I think I see you in ways you don't realize. Like you're the only thing. Whether you're in the winner's circle or soaked after a stupid fall into a creek, it wouldn't matter. It's just you."

She looked up at him, still feeling wobbly and confused, but dead certain that she needed to say something back. There was no way she could muddle through the racing thoughts to pick the most appropriate, so she did the first thing she could think to do.

Rising up on her toes, she pressed her mouth to his. It was soft, a quick slip of lips and warm breath that shot a bolt through to her toes. She felt the surprise shudder through Harris, the surge to respond that he cut off by taking her hands and pushing her gently away, breaking the kiss. Tears renewed, free flowing, and Georgie pressed her forehead into his shirt.

"I don't know what I'm doing," she said against the cotton.

Harris silently undid her helmet, brought her closer to him and wrapped an arm across her shoulders.

"Then maybe we should figure that out."

Georgie didn't think.

She only nodded.

Chapter Twenty-One

THE COTTAGE SAT in a grove of live oaks, situated several paddocks of broodmares away from Tupelo's old plantation mansion. It was one of a fleet of small houses meant to serve as home for a broodmare manager or a foreman, someone who could be needed at a moment's notice. This one was made up of a sweeping front porch, its door freshly painted in Tupelo's distinctive yellow. It hadn't housed a farm employee since Lilliana had died, not since Harris and Lynsey decided there was no more living with Oliver.

That also meant it hadn't been a place Georgie visited frequently. Harris hadn't ever rolled out the welcome mat, no matter Lynsey's badgering.

"Hey," Harris said as she paused there in the doorway. She looked up at him motioning her in. "It's okay."

Swallowing, she followed him inside. He turned on lights until every corner of the cottage blazed to life. Shadows scattered up the walls, revealing general chaos. Plates sat in the kitchen sink, clothes rested on top of the sofa, shoes abandoned in the middle of the floor. It was exactly how she suspected a house shared by Harris and Lynsey would look.

"Lynsey's in class," Harris said, shaking his head like his sister in college amused him. "She left me with strict orders to clean and well . . ."

"You didn't," Georgie finished for him, shutting the front door and bending to unlace her muddy boots, kicking them off on the tile.

Harris shrugged a shoulder.

"Turns out I had to fish you out of the creek instead."

She smacked his elbow, and he gave her a half-smile.

Harris pointed her toward the bathroom. She stood under the warm spray longer than necessary, poking through Lynsey's immense collection of shampoo and body wash before she counted the bruises rising along her skin like blue stains. A shallow scrape ran red and angry down her forearm, flushing in the warm water. Already her muscles sang stiffly, telling Georgie they would like it if she just sat down and didn't move.

After toweling off, she rummaged through Lynsey's drawers and came away with oversized sweats. Georgie tugged them on slowly, looking at her reflection in the mirror propped up over Lynsey's vanity. Puffiness still surrounded her eyes, but for the most part she looked better, even after having fallen head-first into the creek.

Go figure, she thought with a half-hearted smile. Then she opened the door.

Harris sat on the sofa, knees bouncing and eyes focused on some spot on the wall. He stilled when his eyes dropped to her.

"Moment of truth?" he asked.

She sank down onto the sofa, easing her bare feet underneath her legs. Lynsey's sweatshirt sagged over Georgie's collarbone, exposing enough skin that she fiddled with it nervously, pushing it back into place.

"I don't know a lot," he started, knee bouncing again.

"You own my filly," Georgie pointed out. "You know more than I do."

Harris nodded, looking up at the ceiling as though it could provide guidance. "Sometime before the Jim Dandy, your dad contacted Oliver to give him the opportunity to put in an offer on Red Gate and Sweet Bells. My dad has been dreaming about this moment for years. He was practically salivating."

Georgie didn't have to put two and two together. It was right there in front of her.

"You knew then," she said. "Otherwise you wouldn't have come to The Graveyard after the race."

"I knew," he said, shutting his eyes. "It wasn't a done deal, but it might as well have been. I didn't know what to tell you. We hadn't talked in over a month, and I figured if I didn't try to fix things before you found out about this . . ."

"I would have blamed you."

He looked over at her. "Don't you now?"

Georgie bit her lip, tugged at the loose collar again.

"How did you get Sweet Bells?"

"My dad is an asshole," Harris told her. "But an overly sentimental asshole, as it turns out. I don't know why he gave Red Gate's share to me, but it was either take the half-interest or hand the filly straight to Tupelo. I couldn't do that, Georgie."

"What do you think you're going to prevent with your name on those papers?" she asked. "You took me off of Roman when

Oliver had a hissy fit. I doubt you could stop anything Oliver sets his mind to doing with Bell."

Harris made a frustrated noise in the back of his throat, his back stiffening. "I'm offering to put you back on Roman. Screw Oliver's feelings."

"I appreciate the offer, but this is about Bell."

"I can put you back on Bell," Harris said, jaw tensing, like he could make this happen now with only his will. "I know I can."

"Can you?" Georgie asked. "Because I doubt Oliver will feel so sentimental when it's the Breeders' Cup on the line."

"Then ride Roman in his next race," Harris told her. "Give him a reason to agree with me."

Georgie frowned. "You know I have a deal with Nick."

"And I happen to know he's not running Little War again until the Classic," Harris came back quickly. "So if Roman runs in the Gold Cup, what's stopping you from riding him?"

Georgie stared at him for a long moment, because he knew why.

"Why are you so determined?" she asked him quietly.

"Because it took me a long time to figure us out, and I'm not letting anything derail that. Not again."

Georgie ducked her head, looked at her hands. She thought of the desperate way she'd kissed him in the creek, the way he'd stopped her. Maybe he hadn't wanted to, had wanted a better moment when she wasn't a wild thing grasping for solid ground. She tipped into his shoulder, found him watching her intently.

"Think you have us figured out, do you?"

He let out a huffing laugh. "I sure as hell hope so."

She let her weight sink into him, needing that connection,

needing something she couldn't put to words. Georgie lifted her head and simply found him there, so close to her that it was easy to push just a little further.

Her lips met his like a sigh. Soft, careful, like anything else might scatter the moment into the wind. Georgie's muscles loosened, the pain shuffling to the back of her head with her concerns and her worry. It all got shoved aside, leaving only this.

And Georgie liked it.

Harris moved, a hand brushing into her damp hair and cupping the back of her head. Georgie's hands found his chest, found him turning into her, his body taut with some tension she didn't understand because this was good, it was calm, it was Harris filling the hollow left over when all the suffocating feelings disappeared in her chest.

Her fingers plucked at his shirt, scrabbling for purchase as the kiss blew past calm and became consuming. Dimly, Georgie registered her heart thumping wildly in her chest, her fingers pulsing with each beat. Harris was on her tongue, in her mouth, underneath the hem of the sweatshirt and burning across her skin. His fingers found the small of her back, dragged up her spine. She gasped, the heat pooling and sparking, tingling across her skin as she shivered into him.

They fell backward into the sofa cushions, his mouth coming back to hers and Georgie tugging at his shirt. It came off in a harried flash, Harris yanking it over his head and Georgie pulling him back down, his hands bracketing her head, denting the cushions, sending her so far back in time that she wasn't surprised when all she could think about was the leather sofa in the training office, the way he'd kissed her then like he could lose himself in her.

It was a mistake. Georgie had known that when she walked across the road to Tupelo that night, too anxious to sleep and too disgusted to stay in the same house with her parents. Her mother slipped past her without meeting her eyes, and her father nursed his whiskey, the amber liquid sloshing against the glass. It was impossible to sit still with the thoughts racing through her head.

Say something, say something, say something.

Georgie didn't say a word. No one did. The silence pushed her out of the house, across the street, into Tupelo like she was tugged along by a gravitational pull.

Sweet Bells. She burrowed into the filly's neck and breathed against her mane, tried to tell herself to calm down so she could think, develop a plan.

"Dad left for the night."

Harris' voice startled her, made Bell throw her head up and circle anxiously in the stall, all yearling filly nerves lighting up like bottle rockets with nowhere to go. Georgie shushed the filly, put a hand on her neck.

"You told your mom," Georgie assumed, looking at him over the filly's back. His hair was pushed on end, like he'd been yanking at it. He only nodded, sagging against the doorframe.

"She's not . . ." he trailed off, looking distantly down the barn aisle.

"What, Harris?" She ducked under the filly's neck, let herself out of the stall, and put herself in his line of sight. He refocused on her, shaking his head.

"I needed to not be at home," he said, sending her a shaky smile that made her fingertips feel icy. "Not right now. Looks like you're in the same boat, huh?"

The answer got stuck in her throat, because she wasn't sure she could reliably lie to his face. He'd know, because she'd never been good at lying. She pushed into him, wrapping her arms around his ribcage. His arms came up, draping across her shoulders. The weight should have been comforting, but it only made Georgie's stomach twist, made her dig her fingers into his sides and pull her head back.

Before she could find the words that wouldn't come, his mouth met hers. Shock sent her eyes wide before she let them sink closed, her whole body settling into Harris' hands because this was so much better than talking. She met him halfway, pushing aside the doubt that crawled up the back of her head and whimpered when he pulled away.

"What . . ." she started to ask, falling silent when he shook his head, tugged her toward the open office door.

The sofa was buttery soft, slippery under her jeans. She slid along it, Harris' weight keeping her from flying apart as she tugged at his shirt, his belt, undoing the button of his jeans. His hands bracketed her body, pushed into the sofa and got caught up in her hair, which looped like fiery circles between his fingers.

His mouth left hers, his body moving down hers.

"I don't," she tried to say, staring at the ceiling and trying to find the right words. "I don't have . . ."

Harris shifted over her, his forehead resting against her ribcage as a laugh burst out of him.

"Harris," she growled, pushing at his shoulders. What was so funny? This was definitely not what she would call hilarious. He lifted onto his elbows, kissing her quickly.

"That's what I love about you, George," he told her, pushing off of her and grabbing his shirt off the floor. "Always the voice of reason."

She gaped at him, scrambling to her feet. "If I were reasonable, I wouldn't be doing this."

He grinned at her, buckling his belt and swooping up to her. Before she could dodge away his mouth was on hers.

"Let's go up to the house," he said. "We can be reasonable up there, I'm pretty sure."

"Pretty sure?"

His answer was a laugh over his shoulder as they dove into the dark Florida night, Tupelo folding around them with cicada cries and the soft sound of horses. Georgie's heart fluttered eagerly in her throat.

She followed Harris up the steps of the house, waited as he pushed the door open so quietly, padded over the threshold and up to the second floor with her hand in his. Georgie knew where his room was, could navigate to it with her eyes closed, and moved that way on instinct until he stopped dead in the middle of the hallway.

She ran into his back, the haze shaking off just enough for her to recognize that they stood in front of his parents' room, the door yawning open like a beckoning invitation. From within the room, water roared into a tub, slapped at tile, trickled and tinkled like a babbling brook over stones.

"Wait," Harris told her, his voice making the hairs on the back of her neck stand on end. He slipped out of her grip, hovered in the open doorway like an invisible barricade slammed down in front of him.

His name was halfway out of her mouth when he stepped

into the room, leaving her there with the thoughts and the doubt crouching at the edges of her.

She glanced down, noticed the orange prescription bottle sitting in the middle of the hallway. It was empty, all the lithium tablets missing.

This was not where she should be. Georgie felt the house constrict around her, pressing in on her. The urge to sprint back the way she'd come flamed on every nerve. Just as she took a step back, Harris screamed her name.

Georgie jerked, jumping to the doorframe and making herself take the steps across the pristine carpet. Her boots trailed dirt across the room, as she cast a panicked glance for Harris.

"Georgie!"

Lurching toward the bathroom, her boots slushed into water-logged carpet. She slipped, grabbed the doorframe to keep from falling onto the tile of the bathroom floor. Harris crouched in the water, too busy pushing his hands against Lilliana's chest to notice he was soaked and the water kept coming. Lilliana laid across the tile, her dark hair floating in the water like a mermaid. Her hands curled toward the ceiling, the pale underside of one wrist marked with a compass.

The cuts that slashed across it stained the water red.

The world tilted, and Georgie fell.

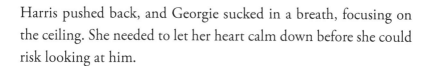

Harris pushed back, and Georgie sucked in a breath, focusing on the ceiling. She needed to let her heart calm down before she could risk looking at him.

"I can't do this," he croaked out, which got her attention. Her blood still thrummed under her skin when Georgie made herself look at him.

"I know." She pushed the hem of the sweatshirt back down, started to crawl back to put space between them. He tilted his head at her like he didn't understand, and grabbed her bare ankle to block her retreat.

"Are you going to ask me why?"

"I think I already know why," she muttered, shaking his hand off her foot. "It's all I can think about."

"Really," he said, voice so full of disbelief that Georgie glowered at him from her side of the sofa. "Because the reason I can't do this is because I'm in love with you. When I told you about that you rather classically told me that's not possible."

She opened her mouth. Shut it. "Oh."

Harris nodded. "I think that sums it up rather nicely," he said, reaching to the floor and grabbing his shirt. He stood, back to her as he yanked his shirt on, covering up the compass tattoo that nestled between his shoulder blades, the little N resting along his spine.

"What did you think I was going to say?" he asked, turning around as she was still trying to understand why Lynsey's tattoo was on his back.

"Your tattoo," she blurted, and he tilted his head at her, like he could make her out better if he changed his perspective. "I was with Lynsey when she got hers."

"While I was off in rehab land, I know," he nodded, pushing a hand into his hair and sitting down again. "She nagged me about it forever. Mom had one, said it helped her remember who she was when she couldn't think straight."

"I remember it," Georgie said, pushing out the words. Harris stared at her, then down at his hands.

"Eventually the hurt fades," he said. "The memories get fuzzy. For a while that pissed me off, having everything I remembered about her blur with the background. I couldn't deal with that. I'm still not okay, Georgie, but I'm not okay with it dragging me down either. It probably took me too long to figure that out."

Georgie watched him, feeling pinpricks of tears in her eyes and willing them away. She was so tired of crying, of being a flaming red mess all the time and not knowing what to do about it.

"Great," she said, swiping at her eyes forcefully. "So I have years of grief and anger to process. That should be productive."

"I'm not saying you should go full-on destruction, bridges burning in your path or anything. It's just that no one would blame you if you did."

"I blamed you," Georgie said. "I should have been there for you like I was for Lynsey, and I wasn't. Even worse, I left everything that happened that day with Mom and Oliver to you. I didn't say a word, like a complete coward, and you had every reason to think I'd betrayed you. My life went on like nothing had happened, and yours . . . ended."

"What makes you think I would have let you be there?" Harris asked.

"Does it matter?"

"Yes," Harris said. "You did what you thought you had to do."

"That isn't true," Georgie argued right back. "I said I'd stand by you and I didn't. I denied everything. I . . ."

"George," he stopped her. "What do you need me to say?"

"That you forgive me," she blurted out, her heart thumping harder.

He stared at her like he couldn't make sense of what she was asking him.

"This is my fault," Georgie ground out. "I pretended my way through two years like everything would be fine when I knew it wouldn't be. Maybe Red Gate was never going to survive, but my dad might still be here if I'd just said something. I should have said something, Harris."

Harris stood up and crouched in front of her, made her look down at him.

"You have to stop," he told her. "Your parents made their decisions, and you were never a part of that. You never were."

"And you?" she asked, wiping at her eyes with shaking fingers.

"I think it's safe to say I'm a raging idiot," he told her, and she smiled on instinct. "See? You don't need my forgiveness, Georgie. You never did."

Georgie exhaled, closing her eyes and leaning her forehead into his shoulder. He lifted his hand, rested it on the back of her neck. For a moment, it felt like what was happening outside of their bubble didn't matter. It was no longer important, just nondescript details that she was sheltered from so long as her eyes stayed shut and Harris' warmth radiated down through her skin.

"Can I stay here?" she found herself asking. "Just for a little while."

His lips moved against her hair.

"You can stay for always."

October

Chapter Twenty-Two

BELMONT PARK IN September was a gray thing, its eaves hanging with dripping rain. The air was wet, pungent with the first tangy scent of fall. Georgie breathed in the damp and trailed her fingers through the dark and light strands of Roman's mane, which was dotted with shimmering dew.

The colt looked like diamonds dusted his coat, glinting and shining as they jogged. Georgie rose and fell with the beat of his trot, letting the welcoming smiles from the other exercise riders warm her when she should have only felt the damp chill. Here there was only the fogging breath of horses and the shushing sounds of hooves sinking into dirt underneath the chatter of riders. It was Georgie's language, and she slipped back into it effortlessly as Roman carried her down the backstretch.

Slowing into a rocking walk, Georgie sat back in the saddle and took a deep breath. Belmont expanded in front of her, the shedrows nestled into turning autumn color. The training track stretched under Roman's reaching strides, the soft sounds of his hooves sinking into the dirt luring Georgie into a calm only the track could bring. She sank into the walk, let her muscles slip and slide, moving along to the gait.

"Look who's back!"

Georgie looked over her shoulder at Dean, his body perched lightly on the withers of Stonecutter. The older colt huffed, head craned up and eyes white-ringed with nerves. Roman cocked an ear inward, chewing the bit and shifting his hind end toward the other colt in warning. Georgie straightened him out, let him throw his head back in agitation. Dean settled into the saddle, pulling Stonecutter into a mincing walk.

"Just yesterday I said I was getting bored with all this winning," Dean said, grinning at her. "Too easy. Granted, I was getting enough of that around here when you were riding this summer."

"Remarkable." Georgie shook her head.

"I know, right?" Dean waggled his eyebrows at her.

"No," Georgie said, "your ability to make everything about you. That's true talent."

Dean scrubbed Stonecutter's neck as they walked the aisle back to the shedrows, the autumn canopy all orange and yellow above them.

"True talent," he muttered to himself, sitting back in the saddle and kicking his feet forward. "Look, I'm sorry about the shit you've been through lately. Your dad, the farm, your filly . . ."

She stilled so totally in the saddle that Roman came to a dead halt, lifting his head anxiously.

"How do you know that?" she asked him. Dean slowed Stonecutter, tilting his head at her curiously.

"There's a fleet of press outside the Tupelo shedrow," he said. "Haven't seen for myself yet, but the news on the track sounded pretty damn huge."

Georgie put her heels to Roman's sides, and the colt bounded forward. Two deer leaps and they overtook Stonecutter before Georgie could bring him back down to a jaunty walk, his ears up and forelock flipping back off his head.

"So it's true, right?" Dean called after her. "Georgie?"

She didn't answer, leaving them in their wake as she veered off the aisle and cruised up to Tupelo's shedrow like a homing missile. Reporters curled around the mouth of the barn, four deep with microphones thrust forward. Oliver stood in the crook of them, hands stuffed into jeans and hair delicately tousled, like this was his version of comfortable equestrian style. He smiled at the group as he talked, shrugging his shoulders like he just couldn't help it.

He just had to save the farm.

"Clear a path," she yelled over Roman's head, scattering the group of reporters on her way into the barn. She walked Roman through the channel, forcing Oliver to step aside on her way down the shedrow. Chatter surged up at her back, but she kept going. The colt's groom took Roman's head, and she jumped down, pulling off the saddle and putting more distance between her and the group of reporters that shifted toward her, eager for words she couldn't give them.

"Georgie!"

She quickened her step, dodging into the tack room. Shoving the door closed with her shoulder, she threw the saddle down on its post and leaned into it, taking a deep breath.

The door opened, and she straightened automatically. Her shoulders relaxed when she found Harris standing there, closing the door behind him.

"Oliver doesn't waste much time," she said.

"Theoretically, he waited three weeks."

"Was probably bursting out of his skin the entire time," she sighed, pulling off her helmet, purple bandana coming with it. "Just couldn't wait to show off his new toys. Probably busily ripping down Red Gate's front sign as we speak."

"He's not," Harris said. "He's just talking today."

"And tomorrow?" she asked, huffing out a breath when Harris just looked at her. "Forget it. There's nothing I can do anyway."

"You don't regret coming up to Belmont, right?" he asked. "Because you seem . . ."

"Distracted," she finished for him. "No, this is what I need. Being at Belmont gives me a handy excuse to not be at home, and since the cat's out of the bag now I might as well be anywhere. It doesn't matter."

"Doesn't it?" he asked, pushing off the door. "Because today is the Gold Cup. If you don't want to be here—if you're not *ready* to be here—then I need to know."

She pushed her shoulders back, looked up at him steadily.

"I want to be here."

"You just nearly ran over a whole pack of reporters and my father," he reminded her. "With my horse. Intentionally. The horse that's running in the Gold Cup later. You know that horse?"

"Yes, thank you," Georgie sighed. "I get it. I'm upset because Oliver has crappy timing, but I want to be here and I want to ride. I felt . . . better. Being out there on the track was where I should have been all month instead of—"

She stopped, wishing so much else had happened. But that was useless. Wishing was worthless. Georgie made her own luck, and she was ready to start again.

"I'm ready," she insisted.

"Good," Harris said. "Because this is just the first part of the plan, Georgie. I need a strong show here to convince Oliver that you're the one they want for Bell in the Classic. I need you to meet me halfway here."

"And I can do that."

He looked at her dubiously, and Georgie wondered if he was only thinking of her less-than-stellar summer on Belmont's track. The articles in the *Daily Racing Form* wondered as much for them both—could she come back on a track that had bested her so phenomenally? After so much had happened? Where was her head? Where was her heart?

Everyone had so many questions for her, and Georgie let them roll off her back like the rain.

You make your own luck.

She looked at the door behind his back.

"Think they're still out there?"

"Absolutely," he said. "Want to make a run for it?"

She nodded.

"Let's go."

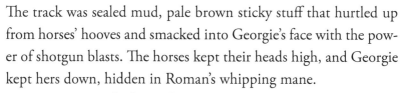

The track was sealed mud, pale brown sticky stuff that hurtled up from horses' hooves and smacked into Georgie's face with the power of shotgun blasts. The horses kept their heads high, and Georgie kept hers down, hidden in Roman's whipping mane.

Roman stretched out, driving down the homestretch. Georgie

took him wide around the leader, straightened him out, and gave him his head. When that wasn't enough, when the older colts kept coming, she tapped Roman hard on the hindquarters and sent her fists deep up his neck. Throwing a cross, she tipped the crop up, flicked it past his eye, and then reached back again and snapped it across his rump.

That set a fire under his hooves, and a thrill up Georgie's spine. Her fingers tingled with it as the colt lengthened his stride and dug in, the rail blurring along Georgie's boot on their way past the sweeping Belmont grandstand. Georgie sipped breaths in rapid succession, letting her arms float up the colt's neck with each stride, moving with his body until Roman drew clear half a length at the wire.

She stood up in the stirrups, let the colt slow and then pulled him down to a trot in the backstretch. The rest of the field turned around in front of her, two-beating it all the way back to the grandstand. Georgie set Roman into a canter, strolling up the outside rail and not even trying to stop the smile that ate up her face.

On her left, people pressed up against the dripping outer track rail. The regulars waved to her, hollered their drunken congratulations. She stroked her hand down Roman's dirty neck and indulged in the rush. Roman walked toward the winner's circle, awash in so much mud he was no longer gray. He was a huffing dirt monster, and Georgie knew she looked no better. Not that it mattered. Her heart was too full now to care.

Harris appeared there in the crowd, the steady grin on his face telling her all that she needed to know.

"How was it?"

Amazing. Phenomenal. Inspiring. I want to do it again.

"Like old times."

"The Old Man was impressed," Harris said, nodding to Samuel further back in the winner's circle, waiting for them to come to him. Lynsey linked her arm in his, her mouth moving a mile a minute with words that Georgie knew were all about her.

They were all planting seeds.

"And Oliver?" Georgie asked, scouting out Harris' father in the small space that was crawling with too many people. She finally found him, standing next to her mother, talking animatedly about something that she was positive had nothing to do with Roman. The thought was a cramp in her side, the dark mark in a brilliant, damp afternoon.

"I'll work on it," Harris said.

That wasn't what Georgie wanted to hear, not with a win like this over older horses. It wasn't like she expected Oliver to hand her Bell's reins without an intervention, but it sure as hell would have been nice. Harris took the colt's lead and walked them up to the crowd as a smattering of applause clattered around them.

After the photo, Georgie leapt back to the ground. Undoing the girth, she pulled the wet saddle off and gave Roman's back a pat as he was led off to the backside, where a bath and a warm stall waited for him. For Georgie, all she wanted was the same until she turned and was met with a smiling reporter.

She blinked at him, looked down at the logo of a horse smoking a cigar embroidered over his jacket's breast pocket. *Uncle Moe.* Jumping back to the impromptu press conference that morning, Georgie wondered if he had been in the crowd when she'd barreled through on Roman, setting everyone alight with questions. Without the logo, he could be any other reporter asking for a quote.

"Georgie, do you have a second to discuss the sale?"

Of course it was the sale. This was *Uncle Moe*, after all.

"Not right now," she replied, voice strained under the weight of her professionalism. "We can talk about Roman, who just won the Gold Cup. Did you see that? It just happened."

He smiled slowly, rubbed a thumbnail between his eyes and shook his head. "Yeah, that's not the biggest event in racing today."

Georgie shook her head. "I can't discuss it."

"I'd really love it if you would," he said, wheedling closer to her. Disgust washed over her, the whole day now cast not with Roman's brilliant victory, but with this, the headline that raged across horse racing and the one thing she didn't want to talk about.

"Then let me clarify by saying that I won't talk about it," she told him, shifting away from him. She had no more races for the day, and obviously he knew that, lying in wait to strike.

"Come on, Georgie," he started, reaching out for her arm like touching her would somehow keep her still for his questions. She recoiled, skittering away from him, boots scraping on the concrete and making heads turn in their direction. Harris and Reece, all that remained of the Tupelo crowd in the winner's circle after the colt was led away, both caught her eye.

She must have looked panicked. Georgie realized that later when they both came roaring to her defense, surrounding her like bodyguards putting walls of muscle and bone between her and the threat. Reece steered *Uncle Moe* to the side, firm hand on his shoulder, English accent clipped to cutting. Georgie took the opportunity to slip into the Belmont crowd, skipping ahead of Harris, dashing down the walkway to the door leading to the basement, and the jockeys' room within. Her rubber soles squeaked on the tile as she finally slowed down in the hallway, her breathing still coming so quickly it felt like she was full of too much air. She held her breath, squeezed her eyes shut, and exhaled.

When she opened her eyes again, Harris stood in front of her. Any remaining glee from Roman's win was wiped away from his face. Instead he was vibrating with energy, dark eyes bright and eager with something she couldn't name.

"What was that all about?" he asked.

"*Uncle Moe* wanted to talk about Red Gate," she told him. Then she laughed. "Can you believe that? After all the things he says about me, he just decides to walk right up. Get the dirt from the horse's mouth. Has to be more efficient that way."

"He won't do it again."

"Who's going to stop him?" Georgie asked, and bit back the rest of her words at his stony look. She rubbed her fingertips against her forehead, groaning at the thought of *Uncle Moe* digging for gossip around her like wherever she walked whispers sprouted like weeds.

"It doesn't matter," she said, shaking her head and turning for the women's locker room.

"Georgie," Harris sighed, stepping toward her and pausing, looking at her like he just remembered he wasn't sure what to do. Touch her, don't touch her. *You don't love me, you can't.*

She wanted to go back in time and slap reason into herself. Harris danced around her, hovering just close enough for her to want him to take the extra step before he backtracked, jumped back, leaving a Harris-sized hole in his wake. She'd gotten used to not having him, gotten used to refusing the thought of having him, and now he was here and she didn't know what to do.

You don't love me, you can't.

Every time she thought about it, she cringed. It didn't seem fair, still slipping into his space, letting him give her a leg up onto Roman in the mornings, skimming so close to him and flittering away like she was caught in the breeze. So she doubled back, thought about his weight on her before he'd pushed away, her words on his lips.

You don't love me.

You can't.

Harris hovered there, and she quivered just within his reach. She didn't say the words she knew she needed to say to bring him closer, and she didn't step away. She only stood within grasping distance and berated herself for being unable to decide.

"You were backed into a corner," Harris said. "You're coming out swinging."

For a minute, Georgie let herself think she was a prize boxer, knocking down her problems instead of taking the course of least resistance. She shifted away from Harris, felt his lack of warmth immediately and wanted to scurry back into the line of his body. Instead she pushed her damp back against the door.

"Phase one complete," she said. "What's the rest of the plan?"

"You'll find out during the Tupelo mandatory celebration," Harris replied. "You just need to follow my lead."

She arched an eyebrow at him, and Harris waved her off. "Hurry," he mock whispered at her. "They'll start without us."

Finding a smile down deep, she pushed into the jocks' room, leaving Harris in the hallway. Belmont Park hummed down around her, cocooning her from the real world. The jocks whistled to each other, shouted out at her as she weaved through to the ladies' room.

Dean snapped his towel at her butt, and she flipped him off carelessly to laughter and hoots. They looked at her like there was something only they knew—the understanding that they'd come back here, no matter what life threw at them. Tension slipped off of Georgie's shoulders, unspooling as she was accepted back into the fold.

The track was a live, warm thing, and it welcomed her home.

Mandatory celebration, as Harris put it, started early. That was the way of things when they all had to be awake and working before dawn. Georgie sat next to Lynsey at the bar, the restaurant around them buzzing with Saturday energy. Lynsey spun on her stool, shimmering dress whooshing back and forth around her knees and cocktail halfway gone.

"I deserve a commendation," Lynsey said, spinning toward Georgie. "By the time we left that winner's circle, I knew I had Grandpa wrapped around my little finger because I am *that* sweetly manipulative."

"I cannot believe I'm saying this but having a sweetly manipulative best friend is definitely awesome," Georgie said, looking out at the restaurant.

"High five." Lynsey lifted her hand, and Georgie slapped her palm against it.

"Now I just have to get the ride," Georgie said, drawing her lower lip between her teeth.

"You did your part," Lynsey told her. "Rode Roman to a win and looked good while doing it. You have more horses to ride, right?"

Georgie stared at her. "Theoretically. No one is beating down the door."

Although there were offers, and Angel, star agent that he was, scooped them up and poured them into Georgie's schedule. The win in the Gold Cup would help, with Georgie's phone already blowing up with Angel's curse-riddled texts about rides and trainers who could go screw themselves in any other situation other than this one, which was to get Georgie back to the top.

Lynsey stopped spinning. "Regardless, I think it's safe to say I still did an amazing job."

"You did," Georgie replied, watching Oliver out of the corner of her eye. He walked from Harris to Claire, shaking his head like something amused him. The restaurant buzzed in Georgie's ears, becoming a low drone when she watched Harris tip back on his heels, like he was forcing himself not to go after his father.

Plan A was dying a quiet death.

Georgie blinked rapidly and jumped off the stool, winding toward Harris. Lynsey scurried behind her, high heels clacking on the floorboards.

"What happened?" Georgie asked him, although she knew by looking at him what happened.

Harris rolled his eyes.

"That father-son sentimentality bullshit met a swift end. The reality is my father isn't interested in listening."

"Has he ever been?" Lynsey quipped, sipping at her drink.

"No," Georgie growled, the buzzing noise turning into a drone. She watched her mother tilt her head at Oliver, smiling in that charming way she had. Oliver smiled right back, guiding her to a table like they were on a date. Georgie set her jaw, pushing into the crowd before anyone could call her back. Winding through packed tables, she prowled up to the intimate two-top containing Claire and Oliver and stopped short, approaching a nearby table with a forced smile.

"Hi," she waved to the innocent couple, grabbing the back of an empty chair. "Taken? No? Thanks."

She hauled the chair away before anyone could tell her no, depositing it between Claire and Oliver and falling into it with a whoosh of breath. They startled, Oliver lifting himself off his elbows and Claire nearly upending her glass of red wine, jumping to settle the glass on the table.

"Georgie! What are you—"

"I think we need to talk."

Claire sent a questioning look across the table to Oliver, who sighed like he was generally willing to do a lot of things, but this was just out of the question.

"I already told Harris—" he started, when Georgie raised her hand.

"You told Harris that putting me on Sweet Bells was unacceptable," she said. "That if you'd had your way I wouldn't have gotten the ride on Roman, but Harris, being the guy he is, went ahead and named me anyway. That must have hurt your tiny, barely recognizable feelings."

Claire gaped at her, and Georgie did her best not to care.

Oliver shook his head, lifting his hands off the table like there was nothing he could do. "Honestly, Georgie, this is already a done deal."

"Nothing is a done deal until the gate opens," she snapped

back at him. "I have ridden Bell through her hardest races, and I've gotten her there. What does Raphael have? A win under wraps? Do you want someone to hit cruise control on her in the Classic, where she'll be up against not only the best older colts, but Roman, Little War, and most probably Hero? Because I wouldn't."

"Raphael is one of the top jockeys in the business," Oliver told her, reaching for his whiskey. "If he can't get it done in the Classic, no one can."

Door shut. Georgie curled her fingers into fists.

"I'm glad for you," Georgie said, pushing her chair back. "Must be awesome to walk around with that sort of confidence."

"I expect my son will give you the ride on Roman," Oliver replied, waving his hand at the restaurant like he knew Harris was around there somewhere, but didn't quite care to know exactly. "Should that fall through, you have Little War. Asking for more is tasteless at this point, Georgie."

Struck speechless was a new feeling, one that had her anchored to the chair when she'd intended to get up, call the whole thing off. Getting the ride on Sweet Bells was impossible, not with Oliver so firmly at the controls. But this?

Georgie leaned forward. "It kind of seems to me that Mabel doesn't know anything about you two, right?"

She looked between Oliver and Claire, watching her mother's wide-eyed mortification and feeling little slivers of heat pierce at her heart. Georgie wanted to stop there, but the words kept falling out of her mouth in a satisfying hiss. "So would it be tasteless to tell her about that, or to keep quiet so you can slink around when you think no one's watching? Because take it from me: everyone is watching."

She got up.

Oliver watched her stand, his face a carefully arranged mask that she'd seen so often on Harris. She knew what was happening on the other side of that emotionless façade, and down deep it was good enough. If she couldn't have Sweet Bells, she could have this.

Her mother scrambled out of her chair, grabbed Georgie's hand and pulled her out of the restaurant.

"What are you doing?" Claire whispered, pushing Georgie through the double doors, out into the fine mist that hung hazy in the street lights. "You can't just say those things, Georgie. It's not . . ."

"True?" Georgie asked, spinning around. "Please don't bother, Mom. I know better. Everyone knows better."

Claire heaved a deep breath. "I don't know what you think you know—"

"Are we really going to play this game?" Georgie asked, astonished. "Dad told me months ago that you'd always had Oliver. That you always would. Whether you are or are not, in fact, actively screwing is not the point anymore, Mom. You're involved. You're *always* involved."

"Then there's nothing I can say, is there?" Claire asked. "I'm guilty no matter what."

"I cannot have this conversation," Georgie said, voice rising. "It's maddening enough to have to look at you two and put up with the things people say, and the doubts that you put in my head. I can't stand here and listen to you tell me it's nothing."

"Then I won't tell you it's nothing," Claire cried, shrill enough to make Georgie stumble. She stopped, gaping at her mother in the mist that drifted slowly between them. Claire blinked, like she was surprised she'd said something so damning, and then she set her jaw.

"With Oliver, it's never nothing," Claire said, lowering her voice. "I know you don't understand, and I know it's not fair, but this isn't about you, Georgie."

"Yes, it is." Georgie felt her heart beating so fast she thought it might rip its way out of her chest and fall at her feet, and she had to rush to breathe. "For the longest time, I let Harris blame me for everything that happened after Lilliana died, and I let him because some part of me thought he was right. I felt guilty. And now Oliver owns my horse and he owns my farm. He has you, my mother."

Claire stared at her, eyes shining.

"And Dad?" Georgie's voice cracked as a chill rushed over her skin. Claire lifted a hand to her mouth, clamping whatever she needed to say inside. That was fine, Georgie thought.

She knew better than to hope for more.

Shaking her head, Georgie turned back to the restaurant, pushing through the door and leaving Claire behind.

November

Chapter Twenty-Three

GULFSTREAM RUMBLED UNDER high heels and shining leather shoes. Women hid behind the sweeping brims of plumed hats, champagne perched between fingers. Cigar smoke puffed blue-gray into the air. The starting gate rolled onto tilled dirt, the purple placard sitting atop it like a royal banner, words in white printed boldly over the numbered stalls.

Breeders' Cup.

Georgie sat on Maghreb, the leggy long shot, who was all wild eyes and goofball antics in the post parade for the Distaff. She rode through the bumps and the spins, the eager way the filly shouldered the pony rider, pressing her muzzle into the pony's neck with all the insistence of a toddler in a tantrum. When they went into the gate, Georgie shushed Maghreb's nervous bouncing, her hindquarters glancing against the gate, metal whining under the impact.

"Hey now, baby girl," she told the filly, rolling her eyes at the assistant starter, who smiled knowingly and patted Maghreb on the forehead.

Then the gates burst open and they were gone, a thunder of

hooves and wind.

Two leaps, four leaps. Maghreb dug and pushed, all reaching legs and trailing tail. Georgie crouched in the irons and held the filly's head straight, drifting in to the rail and settling on the turn. Ahead of them, Absolute Stunner led the way, clods of dirt sailing from her hooves and hitting Maghreb's chest with pattering thuds. Maghreb lifted her head, snorting at the impact. Georgie let her drift up alongside Absolute Stunner, avoiding the rain of dirt. The filly settled, ears pricked at the track sweeping around the next turn, her stride strong and sure.

She was ready.

"Now, baby girl."

Georgie whispered it into her mane as they sailed into the homestretch, and Maghreb eagerly shifted into a stream of legs and blowing breath. Georgie gathered rein, pumped her arms up her neck, asked for more as Maghreb bunched and started to shake free. Absolute Stunner reached out, nostrils blown red with exertion as she tried to reclaim the lead. Her jockey lifted the crop, a clean arc slicing through the air. Georgie couldn't hear the crack of leather on muscle, but she did see Absolute Stunner's head jerk back, her body suddenly gone from Maghreb's side as she glanced off the inside rail with a sharp crack that twanged down Georgie's spine.

Absolute Stunner's jockey flipped over her neck, sailing down to land at their feet and rolling, flopping, arms flailing and legs folding in the dirt. Georgie hissed out a breath, grabbed mane, and pulled Maghreb aside. The spooked filly skittered over her jockey, recovered her footing and launched into a flat out run, ears pricked and trucking down the inside.

There was no time to think about what was happening behind her. Georgie pushed her crossed reins up the filly's neck, her fingers getting caught in mane and her knees burning with the effort to stay in front of a cascade of horses who wanted it just as much.

The wire loomed, and on her outside Blue Arrow appeared like a gray streak, all business with Dean working away like a madman, arms pumping and crop flipping up and down. The gray churned right past them, cruised over the wire by a half-length to win.

Maghreb crossed the finish line second, Georgie standing in her irons and her attention on the huddled body she could barely see behind horses, surrounded by help, an ambulance driving up without its lights flashing.

"Did you see it?" she asked, finding Dean on the backstretch. Blue Arrow stood speckled with dirt globs, licking her lips and pricking her ears while Dean patted her neck, mouth full of praise. At Georgie's question, he looked up, cast a quick look toward the homestretch and diverted his gaze back to the mare beneath him.

"Filly got spooked, went right into the rail," he said, collecting the reins. "Whole damn thing waved like a rubber band. Raphael came out of the saddle and that's all I saw."

Raphael.

Georgie sank into the saddle, her heart plummeting. Her whole body buzzed with so much leftover energy from the race that her ears rang. She swallowed down the sickness that rose up her throat and turned the filly, following Dean back to the silent grandstand and trying not to look at the ambulance.

She jumped off Maghreb as the crowd began tentative applause, and Georgie didn't stop what she was doing to see if it was a welcome cheer for Blue Arrow or relief on seeing Raphael bundled into the ambulance. Handing her saddle off to her valet, she high-tailed it for the jockeys' room, where she could shower the sweat off and feel like a new person. A person who hadn't just watched another living human be trampled right before her eyes.

Shuddering, Georgie pushed into the hallway and came to a surprised halt.

Claire stood there, racing program rolled into a tight spiral in her clenched hands. Every part of her was immaculate, from her flowing dress to her impressively tall heels. A wide-brimmed hat sloped across her forehead, shading her face and her hair, which was gathered into a low ponytail and left to cascade down one pale shoulder. Her fingernails were delicate half-moons, so glossy and polished she hardly looked like she spent a second around horses.

She looked like she'd spent too much time around Oliver, and maybe that was exactly the case.

"Can we talk?" Claire asked, squeezing the program in her hands.

"I don't know." Georgie pushed past her, headed for the jockeys' room. "Is Oliver lurking nearby?"

"It's about Sweet Bells."

Georgie's whole body flushed hot at the words. Sweet Bells, the filly she couldn't ride. Sweet Bells, whom she hadn't touched in weeks, not since she'd raced through Belmont's fall meet by herself and racked up enough wins to put her in most of the races on the Breeders' Cup card. And mainly she'd done that so she didn't have to go back to Red Gate and feel sick every time she woke up on Oliver's land.

Then there was her mother.

"What about Bell?"

She hated that she even had to ask. There were some things that she had learned to take for granted, and knowing every move the filly made had been one of them. Now she was clueless, a spectator on the sidelines.

"You already know," Claire told her, shifting on her feet like her heels were killing her. They probably were. "Raphael won't be coming back to the track after that fall, not for a while. His other horses are already transferring to other riders and Tupelo needs a jockey for Sweet Bells."

"So I suppose Oliver has plenty of options. I'm sure he has an entire contingency list."

"He does," Claire nodded. "But I nominated you."

"And he laughed, right? Just laughed and laughed, because he would never put me back on his horses, not after what I said straight to his face."

Claire shifted again, gave the program another hard twist.

"He agreed, actually."

Georgie stared at her hard, relief and distrust flooding into her and slapping against each other like two tidal waves meeting. Her jaw dropped, and then she made herself ask the question she needed to know.

"Why did he agree?"

"Because I asked. And because Oliver needs a manager for Red Gate."

"You didn't." Georgie pulled off her helmet, a cold sweat breaking out under the bandana she'd wrapped over her hair. She pulled that off, too, still feeling stifled.

"What would you have me do, Georgie?" Claire asked, desperation tinging her voice. "I can keep the house, keep running the farm, keep everything—"

"Except you can't, because it's not yours!" The words exploded out of Georgie. "The farm isn't ours anymore, Mom. It's his, remember? And now he's going to have you, too, in every capacity, and you'll do it because you don't even begin to see how incredibly repugnant it is."

"It is not repugnant to want to keep having a say in the place I helped maintain . . ."

"And systematically drove into the ground," Georgie reminded her.

Claire shuddered into silence, staring at Georgie like she'd been slapped.

"I don't want the ride," Georgie blurted. "If this is the deal, I don't want it."

"There's no choice," Claire told her. "I already did it. It's done. Whether or not you ride Sweet Bells. This is a favor, and it's one that I'm taking."

Georgie pushed away from her mother, heading to the jockeys' room, shaking her head when Claire called behind her. She needed to think, needed some sort of quiet, and she couldn't do that with Claire looking down at her, waiting on her to simply accept the facts of her life.

The jockeys' room was quiet after Raphael's fall, hushed whispers collecting in corners. Georgie blew through it without pausing to notice, her mind churning around Oliver and Claire and Sweet Bells, knowing there was no choice to make and hating it all the while.

She had to ride Sweet Bells.

It was Sweet Bells.

When she finally left the jockeys' room, her mother was no-where to be seen. For a moment, she felt a surge of relief loosen her chest, but when Georgie walked out into the lavender evening she realized that was premature.

Claire sat on a bench by the saddling paddock, the palm trees waving above her head on bending trunks. Her legs were crossed at the ankle, program cast aside in loosened spiral of bound pages. The brimmed hat flopped over her lap, and Claire stared down at it like she wasn't sure what it was or why she had bought it.

It was so not like her, like a life she'd left behind and didn't feel comfortable shrugging back into even for a minute. Georgie shifted on her feet and made herself take the first step.

"Why Oliver?"

The question was slippery, out of Georgie's mouth as she fell down onto the bench like a sack of sand. She'd never wanted to know the why of Claire and Oliver, not when the details and the truth could be so muddy. Now seemed like a good time to push that aside. She had to know. Claire looked up at her, shock stiffen-ing her shoulders before melting away.

"Because," Claire said after a moment, shaking her head. "It was always him."

"And Dad . . ." Georgie trailed off, hoping that this hadn't all been for nothing.

"Of course," Claire said softly. "Of course I loved your father."

Georgie was quiet, watching her mother settle back into the bench, sighing.

"Your dad introduced me to Oliver, back when I was just a bloodstock agent. It was always all or nothing with Oliver. When I was with him nothing else seemed to exist. It was easy to get swept up in him. Still easy, as it turns out."

She swallowed, looking out the saddling paddock. "It was also easy to get swept aside. Your dad, though, he was always a rock. Constant. I needed someone like your dad and when we married it was the best decision I ever made."

Claire swung her gaze to Georgie, her eyes shining with new tears. "And it was wonderful for a long time, Georgie. It was. We had you, and we had the farm. Things worked so well up until they didn't. Things fall apart faster than you think, and when we lost the stallions I went to Oliver for help. That was a mistake, in retrospect."

Georgie twisted her hands together.

"I believe Oliver wanted to help," Claire said over Georgie's scoff. "But the farm never stabilized and your father . . ."

Claire sighed. "Your father was a drinker to start. Maybe he would have drunk himself to death more slowly without Oliver trying to fix things, but in the end it was easy for me to give in. I was just so tired, Georgie. And Oliver made things so easy."

"He is not a good person," Georgie said.

"He loves me," Claire said quietly, and Georgie stared at her hard, a spike of pressure driving itself between her ribs and leaping up to her heart.

"Do you love him?"

Claire shut her eyes and opened them, like she needed to clear her vision.

"Sometimes," she said, and shook her head. "When I let myself forget about everything, yes. I do."

"And now?"

Claire shook her head hard, her face gone puffy and pink from the tears that she was trying to control.

"I made that mistake," Claire said. "I blame myself every day, Georgie, for what happened to Lilliana and *you*. I have tried to put on blinders and move forward, do what I can to make it all right. But now Tom isn't here, and I've been offered a chance to keep some shred of what I had. I jumped at that offer, Georgie, because as it turns out, I needed to keep at least this one thing."

But that wasn't true, not really.

The past was just that, over and done with, leaving Georgie with nothing but the moment she was living in now. She could choose how to live that moment, and she chose to reach across the space to find Claire's fingers, squeezing hard.

"You still have me," Georgie said, her voice breaking.

Claire burst into tears, and Georgie dropped the duffel at her feet, crossing the bench to curl into her mother's body and hold her tight.

"I'll ride Sweet Bells in the Classic."

The words still stung on her lips, knowing what Claire had given up. Or what Claire thought she was gaining. Georgie stood at Gulfstream's rail as the sun slipped below the horizon, trying to come to terms when she looked down and found a copy of *Uncle Moe* caught there on the railing with its edges flicking in the breeze.

Red Gate sold to Oliver Armstrong, it said after she smoothed it out. *Who will bid on Georgie Quinn?*

The cartoon underneath showed Georgie in bold, caricature lines. Men held up numbered placards and shouted at the auctioneer who would seal her fate. Georgie didn't read it, let the piece of paper rip out of her hands with the breeze as she stood on Gulfstream's backside and watched it roll into Harris' approaching feet.

He picked it up, the corner of his lips lifting in a smile as he folded the paper in on itself and pushed it into his back pocket.

"Keeping that for your scrapbook?" Georgie asked, leaning against the outside rail. The racetrack swept at her back, tilled dark dirt and the well-lit grandstand flushed pink.

"It will get its own page," Harris said, stopping in front of her and handing her a package sloppily wrapped in silver paper. "I'm sure I can find sarcastic stickers to go with it."

"I don't doubt it," she said, eyeing the package. "My birthday was in July."

"It was," he agreed. "I ignored it at the time because we weren't really speaking, but now that we are and in light of recent news, I thought you'd like this."

Georgie took the gift tentatively, felt the contents rustle inside as she shifted it to run her fingers under the tape, pulling the paper free and lifting the lid. Blue and red shimmered up at her, and Georgie dropped the box, let the paper drift out of her hands as she grasped the silks.

"Red Gate's silks," she said, holding them out to get a good look. Red and blue alternated in quarters across the torso. She hadn't seen them in so long that the sight brought little pinpricks behind her eyes.

"Came with the farm," Harris said. "I brought them down, just in case."

"That's incredibly Boy Scout of you." Georgie lifted the colors to her face, breathing them in like they might smell like something she recognized. Like Red Gate, during its heyday, when their horses raced across the wire first. Georgie assumed Oliver would frame these silks and put them on his office wall. It was just his style, and Harris giving them back to her was just like his.

"Who will you get to ride Roman?" Georgie asked, the gray colt rising into her thoughts when she had Red Gate's colors in her hands. "It's so last minute."

"Like I don't have a wait list of jockeys begging to ride Roman." Harris shook his head at her, that half-smile appearing. "It's covered, Georgie. Just like Little War is covered. You just have to focus on giving them both a run for their money."

Georgie shook her head, looking down at the silks. "With Sweet Bells? I can definitely manage that."

She shrugged into the silks, let them hang unbuttoned over her slight frame. It felt like being cocooned by memories, and all at once the bubble rising in her chest overwhelmed her and tears sprang into her eyes.

"Hey," Harris said softly, easing toward her to rub the wetness away with his fingers.

"You didn't have to," she started, and he shook his head.

"I kind of had to after I convinced Oliver to let you wear these during the Classic. I'm still sure I only managed it because he was in a frighteningly good mood, considering everything that went down after the Distaff."

She shivered, her breath catching in her chest.

"Why?" she asked, looking up at him.

Harris frowned, running his fingers down the edge of the silks as they shifted in the breeze. The colors were vibrant in his hands. "Because Sweet Bells is half mine, but really she's yours. She'll always be yours, if you want her."

"What are you saying?" she asked softly. Harris smiled, let the silks trail out of his fingers.

"That when Bell is done with all of this, I want you to have my interest."

"Harris," she started, her voice going all gravelly. He shook his head.

"You made Sweet Bells and Roman what they are, Georgie. Without you, who knows where we'd be today?"

Georgie swallowed thickly, huffing out a little laugh.

"I'm pretty sure you'd still be here," she said. "Just not with me and these silks."

"But I've got you and these silks," Harris said, looking at her like he needed convincing. "Don't I?"

In answer, she rose up to her toes, tipped her lips into his like it was the easiest thing in the world to kiss him there on Gulfstream's backside without thought or panic that it wasn't right. They rested there like that, Georgie sliding a hand to his chest, her fingers digging slightly into the soft fabric she found there. His hands glided up to the collar of her silks, grasping it to keep her there, anchored against him. When he pulled back she let her head dip, wondering what he'd say this time. Wondering what he'd do. They didn't have the best track record with kisses.

"I'm not the guy you wanted," he said, still holding onto her collar. He slipped a hand to the back of her neck, and she made herself meet his gaze. "I'm not him, George. You said you wanted to find me again before the Preakness, and that haunts me because I don't think there's anything there to find anymore. This is me, and . . ."

She shook her head, pushed the flat of her hand against his chest hard enough to make him stop talking. This was not what she wanted, Harris telling her that he wasn't enough after two years of waiting and wondering if he'd ever be able to find it in himself to look at her again that way, like he had before everything had changed.

"I love you," she said, and his words came to a screeching halt, his eyes widening. "Do you still love me?"

"Idiotically," he answered readily, stupidly.

"We've been living in that moment for too long." She eased up closer to him, put both hands on his jaw and leaned up. "Can we live in this one now?"

"I can do that," he nodded, laughed as she kissed him, the newness of it bursting into her veins and warming her down to her fingertips. She opened her mouth to him, opened her hands, opened herself. Let him in and laughed.

Chapter Twenty-Four

IN THE MORNING, Georgie whispered her secrets into Sweet Bells' mane, her lips catching on the coarse strands. Around them, the track was a thunder of hooves and floating bodies. Horses trailed through the mist, purple saddle blankets indicating their worth, how deserving they were to be there. Georgie pushed herself back into the saddle, wiped a hand on her worn jeans, and couldn't stop the grin that flickered onto her face as she approached the gap, the filly huffing with each step like a prize fighter eager to find someone to knock down.

Hero galloped easily along the inside of the track, her golden coat flaming in the morning sun. Photographers' cameras followed her like flowers seeking light, little clicks of shutters popping. The entire day would come down to this. Hero against Sweet Bells, two fillies going for broke in a race designed for colts against colts.

The grandstand hummed to life early, races spiking through the anticipation every forty minutes like clockwork as the day spiraled toward the Classic. Georgie dressed in clean silks after each race, washed the dirt off her face, and presented herself back in the paddock for a new horse, each clang of the opening gates leading to the day's natural conclusion. Sweet Bells and Hero, Roman and Little War, all only moments away from lining up in the dirt. The horses would be walking over from the backside, their coats shining in the setting sun. Sweet Bells would be pawing the ground with each step, the crowd's noise thrumming along her back.

Georgie pushed into the changing room, where Silvia Zambrana rested in child pose on her pink yoga mat, Little War's silks stretched over her shoulders. Georgie smiled to herself and peeled off the silks left over from an out-of-the-money finish in the Turf. The loss didn't matter. Georgie shuffled it off her shoulders and stared at the red and blue colors of Red Gate waiting for her. Splashing water over her face and retying the bandana over her hair, Georgie went back to the silks and shrugged them on over her protective vest. Snapped the buttons, tucked in the tails. She pulled the elastics around the sleeves and stared at herself in the locker mirror.

She had to swipe at her eyes, told herself to quit it. Georgie splashed water over her eyes again, toweled off, and grabbed her helmet, replacing the slip cover to complete the colors. Blue and scarlet red.

It was like looking back in time.

When she walked out of the jockeys' room, camera flashes lit up the hallway to the paddock. Georgie flicked her crop up behind her arm, looked searchingly out across the paddock to the number six spot, where Sweet Bells stood with Reece, tightening, tucking, stretching, making sure she was ready to run. It felt good to see her there, standing in the middle of the preparations with her ears up, watching the goings on like this was every day.

Roman stood near the great big filly, his gray coat shimmering as he lifted his head up and down, dragging his groom along for the ride. Little War danced in a circle behind them, ears tipped back, waiting for the call. Harris and Nick stood next to each other, watching their horses and laughing, like neither one could believe they were here as Lynsey shook her head at them, amused as always.

On the other side of the fountain, Hero stood calmly, swishing her gold tail around her hocks and licking her lips. She pricked her ears at the crowd that flowed around the paddock like a steady stream around rocks. Nothing new to her.

Georgie dodged around runners, owner contingents, smiled at well-wishers and the softball question lobbed from the crowd.

Who's going to win the Classic?

"Sweet Bells," she answered with a laugh, dancing around people and horses all the way up to the big filly, who stood with neck arched, pawing at the ground impatiently. Reece finished adjusting the equipment, moved on to Roman with a sharp nod of his head.

Only minutes now.

Nearby, Claire stood on the fringes of the group, looking around the paddock like she was watching something for the last time. Georgie stopped in front of her and touched Claire's hand. Her mother shivered.

"It's incredible," Claire said, looking around at the packed paddock, the people pressed at the rail, posters lining the paddock that said *Hero* and *Sweet Bells* and *Georgie*.

"Thank you," Georgie said, getting her mother's attention.

"For what?"

Georgie squeezed her mother's hand.

"For Sweet Bells, of course."

Claire shook her head, reached to cup Georgie's cheek. On the other end of the paddock, the judge lifted his voice to call for riders up. A thrill shot down Georgie's spine as a ripple moved over the crowd. It was a wave of anticipation, and she had to move with it.

"I'll see you after the race," Claire said. "Good luck."

Georgie spun to Sweet Bells as the filly did her stutter step dance, one foreleg out, the other to the side, her neck bowed to the ground as she pawed and huffed. The paddock shifted, horses moving toward the track in a loop around the fountain.

Putting a hand on the filly's withers, Georgie looked back and found Harris behind her. He leaned down, hooked a hand around her leg. She left the ground like a floating thing and settled soft and airy in the saddle.

"So," Harris said as he walked next to her boot, Georgie collecting the reins. "Who do you like?"

Georgie glanced behind them, saw Hero walking like she was carrying a princess, all well-mannered and beautiful. She looked ahead at Roman, swishing his tail and bobbing his head, all wiseass excitement as he fed off the crowd. Little War bounced into the air, all four legs curled off the ground.

Sweet Bells snorted, tapped a hoof against the walkway twice and danced to the left, shimmied to the right, blew out a snort like she was just so ready for this.

Cracking a smile, Georgie leaned down over the filly's shoulder so she could kiss Harris soundly on the lips.

"We are definitely winning this thing."

Harris put a hand on her boot, squeezed through the thin material. Georgie twined her fingers with his and rested over Bell's neck, rocking to her filly's proud victory walk to the track.

Bell set foot on the harrowed dirt, where Harris couldn't follow. Georgie shot him a grin over her shoulder, watched him standing in the chute to the track as the rest of the horses walked past him, their coats gleaming as the late afternoon sun beat down on the track in waves. He nodded once, and disappeared back to the grandstand.

Back to Tupelo.

Georgie was alone with Bell, who danced past the low roar of the grandstand and then kicked into a canter when Georgie asked. With a nod, the pony rider let them go. They jumped into a slow gallop past the starting gate and away from the grandstand, warming up muscles and legs. Georgie let the filly lower her head into the gallop, skimming by the outside rail and up to the backstretch, where it was quiet. Where they were alone to look back on Gulfstream sitting tall behind them.

Slowing the filly to a halt, Georgie turned her in toward the grandstand and ran her hand over Bell's pitch black mane. She could hear the track from here, a moving, living thing staring back at them. Bell bobbed her head, and Georgie felt her breath underneath her knees. It was sure, steady, a soft welcome home.

I missed you.

Georgie put her hand on Bell's shoulder, patted her softly. *I missed you, too.*

They ambled back to the starting gate, entered it to a whoop of crowd approval. Georgie leaned into the filly's neck, her fingers twisted up in mane, her heart and a question in her throat.

"Ready to go?"

The filly quivered, ears tipping back.

The gates opened.

About the Author

Aside from her Texas beginning, Mara Dabrishus spent the first two decades of her life in the Arkansas Ozarks. She primarily writes young adult fiction about her first love—horses—although she's also been known to write speculative and paranormal fiction. Her stand-alone novel, *Finding Daylight,* was a semi-finalist for the Dr. Tony Ryan Book Award and her short stories have been recognized by *Writer's Digest* and starred in *Kirkus Reviews,* as well as having won the *Thoroughbred Times* Fiction Contest.

When not writing, she's a librarian at a small college outside of Cleveland, Ohio. She lives with a husband, two ridiculous cats, and a small infant daughter.

Acknowledgments

Novels are never written alone. *Finding Daylight* took the help of many people, all of whom deserve more thanks than I can give them here. Nevertheless, here is my attempt to try. Carrie Starkey, my long-time beta reader, gave me her unflinching opinions. Linda Shantz, my horse racing expert, kept me honest. Erin Smith, my incredible editor, coaxed me into writing the story that wanted to be told. My additional thanks goes out to my writing group of immensely talented horse book authors: Maggie Dana, Tudor Robins, Kim Ablon Whitney, Natalie Keller Reinert, and Kate Lattey. And, as always, my thanks to my family and my patient husband. Without them I simply wouldn't be here, writing away.

Keep In Touch!

Support the Stories
Your opinion is important! If you enjoyed this book, please consider leaving a review on Amazon or Goodreads. Just a few words really help to keep me writing so you can keep reading!

Contact Me:
I love hearing from my readers!

Website: http://www.maradabrishus.com
Facebook: https://www.facebook.com/maradabrishusauthor
Twitter: https://twitter.com/marawrites
E-mail: mara@maradabrishus.com

Made in the USA
Lexington, KY
25 September 2018